MW01610944

FIGHTING FOR ELLA (SPECIAL FORCES: OPERATION ALPHA)

PREY SECURITY: ATHENA TEAM
BOOK FOUR

JANE BLYTHE

Dear Readers,

Welcome to the Special Forces: Operation Alpha Fan-Fiction world!

If you are new to this amazing world, in a nutshell the author wrote a story using one or more of my characters in it. Sometimes that character has a major role in the story, and other times they are only mentioned briefly. This is perfectly legal and allowable because they are going through Aces Press to publish the story.

This book is entirely the work of the author who wrote it. While I might have assisted with brainstorming and other ideas about which of my characters to use, I didn't have any part in the process or writing or editing the story.

I'm proud and excited that so many authors loved my characters enough that they wanted to write them into their own story. Thank you for supporting them, and me!

READ ON!
    Xoxo
    Susan Stoker

ACKNOWLEDGMENTS

I'd like to thank everyone who played a part in bringing this story to life. Particularly my mom who is always there to share her thoughts and opinions with me. My wonderful cover designer Amy who did an amazing job with this stunning cover. My fabulous editor Lisa for all the hard work she puts into polishing my work. My awesome team, Sophie, Robyn, and Clayr, without your help I'd never be able to run my street team. And my fantastic street team members who help share my books with every share, comment, and like!

And of course a big thank you to all of you, my readers! Without you I wouldn't be living my dreams of sharing the stories in my head with the world!

CHAPTER ONE

February 5th
  9:09 P.M.

THIS WAS WRONG.

The worst thing she'd ever done.

A betrayal of three of the people she cared about the most in the world.

Yet Ella Whitlock didn't stop what she was doing.

She couldn't.

She'd made this decision and had to finish what she'd started even if she was having second thoughts.

Or third.

Or, heck, thousandth thoughts.

The truth was, she didn't really have a choice.

As much as it pained her to know that her three Prey Security Athena Team members would forever hate her for turning on them, Ella knew that this was something she had to do.

Besides, she comforted herself, it wasn't like she was going to walk away from this alive.

Raul Castillo didn't leave loose ends, and she was a major loose end.

Shoving thoughts of her three best friends, Scarlett Madden, Lucy Elrod, and Cassidy Caddel, from her mind, she punched in the code for the safe where the four of them had hidden the only vial of the Reactivator that existed. The drug was a wonder drug that she and her team had been working on creating for the last four years. It worked to dull pain receptors, slow bleeding, encourage faster healing, and give the patient a much-needed burst of adrenalin.

They'd intended for it to be used to save the lives of men and women serving in the American armed forces. Intended for it to save lives. Ella was confident that it would have as well, but now everything was ruined, messed up beyond repair, and she was stuck sneaking out this vial from Prey's lab.

No one knew that this small safe existed. They'd hidden it in the back of a little fridge they kept in the lab. Unless you knew it was there you would never suspect what it really was. Which had made it the perfect place to hide this vial of the drug when it became clear that they were getting close to perfecting it.

Not that any of them had imagined the disaster of the last month happening.

Who could have predicted it?

As Ella slipped the vial into her pocket, snatched up her purse, and hurried from the lab, she felt like her heart was being ripped in two. Loyalty to her friends warring with her need to do this.

There was no easy choice.

There was no choice at all.

When she'd taken the first step down this road, she'd committed herself to it.

To treason.

Because that's what it all boiled down to.

She was taking a drug that had been intended to save the lives of her fellow citizens to hand it over to a Mexican weapons trafficker. Raul Castillo was at the top of the food chain in the weapons smuggling game. No one even came close. With all his money and the stellar reputation he'd built, he was on several countries' wanted lists, but so far the man continued to evade capture.

Now she was going to meet him.

The address she'd been given felt like it was burning a hole in her mind.

No trail.

That had been impressed upon her in the most painful of ways. In fact, each step she took reminded her of how important it was that she made it out of there without anyone stopping her. Then all she had to do was take a cab to the airport, hop on the flight to Mexico, and disappear for good.

And it would be for good.

This wasn't something she would be able to come back from.

Didn't even want to, not really. Because coming back from it would mean facing the people she had betrayed, and she was too much of a coward to do that.

So instead, she walked through the halls of Prey's West Coast offices for the last time. As she did so she tried to commit everything to memory. The crisp white walls, the heavy oak doors to each room. All the fun times she'd had there, giggling and laughing with her friends, and all the good work she'd done examining evidence that helped Prey catch and eliminate dangerous targets.

Here she'd done a lot of good, and Ella hated that it was ending the way it was.

But she'd made her choice and had no option but to stick with it. What was done was done and now she had to live with the consequences.

At this hour the building was quiet. The six former SEALs who ran this branch of Prey were all at home with their wives and kids. Scarlett, Lucy, and Cassie were all home with the men they had fallen in love with. All three of them were still healing from the injuries they had received at the hand of Raul, and she hated that they had been hurt. She wished there was something she could do to change what had happened and what happened next.

"You can't," she whispered aloud.

It was true.

It sucked, but it was true.

Rounding the corner, she stifled a scream when she walked headlong into someone. Panic thudded through her body.

No.

She couldn't get caught.

Not yet.

She'd been sure that she would have enough time to make it to the airport and get on that plane before anybody realized that she'd taken the vial of the Reactivator and disappeared.

Someone would figure it out. She knew that. There were cameras everywhere inside the building, even more had been installed after Scarlett had been abducted at the beginning of the year.

Almost exactly a month ago.

How had so much changed in one month?

"Ella? Is everything okay?"

Relief washed over her at the sound of the voice. It was one she recognized but didn't belong to one of her team-mates, one of the guys, or any of the SEAL teams working with Prey on this mess.

"Dora," she said, pressing a hand to her chest to try to calm her racing heart. "You scared me. I thought you went home already."

"Catching up on some paperwork," Prey's receptionist replied. "With everything going on, we've gotten behind on some other things, and I've been trying to get us caught back up."

"Oh, umm, that's good, a good idea," she mumbled. Dora was a nice enough woman, but right now, Ella just wanted to get out of there. Her nerves couldn't take any more of this, it was too stressful, and she wasn't cut out for this kind of life.

Why hadn't she listened to her parents?

Why hadn't she followed the rest of her family into music?

If she had, she never would have gotten herself into this.

So many people hurt, so many lives still hanging in the balance. She just wanted this to all be over, even if that meant losing everything.

"I was just doing a little research myself, but I'm heading home now," she said, trying to infuse as much normalcy into her tone as she could but pretty sure she failed. Failed abysmally.

"I'll see you tomorrow then," Dora said with a warm smile and Ella's confidence rose a little. If she'd fooled the recep-tionist, then maybe she could pull this off.

Maybe.

A huge, gigantic maybe.

After waving goodbye to Dora, she did her best to keep her steps even and slow. If she went running out of there, she'd only tip her hand and give away what was tucked inside her purse. If she wanted any chance at pulling this off, she had to play it cool, not alert anyone who might be watching the security cameras that anything was wrong.

Thankfully, no one on Athena Team was a suspect. That was the only thing she had working in her favor, and that was only going to last a little longer. As soon as one of her teammates checked on the safe and found the drug gone, they'd know. Know it was her. Know she was a traitor.

Betrayal was bitter on her tongue as she stepped out into the cold night. Since the whole subterfuge thing wasn't her strong suit, she already had a cab waiting. The quicker she got out of the country the better.

The ride to the airport felt far too long. Even though she tried her best to fight against the urge, Ella kept failing and glancing out the windows, constantly expecting the shrill wail of sirens and flashing lights as police cars converged on the cab. Unless she could get out of the country, she was looking at spending the rest of her life locked up in a tiny cell.

If she was lucky.

If she wasn't, she'd be shipped off to some CIA black site that hardly anybody knew about. There she'd have no rights, no way out. Her life would just be surviving torture after torture until, eventually, her heart gave out and she died.

She'd be praying for death if that was her future even though it was one she would deserve.

Because she deserved whatever she got, she wasn't so far down the path she had chosen that she wasn't painfully aware of that fact.

But even though she knew she was doing the wrong thing, she paid the cab driver, entered the airport, and checked in. Right or wrong, nothing was stopping her from getting on that plane and fleeing the country.

Nothing.

* * *

Of all the ways Miguel Aguilar thought this whole mole at Prey mess would play out this was absolutely at the bottom of the barrel.

The only person at Prey who was less likely to betray their country than Ella Whitlock was possibly Cassie, and that was only because the woman was so young and so innocent it was impossible to believe that she had a single bad thought in her head. Ever.

But Ella was a close second.

Long blonde hair, dark lashes framing wide green eyes, the prettiest smile he'd ever seen. Ella was gorgeous, sweet, and smart, exactly the kind of woman he usually loved sweet talking into his bed. Not to hurt them, he was always clear that he wasn't looking for a relationship, nothing serious or permanent. He was a playboy and lived up to that reputation, but he also liked a challenge. Putting in the work to woo a sweet woman into his bed was always harder than going after the ones who wore their sexuality confidently.

If things were different, if his brother hadn't fallen head over heels for one of Ella's teammates, then maybe he would have tried his luck with her. See if he could have convinced her to give him one night, where he'd make her feel things she'd never experienced before.

Call him arrogant, but he was good in bed, knew his way around a woman's body, and knew every button to press to

7

make them lose their minds to bliss-filled pleasure. He would have done the same for Ella, only now things had changed.

Drastically.

"Are we sure about this?" he asked, looking around the conference room at Prey where no less than three SEAL teams were crammed around a table, along with six former SEALs who now ran Prey's West Coast office. There was a lot of testosterone in the room and a lot of anger, too.

All of it was directed at a woman who wasn't even there.

Who had fled the country supposedly with the only vial of the Reactivator in her possession.

Her plane ticket said she was bound for Mexico, and they all knew that Mexico was where the weapons trafficker who had bought the Reactivator from a mole at Prey was based.

It all looked so simple on paper. Ella had taken the drug and left the country. She worked for Prey, had been in the know from the beginning, and had the opportunity to alert Raul Castillo every time he was about to be raided, which was the only explanation of how the man constantly managed to evade capture.

He'd seen the empty safe with his own two eyes. All three other Athena Team members claimed that was where they kept the drug, the only other person aware of its location was the great Eagle Oswald himself. CEO and founder of Prey Security, the man had been a SEAL until an injury forced him into retirement. A billionaire, he'd decided to use his money to create a security firm that was the best of the best. There was no way a man with more money than he could ever use would need to sell a drug his company owned anyway for a measly five million dollars.

Five people knew where the drug was. One had been on the other side of the country when it was taken, the other three were at their homes with their boyfriends, so that only left one person who could have taken it.

One person who was here in the building.

Who was seen in the lab slipping it into her purse.

Who was seen walking through the halls.

Who was seen climbing into a cab.

Who had gotten on a flight out of the country.

Ella Whitlock.

It was her.

They knew it.

There was enough proof to have her locked away for the rest of her life for that alone, aside from everything else the mole at Prey had orchestrated.

Yet...

Miguel couldn't shake the feeling that something didn't feel right. Something didn't sit right about this whole thing, he just couldn't figure out what it was.

"Don't see any other option," Owen "Fox" LeGrand muttered. As the leader of the SEAL team and, by default, the leader of the West Coast offices and the two teams that worked out of it, it looked like he was taking this the hardest.

Although none of the others looked much less angry.

This was a hard betrayal for all of them to swallow.

Ryder "Spider" Flynn, Eric "Night" McNamara, Logan "Shark" Kirk, Grayson "Chaos" Simpson, and Charlie "King" Voss looked like they were seconds away from jumping onto planes and heading off to Mexico themselves to drag back their little traitor. It was a blow they would never really recover from, Miguel could only imagine how hard it would hit if one of the men on his team betrayed them.

Scarlett, Lucy, and Cassie all had red-rimmed eyes. All three of them sat with their men by their sides, a mixture of shock and anger on their faces. Of everyone, they had been betrayed the most. Not only had they trusted Ella as part of their team, worked with her every day, and created the drug with her, but they had all suffered unimaginable horrors at the hands of Raul Castillo.

Horrors they hadn't even had a chance to recover from yet.

Now they were faced with this and seeing the pain in their faces ignited a powerful anger inside him.

His big brother Luis had fallen in love with Cassie, which made her a little sister to him, which made her two team-mates feel like family as well.

Nobody messed with his family and got away with it.

"Ella knew about the drug from the beginning," Fox continued, addressing Tate Laurier—who had fallen in love with Scarlett Madden when she had been set up as the one who sold the drug to Raul in the first place—and Luis' SEAL team, and a team led by Blake "Rocco" Wise, as well as Miguel's own team. "Those emails that had Scarlett's name on them, the other name on some of the others was hers. We all thought it was just the mole trying to set up the entire team so whoever ended up being kidnapped would take the fall."

Now they knew differently.

The emails with Ella's name were the original ones, the ones with Scarlett's name were the plants.

"Her computer skills are top-notch, almost comparable to Raven and Olivia's," Fox added. Raven was Eagle's sister, and Olivia was his wife, both were computer geniuses. "So she would have been able to set up the bombs, plant the emails, hack our systems, and tamper with the plane that almost killed Zander and Lucy."

At that, Zander Madden, Scarlett's twin brother and a former Delta Force operator who had supposedly died, tugged Lucy closer, wrapping his arms around her. Anger marred the man's features, and there wasn't a single person in the room who didn't mirror that same expression.

"When I was watching Scarlett, when I was struggling with my own doubt about what happened with my dad, I wondered if she could have been coerced somehow," Tate said, leaning in to touch a kiss to Scarlett's temple. "I wasn't about to make the same mistake twice. As soon as we got the call that Ella was seen on camera taking the Reactivator, I made sure that someone was sent around to check on her family. They're all fine. They haven't been threatened in any way, so Ella didn't take the drug to protect anyone."

"She took it because she's the one who wanted to sell it all along," Fox said, disdain in his tone.

"But I don't get why Raul would go after the others then," Miguel said. That was what was bothering him. While they didn't know for sure, they suspected the mole had sold the drug under the provision that they would help get one of the Athena Team members abducted since the mole themselves didn't have the formula. But if the mole was Ella, then surely she knew the formula, so why the need for all of this ... drama?

Abductions, plane crashes, bombs, it was all so much for someone who could have just taken the vial and the formula and gotten on a plane to Mexico, handed it all over to the weapons dealer, and then taken their payout and disappeared.

By the time anyone realized what was going on they could have been in the wind.

They could have gotten away with it.

Instead, Ella—if they were to believe the evidence—had hung around, orchestrated abductions of each one of her teammates, only to then disappear with the drug.

It didn't make sense, and Miguel didn't like things that didn't make sense.

"We did wonder if perhaps there was more to it than that," Fox replied. "Wondered if it was personal. If the mole

11

had a grudge against Athena Team and wanted revenge of some sort and not just the money from helping Raul get his hands on the drug."

If that was the case, Ella wasn't just a traitor, she was an evil psycho who enjoyed inflicting pain and terror on the people who cared about her.

CHAPTER TWO

February 6th
8:36 A.M.

THIS WAS IMPOSSIBLE.

Ella had followed the instructions, she was sure she had. Only she didn't have a written copy of them, all she had to go on was what she remembered. Unfortunately for her, following directions was not something she had ever been good at.

Still, how could she be this lost?

Everything else had gone so smoothly. She'd gotten the drug into the cab, to the airport, and onto her plane without incident. Throughout the short flight, she had been constantly on edge, wondering if there were going to be cops waiting for her on the other end, ready to take her into custody and then drag her right back home where she would have to face the music and pay the price for the choices she'd made.

But no one had been there.

Since this wasn't a vacation, she hadn't packed a suitcase, just stuffed a change of clothes into her bag. Thankfully, she always used quite a large bag, so there was space for the clothes and a few toiletries without the need to bring along a larger bag which would have tipped someone off that she was at Prey to get the drug.

After making it through immigration without incident, she'd headed outside and to the parking lot where she'd found the vehicle Raul said would be waiting for her.

With hands shaking so badly it was a wonder she'd been able to drive at all, she'd made it through the city and out into the jungle, and that's where things had fallen apart.

She was lost.

Completely and utterly lost.

The roads—well, what counted as a road but was really nothing more than tracks through the ever-thickening jungle —were almost impossible to make out now, and Ella was sure that sooner rather than later, they were going to disappear into nothingness.

What was she supposed to do then?

She'd ditched her cell phone at the airport, and there hadn't been one in the car, guess Raul hadn't wanted her to have second thoughts and call someone to confess everything. That meant she had no way to call him now, no way to bring up a map, although the chances of GPS working out here had to be slim.

Her bad day suddenly turned even worse when the car slowed to a stop and the engine died.

"No, no, no, no, no," she wailed, turning the key over and over again in hopes that the engine would kick back on.

But it didn't.

Couldn't.

Because the problem wasn't the engine.

The car had run out of gas.

It didn't matter how many times she turned the key in the ignition, there was no juice to make the car go. Raul must have wanted a safeguard that she was going to drive to where she'd been told and nowhere else and limited the amount of gas in the car to just enough to get her there.

Obviously, he hadn't counted on her being directionally challenged.

What was she supposed to do now?

If she didn't get to Raul Castillo, bad things were going to happen, she had to get the drug to him like she'd promised she would. But how was she supposed to do that now?

The car wasn't going anywhere, meaning she would have to walk.

That would be one thing if she knew where she was going, but she didn't. She had no idea where she'd made a wrong turn and wasn't even sure she knew how to backtrack and find her way to one of the bigger roads where she might be able to find someone.

Even if she could manage to do that, she'd have to hope that the driver she found knew where Raul was and was willing to take her there.

This was a dangerous part of the world. Aside from the fact that the weapons dealer had a house somewhere close by there were cartels, who would do only one thing to her if they found her wandering around in their territory.

Images of her being held down and raped flashed through her mind along with a series of images of what her three friends had been through. Raul had in his possession an arousal drug that was said to keep a woman in a painful state of arousal for hours. According to her friends, all three of them who had fallen victim to the drug's influence while Raul's prisoner, had said it felt like there was something inside of you clawing to get out and that you would do almost anything to find relief.

JANE BLYTHE

That's what they had suffered at the hands of the man she was now going to meet.

If anyone ever deserved to burn in Hell for all eternity for their sins, it was her.

She was the lowest form of low. The worst of the worst. And yet, with a weary sigh, she unsnapped her seatbelt, grabbed her purse from the passenger seat, shoved open her door, and climbed out of the vehicle.

Despite the risks, she was going to have to figure this out on foot.

The only other option was to sit in her car and just wait there until she died of dehydration. Even with the muggy heat that would take days, and she wasn't brave enough to sit there and wait for death to come for her.

Still, she eyed the car once before starting to walk. Maybe that would be the better option. It was certainly what she deserved. Maybe even more than she deserved.

But she couldn't do it.

Instead, she turned and trudged off into the jungle. Ella still had no idea where she was going. Obviously, somewhere along the way, she'd taken a wrong turn, but she had no idea where.

If she kept going forward, there was a chance she might be able to still find Raul's property. She couldn't have gotten so far off track that she wasn't even in the vicinity. At least that's what she assured herself as she climbed over a fallen tree trunk.

Even if she made it through the jungle and by some miracle got to his place, he wasn't going to believe her when she said she'd just gotten lost. There would be some punishment she'd be forced to endure, and she had already decided she would take it without complaint.

It was the least she owed her friends.

Being lost aside, there was every chance she wouldn't

even make it through the jungle. There were so many predators out there, both animal and human. Plus, she had zero supplies and wasn't even dressed to be traipsing through the jungle. At least she'd swapped out her usual dresses and heels for a sensible pair of jeans and sneakers.

Despite the early morning, it was already hot and humid. Hot enough that she shrugged out of her hoodie and tied it around her waist. Tonight, when the temperature dropped, she'd need it again, but right now it was too warm to keep it on.

After only several minutes of walking, Ella was already thirsty, but she'd finished the bottle of water from the plane in the car before she realized she was lost and had taken a wrong turn somewhere along the way.

The outdoors was not her thing, she was an inside girl. When she wasn't working or hanging out with her friends, she was either reading or practicing. Coming from a family of classical musicians, it had always been assumed that she would follow in their footsteps. It wasn't that she wasn't talented enough, she'd been a child prodigy, playing multiple instruments before she could even read and write. Cello was her favorite, and even though she'd chosen a different path for her life, she still occasionally performed in front of large audiences, her fame as a child meaning she got plenty of invites.

Music was her happy place. Not that she had ever once second-guessed her decision not to make music her career. She'd made the right choices, the best ones for her, and she'd done a lot of good work at Prey.

Too bad it was all tainted now.

All anyone would ever remember of her was that she had taken a drug she'd designed with her friends and sold it to a weapons dealer. Nobody would care to dig deeper and find out the whys.

That hurt.

Maybe more than it should given that Ella was aware that she was the bad guy in this situation. If her friends didn't believe in her then that was her own fault.

Things didn't have to go this way. She could have made a different choice, but she hadn't. She'd made this choice and now had no other option but to follow it through to the end.

Whatever the end looked like.

Whether she wound up getting killed by an animal, dehydration, exposure, a cartel, Raul, or one of his men, it didn't really make much difference.

Whatever she got she would deserve.

* * *

FEBRUARY 6TH

11:37 A.M.

THE USUAL RUSH he got when off on a mission with his team was lacking today.

If anything, Miguel would rather be anywhere but there.

Despite knowing the mountain of evidence against Ella, he couldn't shake a sense that something wasn't adding up.

Sure, the Prey guys had an explanation for why Ella would set up her friends and get them abducted when she already had the formula for the drug. Even if she had a grudge against them, and so far, no one seemed to be able to come up with a logical answer as to why she would have a grudge and what exactly the grudge would be, that didn't explain the three other Athena Team members own accounts of their kidnappings.

From Scarlett to Lucy to Cassie, all three women repeated versions of the same story. They'd been taken,

18

imprisoned, and tortured into giving up the formula for the drug. If Raul had access to the formula through Ella, why torture them?

Why specifically torture them to get them to talk?

If it was just about revenge for some perceived slight that had Ella setting up the abductions, there was no need for Raul to try to get them to give up the formula. He still could have tortured them, but why was the man so intent on getting the formula if he already had it?

It didn't make sense.

Straight up didn't.

The theory that the abductions were because of a grudge Ella had against her teammates only worked if you just took her into consideration. As soon as you added Raul to the equation, the whole theory became as shaky as a stack of dominos.

And like dominoes, he felt that everything was about to come tumbling down.

Right now, though, it wasn't his job to figure out if Ella was guilty of all the crimes she had been accused of. There were a few things that weren't up for debate. She had taken the Reactivator from a hidden safe inside a fridge in the lab. She had fled the country on a flight to Mexico. She had gotten off that flight and then disappeared.

With this new revelation about Ella, everyone at Prey had dropped what they were doing, and all energy and resources were focused on finding her. While he and his team had taken one of Prey's private jets down to Mexico, every single one of Prey's tech people was going over footage of the airport in Mexico, trying to find a glimpse of Ella so they could figure out where she was heading next.

And they'd found her.

The woman hadn't put on any disguise and hadn't even changed clothes from what she'd been wearing in the lab when she took the drug. She was seen exiting the building wearing her jeans and a pink hoodie that made her stand out. No hat, no glasses, the woman didn't even duck her head as she walked even though she had to know her image was being captured by CCTV cameras.

Why?

Prey was the best, a world-renowned company, she had worked for them for the past five years, so had to know they would be looking for her and even knew where to look. The ticket was in her name, she knew they knew where she was heading, yet she didn't take a single preventative measure to try to hide herself.

If he didn't know better, he would almost think that she *wanted* to be spotted.

Wait.

Did she?

Miguel was so confused. There was evidence that suggested for sure that Ella had stolen the drug, he wasn't arguing with that, his problem was the why. Unlike everyone else, he wasn't buying that she just up and decided to sell the drug and have her teammates horribly tortured. No way was he going to accept that until someone could give him a legitimate reason why she would want to do that.

If something didn't make sense, then chances were, it wasn't true.

They were missing something here.

Ella was smart enough to cover her tracks and yet she wasn't. She had brazenly taken the drug out of the lab and walked it through the building, knowing she would be captured on camera. She booked a ticket in her own name and made no attempts to hide her appearance, it felt like she was leading them on a journey, hoping they would follow along.

The only reason he could see that she would do that was if she needed help but was unable to ask for it.

She wanted Prey to know where she was, which seemed obvious to him even if it didn't to anyone else, and he wasn't sold on the idea that someone hadn't threatened her or somebody she loved.

Sure, her family had been questioned and not a single one of them mentioned being threatened, but that didn't mean that Ella hadn't been told that the people she loved would be harmed if she didn't comply with orders.

Was that a real possibility?

Miguel believed it was, and he didn't think it was just because he thought the woman was hot and would have loved a shot at her.

There were plenty of women out there and given the development of his brother hooking up with Ella's friend, he likely wouldn't have pursued her anyway.

Guilty or innocent, it wasn't up to him to decide.

If she was innocent, then he hoped she was able to prove it for her sake. And if she was guilty, then he hated to say it, but she would deserve whatever was coming her way.

You do the crime you do the time.

That was a favorite saying of his foster parents, and it was one he thought of regularly in his line of work. As a SEAL, he saw a lot of evil and he'd never once felt bad for anyone who had suffered the consequences of their actions.

Life was full of choices, and if you made bad ones, what else could you expect but bad outcomes?

Regardless of her guilt or innocence, Ella had to be found and brought home. He would have no control over what happened to her once she got there, but if she was honest then perhaps she would be able to work out a deal of some sort, save herself some prison time. Although, if Eagle Oswald was out for blood, then the woman didn't stand a

21

chance. He had power, influence, and money, and Ella had stolen from his company. If he wanted her punished to the fullest extent of the law, it would happen.

"Hey, there's a car up ahead," one of the guys on his team suddenly announced, and Miguel stopped with the internal debate over Ella and what she had or hadn't done and looked out the front window.

Sure enough, sitting in the middle of the track they were following through the jungle was a vehicle.

"I think it's hers," he said. Once they had the license plate of the vehicle Ella was traveling in, the Prey people were able to direct them along the same route that she'd taken. Heading in this direction was the last time she'd been spotted, and since there were no more cameras out there, he and his team had spent the last couple of hours traveling along various roads in the hopes they'd find either Ella or wherever she was heading.

Weapons in hands, they jumped out of their vehicle and approached Ella's warily. She was an unknown, they had no idea how much she had participated in the events of the previous month, where her loyalties lay, how desperate she was, and what her motivations were. There was every chance she would try something stupid, and while he didn't want it to come down to that, sometimes threats had to be eliminated.

As he approached, it quickly became apparent that the vehicle had been abandoned.

There was no sign of Ella or anyone else.

A quick check showed she had taken her purse with her, so she still had the drug, but had she left because she'd met up with Raul, or had there been another car there waiting for her to change to it so it would make her harder to follow?

"Ran out of gas," one of his guys announced.

"Did she get into another car or is she walking?" another asked the same questions he'd been pondering.

Scanning the area, he quickly noticed signs that someone had recently disturbed the undergrowth heading in the same direction the road went. "I think she walked," he said, indicating what he'd found.

It was time to go hunting. Playing the what-if game wasn't useful. It wasn't his job to figure out what crimes Ella had committed, all he had to do was find her and deliver her back home to face the metaphorical firing squad.

Miguel just hoped that she deserved what she got.

CHAPTER THREE

February 6th
12:14 P.M.

EVERY TIME she wiped a bead of sweat out of her eyes another one took its place.

Another dozen took their place.

It was so hot there, and she was already exhausted.

Ella knew it didn't help that she hadn't slept in almost forty-eight hours, had barely eaten anything, and had drunk nothing but a little water from the plane. Plus, she'd been living hopped up on adrenalin and living with a constant argument going on in her head as to whether she was doing the right thing or not.

It was so easy to make that decision in the moment.

To believe that you were doing the right thing, the only thing you could do, that you had no other choice, that life wasn't fair, that even though it didn't feel good this was what you had to do.

But in the cold light of day, it was even easier to second-guess everything.

Had she had other options?

Yes.

They were risky, and she'd decided they were too risky, but they had been there.

If she'd taken one of those other options, would she have regretted it?

This way it was her in the firing line, she would be the one to take the fall. It would cost her everything in the event that she survived the fallout, but at least she would be the one suffering.

And in the end, that was why she'd started down this road.

No one else was going to pay the price for her sins.

No one.

Certainly not people she loved.

Needing another break, Ella paused and checked the ground around her before sinking onto it. The last thing she wanted was to find one of the venomous snakes or poisonous spiders that lived in the Mexican jungles. Plus, there were scorpions here as well, and several species of big cats, not that she wouldn't immediately notice one of them if they were hanging around.

Exhaustion weighed heavily on her as she hung her head. Even though she was there, surrounded by the oppressive heat, the sounds of birds in the air, the feel of the hard ground beneath her, and the rough bark of the tree she was leaning against pressing into her skin, all of this felt so surreal.

Was she really in Mexico?

Had she really stolen the Reactivator?

Was she really going to meet up with the notorious

weapons trafficker if she could find her way out of the jungle?

How had this become her life?

There was no way she could have predicted that she would wind up basically a traitor on the run, being hunted as a wanted criminal. She'd always been the good girl. The youngest of four girls and parents who were internationally renowned classical musicians, she'd always assumed as a child that she would follow everyone else into music. Two of her sisters were famous opera singers, and the other was a pianist who entertained thousands of people every year in performances in the best concert halls in the world.

She loved music, loved mastering a new instrument, and had even enjoyed scales even though most kids her age hated the monotony of them. If her life hadn't changed the summer she turned eleven, she would have become a musician.

It was on a flight to China, where she had been set to perform in a packed-out theatre that it happened. Two men tried to hijack the plane. Had almost succeeded. They'd taken over and diverted the flight, then when it eventually landed, a team of US Navy SEALs had managed to take control and save all their lives.

That was when she knew.

Music was beautiful, and it wasn't something she wanted to give up, but she wanted her life to mean more. So, she'd gone to college and studied a range of things from chemistry to ballistics to computers, eventually getting a job at Prey Security. She'd been so proud when it was offered to her that she could hardly believe that *she* had been offered a job with the best security firm in the world.

It was her dream job, and now it had all come crashing down around her.

Tears leaked out of her eyes, mixing with the sweat and

making her eyes burn. Even though she rubbed at them to erase the sting, she couldn't help but feel like she deserved it.

She deserved to hurt for what she'd done.

A sob was building inside her, and it was precariously close to bursting out, only she heard something.

Her entire body went still.

She was barely even breathing.

Was someone out there?

Friend or foe?

Who was she kidding? Ella knew she didn't have any friends left. All she had was a whole range of foes who wanted different things from her and would treat her differently if they got their hands on her.

What should she do?

Should she stay there and try to hide? Make herself as small as possible and hope whoever was out there walked past her?

Maybe she should try to run? If she snuck away in the opposite direction from the sounds she could hear, there was a chance she could get away.

But even if she hid or even if she ran it didn't solve her problem.

She was lost out there in the jungle. She couldn't survive long on her own. She still had to try to find her way to Raul Castillo's place if she didn't want everything to be for naught. What choice did she really have?

Sighing, Ella shoved back the tears and wearily pushed to her feet. No sooner had she done that than she saw two men dressed all in black, weapons slung over their shoulders, walking through the jungle a mere ten yards or so from where she'd been sitting.

"Hello?" she called out, ignoring the fact that they could belong to a cartel and hoping they were Raul's men. Not that that was much better.

Both of them turned toward her with weapons raised, but when they saw her horrible smiles that made her skin crawl lit their faces, and those weapons were once again lowered.

"Well, well, well, what do we have here? Little blonde mouse that was supposed to have arrived already, hiding out in the jungle," one of them said as he stalked toward her.

Right now, she felt very much like a little timid mouse, trying to make herself as small a target as possible because she knew she couldn't run from the predator hunting her.

"I-I got l-lost," she stammered, taking a step back, but she crashed into the tree trunk she'd been resting against, trapping her in place. Running was a bad idea. These men would catch her, and if she made one wrong move, the consequences could be disastrous.

"Got lost did you, little mouse?" the other man chuckled as he followed his friend.

"Mr. Castillo said if we found you then we were welcome to have a little fun with you before bringing you in," the first man said as he reached her and circled her neck with one of his large hands, effectively pinning her in place.

"I ... I ... that wasn't ... we had a deal ... you can't ..." Ella babbled as the man's hand roughly grabbed one of her breasts and squeezed it so hard she couldn't help but cry out even though she knew there was no one to hear her cries, and no one to care even if they did.

"We can do whatever we want, little mouse," the second man said with a laugh. "Who is going to stop us?" He waved his hands around at the empty jungle. The only other living beings there were the animals, and they certainly didn't care what these two men did to her.

"P-please, please d-don't h-hurt me," she begged, but all it did was make both men laugh.

"Don't worry, little mouse," the second man said as he

shoved a hand between her legs and groped at her. "We'll make sure it's good for you. It won't hurt."

"Well, maybe it will hurt when I take you here," the first man said. The hand that wasn't still around her throat moved to her backside, and he poked at her hole back there through her jeans.

Ella whimpered and it was such a pitiful sound even to her own ears that it was no wonder the two men merely laughed again.

She was pathetic.

Couldn't even remember the directions that would have gotten her to Raul's house. Not that she would have been all that much safer there, but she for sure wouldn't be about to be stripped naked and simultaneously raped by two men.

The worst part of it, though, was knowing that it was all she deserved.

Didn't she know better?

If you played with fire, you got burned. And she was about to be scorched.

* * *

FEBRUARY 6TH
12:31 P.M.

HE HAD NEVER TRULY UNDERSTOOD the saying that someone saw red.

Not until this moment.

When Miguel heard the commotion, he quieted his steps, slowed his pace, and snuck up quietly to see what was going on.

As soon as he saw a woman with long blonde hair shoved up against a tree and two men dressed in black fatigues pawing at her and trying to yank her clothes off her, he was filled with a rage so powerful he was surprised he didn't turn into the Hulk right then and there.

The woman was Ella. He knew that, knew that these men were likely some of Raul Castillo's, that she had gotten herself into this mess when she agreed to sell the weapons trafficker the drug and snuck out of the country to do it. Knew that if she had made different choices, she wouldn't be in this position right now.

But none of that mattered.

Whether she was some criminal mastermind, who had conspired with a dangerous man to have her friends tortured or not, no woman deserved to be raped.

None.

Tears streamed down Ella's face, and her eyes were two big green orbs of terror, she was so focused on the two men trying to strip her naked that she didn't see him approaching. Likewise, the two men were so engrossed in their captive victim that they weren't paying attention to anything else.

One quick slash of his K-BAR and the first man dropped, blood gushing from the fatal wound he'd just inflicted. Before the second man could even process what was happening and do anything about it, Miguel delivered another strike, this one straight into the man's chest, piercing his heart.

Yanking his blade free, he ignored the two men dying at his feet and instead focused on the woman standing in front of him.

She didn't look like a criminal mastermind. That was his first thought. She looked like a woman a second away from a panic attack. Not that it meant she wasn't guilty of the crimes she had been accused of. There was no way for her to know that the men who worked for Raul would turn on her like that and try to rape her, although honestly, she should have known better and expected that kind of behavior from men like them.

Still, she'd had a close call, and he couldn't not feel sympathy for her in this moment even if she had brought some of this upon herself.

"Hey," he said softly, trying to draw her attention away from the men bleeding out on the ground before her. "It's all right, they can't hurt you."

Those wide green eyes shifted slowly to meet his and fresh fear bloomed on her face. She made a small, squeaking sound of terror, and then her gaze darted about and he could tell she was thinking about making a run for it.

If she tried, she wouldn't get very far.

Even if her T-shirt wasn't shoved awkwardly up, exposing her simple white cotton bra, and her jeans unzipped and shoved halfway down over her hips, there was no way she could outrun him. If it came down to it, he'd restrain her, but he'd rather not have to zip-tie a woman who had mere seconds ago almost been brutally raped.

"Don't run, Ella," he said, keeping his voice calm and soothing. "Don't make things worse, yeah?" *Don't make me have to cuff you.*

At the sound of her name, she went stock still, her gaze landing on him again. The terror in her eyes didn't vanish, but it did dim a little, and he relaxed. She wasn't going to run. She knew she wasn't getting out of there and wouldn't try anything stupid.

"My name is Miguel," he continued talking although he didn't move any closer. Right now, Ella was like a spooked horse, one wrong move on his part and this could get bad really quickly. "I'm a SEAL, I'm Luis' brother, you remember me? We've met once or twice."

A shaky nod was all the response he got, but at least she was still standing there.

"You know why I'm here don't you?"

Another shaky nod although he wished she'd give him something. A protestation that she was innocent, that she'd done nothing wrong, that there was a logical explanation for why she'd taken the drug and come to Mexico.

"Do you know who they are?" he asked. While he was assuming they were Raul's men they could belong to one of the cartels in the area.

A third shaky nod, but this time she swallowed visibly. "Th-they w-were Raul C-Castillo's m-men," she stammered as her teeth chattered.

His heart dropped.

Maybe he'd been hoping she was going to tell him she had no idea who they were, that she wasn't here to meet with the weapons trafficker, that none of this was as it seemed.

He'd wanted proof one way or the other that Ella was guilty of what she had been accused of, and it seemed he'd gotten it.

"Th-they were g-going to r-rape me," she said as though she couldn't believe it had been mere seconds away from happening.

"But they didn't," he reminded her. Only because he'd shown up when he had. If he'd been just a minute or so later, it would have been too late to stop it.

"B-because of y-you. Th-thank you," she whispered. Fresh tears shimmered in her eyes as she looked up at him with true gratefulness, and it hit him right in the heart that even though she knew he was there to bring her in, she was still able to express gratitude.

Miguel nodded in acknowledgment because it felt weird to say the traditional you're welcome when he was going to have to take her into custody and return her home to face an uncertain future. "How about we fix your clothes? Then you can drink some water and maybe eat something, and then I'll take you to join up with my team."

Terror flared in her eyes at the mention of his team, and he knew reality had to be sinking in. Yes, she'd been spared being raped, but it wasn't like she was in a better position than she'd been in moments ago. Just because no one was going to sexually assault her when she was taken into custody didn't mean it would be a pleasant experience.

She'd be strip searched and locked up in a tiny cell. Depending on who wound up taking custody of her, there could be some forms of torture involved. Some agencies had their own way of dealing with things, and given she worked for Prey, and the kind of work Prey did, there was a chance she had sold other intel to people who would use it to hurt their country. That information would have to be obtained, and there was a chance it would be by any means necessary because if she had done that, they needed to know and deal with it accordingly.

While he wanted to offer reassurances, he couldn't.

It would be pointless.

They were both aware of the mess she was in.

At least she didn't try anything stupid. Just gave him another one of those shaky nods, then lifted trembling hands and tugged on her T-shirt, pulling it down so it covered her. But when she went to pull up her jeans she couldn't get her shaking hands to cooperate and do the zipper up.

"Can I?" Miguel asked, waiting until she had an internal battle and then nodded before he closed the short distance between them. Trying to touch her as little as possible, he eased the jeans into place and then zipped them up.

This close to her, he could feel the tension coming off her in waves. He wanted to be able to do something to fix this for her, or, at the very least, make it as painless as it could possibly be.

"Ella," he said softly, hooking a forefinger under her chin and nudging gently. "Just be honest, okay? I know this sucks, and I don't know what led you to make the choices that you made, but if you're honest, then they may go lighter on you."

Instead of giving him one of her shaky nods, it was like all the fight drained out of her in one long, weary sigh. A sigh that felt like it came from the depths of her soul, and he wondered just what had made her turn on the people she worked with, people to all accounts she had a good relationship with.

"Could I ... could I just have ... one second to myself?" Ella asked in a trembling voice.

He should say no. She was a prisoner and he was tasked with bringing her in. He should search her to make sure she wasn't armed, cuff her hands, and take her back to his team.

But she was also a victim.

The dead men at their feet were the only reason he agreed. After this, she wasn't going to get to be alone for a long time. Not until it was ascertained that she hadn't handed over more sensitive information to their enemies. And then that time alone would be spent in a locked cell.

It couldn't hurt her to have one last moment of freedom before her world came crashing down around her.

"I'll be just over there," he said, turning and walking a short distance away.

A few seconds later he knew he'd been gullible and had made a mistake when he heard the sounds of her making a run for it.

CHAPTER FOUR

February 6th
  12:39 P.M.

RUNNING WAS STUPID, but what choice did she have?

Ella hated that it made her look more guilty, but let's face it, she *was* guilty of stealing the Reactivator and coming to Mexico. Worse than that, though, she felt like she'd betrayed Miguel.

The man was hot.

Hands down the sexiest she'd ever laid eyes on.

In fact, she'd been secretly crushing on him from the moment she first saw him. But he was a one-and-done kind of man, a playboy, and she wanted the whole white picket fence dream, so she'd never thought it would go anywhere.

Then his brother started dating Cassie, who was like a sister to her, and she'd really known for sure it would never go anywhere. The last thing she was going to do was allow herself to become one of Miguel's conquests, get her poor little heart broken, and then make things awkward for the rest of their lives because Cassie and Luis' love was the kind that lasted forever.

It wasn't just that Miguel was hot that had regret simmering in her veins as she ran through the jungle, leaving him behind. It was the fact that he'd just saved her from being raped. More than that, he'd been kind and compassionate. Even going so far as to allow her a moment to gather herself after what had almost happened.

That wasn't something he had to do.

He'd done it only because he was a good guy.

What was she?

A wanted fugitive accused of betraying her country.

Please forgive me, Miguel.

She wished she'd been able to tell him everything that was going on. The truth. The whole truth. Even nothing but the truth.

But she couldn't.

Not yet.

Not until she was sure they were safe.

Once she knew that her family wasn't going to be harmed, then she would make sure that everyone knew the truth. That she wasn't the mole at Prey and hadn't betrayed anyone. She had been ambushed at her house the night Cassie had disarmed the bomb on the cruise ship and been shown a video of someone setting a bomb under her parents' house. A house where one of her sisters also lived with her husband and three small children, including an infant only five months old.

How did she have any choice *but* to do as she'd been ordered?

How could she risk the lives of the people she loved?

Even knowing the risks, she'd fought, but four men had been there. Four really big men who had held her down while one of them lit a cigarette and burned the soles of her feet as he detailed how he would go straight to her parents' house, torture them, her sister, brother-in-law, two nieces and her baby nephew before sitting back and watching them all die as the house exploded.

That was when she realized that she had been left with no choice.

Obedience was the only thing that would protect the people she loved.

Maybe that made her selfish to prioritize her own family over everything and everyone else.

But it didn't make her stupid.

Hearing footsteps thundering through the jungle behind her, Ella knew she had no chance of outrunning Miguel. Nor could she expect any warmth and compassion from him when he caught her. Perhaps if he hadn't caught her almost being raped, he wouldn't have been as nice, maybe he would have just tackled her and put her in handcuffs, but she knew for sure that's what he would do this time.

Eyeing a tree up ahead, she wondered if she could hide since she couldn't outrun him.

Even if her feet weren't injured, she still wouldn't have had any hope of getting away from Miguel and this might be her only chance.

If she was caught now, Raul would order the mole to detonate the bomb under her parents' house. All she had to do was play this out until she knew the bomb had been removed and then she could do what she'd come here to do.

Betray Raul Castillo and the mole.

Whatever it took, she was bringing them both down.

If that meant she went down with them, then so be it. At least they would pay for hurting the people she loved, for threatening her family, and trying to steal a drug that she and her team had created for good.

Grabbing hold of the lowest branch, Ella dragged herself

up onto it. Then up onto the next. And the next. And the next. She climbed until her arms trembled with exhaustion, and she was high enough up for her stomach to churn.

She didn't like heights.

Had never climbed a tree in her life.

But she'd done it.

Up there she was safe. Miguel wouldn't think to look for her in a tree, he'd assume she was still running and keep running after her. Then, when he'd gone past her, she could climb back down and keep walking, hoping she found Raul's place before Miguel or one of his teammates found her.

Or before another of Raul's soldiers found her.

A combination of fear, sadness, and exhaustion had more tears tumbling down her cheeks.

She just wanted this to be over.

However it wound up ending.

A minute or two after she'd settled high up the tree she saw him. Miguel. Slinking past her hiding place. While he was moving quickly, he'd slowed his pace a little, probably wanting to trick her into thinking that she'd outrun him so that she would slow her own pace and he could pounce on her like the predator that he was.

It was okay. She didn't blame him for it. All he knew was that the mole was someone at Prey with insider knowledge and she certainly fit that bill. Miguel didn't know her and didn't know that she valued loyalty. He didn't know that she loved the people at Prey like a family and would never allow the Reactivator to fall into the hands of a man like Raul Castillo.

But her Prey people, surely, they would figure out the truth.

After all, she'd made it as obvious as she could while still following Raul's instructions.

If she alerted anyone at Prey, the bomb would be set off,

killing most of her family. But if she played along, she could buy time. So, she hadn't tried to hide the fact that she was taking the drug. She had booked a ticket in her own name, had worn clothes she knew were ones her people would recognize as hers and had not tried to disguise herself.

She knew they would follow her, *wanted* them to follow her, she'd just thought she'd have a little more time before they got there. She had to get the fake drug to Raul and have him disarm the bomb before she could let her people know to come in for her.

Patting her bag as she watched Miguel disappear into the jungle, she reassured herself that the fake Reactivator was still tucked safely inside.

There was no way she would risk bringing the real drug with her to Mexico.

The real vial of the drug she'd taken from the lab at Prey was sitting inside a storage locker at the airport, waiting for her to be able to activate the tracker she'd bought with her, have her people come in, and then go back and retrieve it. As soon as the bomb was gone and her family was no longer in danger, she fully intended to tell Prey everything and watch with satisfaction as the threats to her team were taken into custody.

Ella was desperate but not stupid. She'd thought through every scenario she could in the twenty-four hours she'd been given to get on a plane and done her best with what she had to work with.

But going it alone was exhausting. She wanted her team back. Wanted her Prey people around her. Heck, she even wished Miguel would come back just so she wasn't alone.

"Soon," she assured herself as she tentatively began to climb back down the tree. "Soon this will all be over. You'll trick Raul into thinking he has the real vial of the Reactivator. Your family will be safe. Prey will come. Raul will be caught. He'll give up the mole's name and she'll be caught, too. Then life can go back to normal, the way it was before this whole mess started."

Only as her feet touched the ground, Ella got the feeling that nothing was ever going to be the same again.

She was playing a dangerous game, she knew that, and she was banking on the fact that Prey would have faith in her, that they'd listen to her when she explained everything and understand that she had been in a no-win situation and had done the only thing she could to keep everyone alive and safe.

But what if she was wrong?

What if she was wrong about everything?

What if things were only going to get worse and not better?

* * *

FEBRUARY 6TH
1:11 P.M.

SHE THOUGHT she was so smart.

Miguel couldn't help but chuckle to himself as he slunk through the trees following his little runaway blonde.

When he'd caught sight of her trying to climb up the tree —something she definitely needed pointers on since it took her far too long as she almost fell at least half a dozen times —he'd known exactly how to handle this. It was obvious that Ella was not cut out for the life of a fugitive. She'd just assumed that she'd made it up the tree without getting caught, then when he'd snuck right past her, making sure she got a good look at him before moving out of her sight again, she had assumed she'd gotten what she wanted.

But this was his job, and he was good at it.

No way was he going to get trumped by some lab girl turned traitor or whatever the hell Ella was.

Because despite everything he knew as fact, and that she'd run from him, he couldn't shake the feeling that something hadn't added up.

It was her eyes.

In them was no calculation, no attempts to play him, nothing sinister or evil. In a decade as a SEAL, he'd seen plenty of evil people, looked into their eyes as they maimed and killed, looked into their eyes as they lay dying, and saw no remorse.

Ella wasn't like them.

When he looked into her eyes he saw desperation.

Whatever had led to her agreeing to give the Reactivator to Raul Castillo, it wasn't greed or power. She wasn't doing this for the money, that much he would bet his life on. What he didn't know was how much good her motivation would do in saving her from her fate. Even if she'd been black-mailed or threatened, she'd still brought the drug to the enemy and that was going to get her a prison sentence.

For now, though, he wasn't going to let on that he was following her. He hoped she would wind up leading him right to Raul, although from the looks of things she was completely and utterly lost.

Still, those had been Raul's men who had tried to rape her. He'd seen their tattoos, so Raul's place was around here somewhere, and once he found it, he was going to make sure the weapons dealer didn't slip through their fingers once again. He'd already been in contact with his team, told them to hang back, that he was on Ella's trail, and once he had confirmation that she was with Raul, he'd let them know and they could raid the place and bring the trafficker into custody.

Maybe he could even spin it somehow that Ella had helped.

Miguel had no idea why, but for some reason, he didn't want to see the woman spend the rest of her life in prison for something it was clear she didn't want to be doing. If he could try to make it look like she'd worked with him to bring down one of the world's most wanted men then that could go a long way toward reducing her sentence.

When Ella stopped up ahead of him, he stopped, too, although there was no need to make much of an attempt to hide himself. The woman spun in a slow circle but didn't do a thorough search of her environment to ensure she wasn't being followed. She was too trusting, too innocent, too inexperienced, which was why he knew she had no nefarious purpose for being out there.

"Why didn't you ask someone for help, honey?" he murmured. If she'd been threatened or blackmailed, she should have trusted her Prey family to have her back. Yet she hadn't. What did Raul Castillo have on her that she would betray the people she cared about?

Maybe she had a gambling or drug problem? Although the background check they'd been given said she was clean with no financial troubles. In fact, while she wasn't rich, she had quite a nice little nest egg from her career as a child prodigy cello player, and from the concerts she still sporadically gave. While she wasn't worth five million, she had enough that he couldn't see she would risk everything to sell the drug she helped create for that amount.

Perhaps it was a family member she was trying to protect?

Prey was going through every member of her family with a fine-tooth comb looking for a reason why Ella might have done this. No one wanted to believe they'd had a traitor in their midst and nobody had picked up on it.

With a small sob he could hear from there, Ella turned and started walking in another direction.

Miguel followed.

For a solid hour, they traipsed through the jungle. Ella walked with no purpose, just wandering aimlessly as lost people were prone to do. If she was going to play traitor, the least she could have done was work on her skills.

These were dangerous people she was playing with, and she should, at the very least, be aware of her surroundings enough to know that she was being watched. By multiple someones now, not just him.

But from the startled shriek that fell from her lips when four men dressed all in black emerged from the trees, it was clear she'd had zero idea they'd been nearby. However, Miguel sensed another few watching them, hanging back to make sure they weren't walking into a trap.

At least Raul had the good sense to be careful even if Ella didn't seem to possess an iota of sense. Desperate people often didn't though. She was too focused on her own reasons for being there to consider anything else, and if she wasn't careful it was going to get her killed.

"Wh-who are you?" Ella asked, shrinking into herself. Even from there, he could see that she was shaking. After almost being raped by Raul's men it was no wonder she was terrified to be back in their presence, but what had she thought was going to happen when she walked into the lion's den?

"Aww, you don't recognize your friends?" one of them sneered, taking a step toward Ella.

Miguel tensed.

Just because he wanted Raul Castillo in custody so that his brother and Cassie could finally get some peace and she could start healing, he wasn't going to allow Ella to be assaulted.

Odds weren't great, though. There were at least ten men in the area, and they were all focused on Ella. So far it didn't seem like anybody was aware of his presence, and he was going to use that to his advantage.

"Boss said to bring her to him when she got here," another of the men said, stopping the first before Miguel had to come up with a plan to intercede, eliminate all the threats, and still get access to the weapons trafficker.

The first man shrugged. "I don't mind waiting," he said, and Ella went all kinds of pale, almost to the point where he was worried she was about to faint. Guess she had thought she had enough sway being the one with the formula to keep her safe from Raul's men. Which was kind of ridiculous given that she knew what had happened to all three of her friends while they were prisoners of the man.

"You got the drug?" a third man asked.

"Y-yes," Ella whispered, sounding as faint as she looked.

"Then let's bring you in. Boss is angry you're late," the guy who had intervened and stopped her from being assaulted now told her as he grabbed one of her arms and began to drag her off.

A deep-seated protective rage ignited inside him at the sight of the burly man putting his bands on Ella. Just because he knew that despite her reasoning, she'd brought some of this upon herself, he didn't like seeing her manhandled. It didn't sit right with him.

There was no way he would let her get dragged off without him.

Moving quickly now, he zeroed in on the closest presence and found another of Raul's guards with his back to Miguel heading off in the same direction Ella was being taken.

Pouncing on the man before he even realized he wasn't alone, he snapped the guard's neck and let the body drop to the jungle floor. Then with quick, efficient movements, he undressed him and swapped out his own clothes with the guard's. There was no way he could fake the tattoo, but with the jacket pulled up he could cover most of his neck and hope nobody noticed. With his Hispanic looks and ability to speak several languages, including Spanish, fluently, he should be able to fit in long enough to confirm Raul's presence and call in his team.

At least, he hoped he could.

Because he was all that was standing between Ella and whatever Raul Castillo was going to allow his men to do to her when he got what he wanted from her.

The pretty blonde thought she had enough leverage to keep herself safe, but he was pretty sure she couldn't be more wrong.

CHAPTER FIVE

February 6th
   3:22 P.M.

THIS WAS the craziest thing she'd ever done.

Hands down.

There wasn't even a runner-up.

Ella had always been a good girl. She was the kind of kid who went with the flow and never made waves. She loved her music and worked hard at it because she wanted to be good like her parents, grandparents, and siblings. With schoolwork she had the same attitude, she liked to do well at everything she put her mind to. While she hadn't had a huge circle of friends, she'd had a couple of close ones in school, and they were all good girls too. It was rare for her to get into trouble about anything.

Until now anyway.

It was still surreal.

Just a month ago her life was perfect. Well close enough. There were still things she wanted and didn't have, mainly finding someone, falling in love, and having a family of her own. The desire for that had grown over the last few weeks as she saw each member of her team find their other half.

She wanted that.

Had always wanted that.

But now that dream had shimmered so far out of her reach that she knew it would never happen for her.

When she'd gotten on that plane, Ella knew there was a good chance that she would never leave Mexico alive. Not only did she not trust Raul Castillo as far as she could throw him, but she didn't trust the mole either. If her plan worked and she'd been able to alert Prey to Raul's location, and he was arrested, she'd hoped that her Prey family would know that she would never have betrayed them and that life would just go back to the way it had been before, only without a threat hovering over the heads of Athena Team.

Now she realized how naïve she'd been.

Of course, she couldn't walk out of this unscathed.

Miguel had been there to take her into custody. Even though he'd been nice about it, it had been obvious that he believed she was a lowlife criminal who had betrayed her country and that she deserved to spend the rest of her life locked up.

When she told the truth, would people believe her?

Her Prey family had to. Didn't they?

They knew her better than her own family since she spent more time with them, they had to know she would never do anything to betray them.

That was what she was clinging to at least.

But it did little to ease her anxiety as she sat in a nice, open, airy lounge room, waiting for Raul Castillo to make an appearance.

After the second group of men had found her and she'd been walked another quarter mile or so through the jungle to a mansion hidden deep amongst the trees, she'd been offered a quick visit to the bathroom before being brought to this room and left here. Not alone. There were guards at both doors, and one at the doors that led outside to a pretty little patio.

There was no way she was getting out of this room.

Not that she would even if she could.

Her family's lives were worth more to her than anything else.

Because of that, she would see this through. Sit there and wait for a man who terrified her to show up. Pretend that she had the vial of the drug Raul so desperately wanted. Get the threat against her family eliminated.

Pray it all worked.

Pray she hadn't made a mistake in not going to Prey.

Ella had wanted to. She had a much better chance of making this ploy work with them looped in on her plans, but how could she risk it when it was the mole who had set the bomb under her parents' house and the mole worked at Prey? If she tried to alert someone, there was a chance she would have tipped off the mole who she knew wouldn't have hesitated to set off the bomb.

No.

This was the only way.

And it was too late to second-guess herself now anyway. She was in Mexico sitting there in Raul's house waiting for him. Already she was too far down the path she had chosen to turn back.

Regardless of how this ended up, she had to play it out.

Still, that was easier said than done when the sound of approaching footsteps told her she was about to meet the man who had caused her friends so much pain and suffering.

When Raul stepped into the room, looking all cool and crisp in his white shirt and black suit pants, a surge of anger wiped away some of her fear. Just because she wasn't cut out for this kind of high adrenalin, life-threatening stuff didn't mean she wasn't protective of the people she cared about. Scarlett, Lucy, and Cassie were like sisters to her, she loved them, and this man had hurt them.

How could that not make her angry?

"Ms. Whitlock, would you like something to drink?" Raul asked like she was a willing guest in his home instead of being there only because she was being blackmailed and threatened.

"I don't want anything to drink. I'm not here for fun, Mr. Castillo," she returned, pleased with herself when her voice came out frosty, the thread of anger she felt evident.

Apparently, that amused Raul because he was grinning as he took a seat on the white leather couch opposite the one she was sitting on. His gaze was greedy, though, when it landed on the bag she held clutched on her lap.

As anxious as she was to get this wrapped up and get the threat to her family eliminated, it looked like the weapons trafficker was every bit as anxious.

"Is it in there?" Raul asked, obviously happy to drop the caring host act and get down to business.

Tightening her hold on the bag, Ella nodded. "I have it in here. But once I give it to you, you have to tell your partner to remove that bomb. I won't give you the formula until I know that my family isn't going to get hurt." This was a gamble, but it was the only leverage she had, and she had no choice but to play it.

Of course, Raul had his own scientists, the ones who he had intended would follow the formula and make him the drug. Given a bit of time, they would realize that this drug was nothing more than a random combination of whatever she could put together at short notice so she had something to bring with her.

All she needed was a short window, though.

As soon as Raul got the mole to disarm and remove the bomb from underneath the house, she could alert Prey to her location and this would all be over.

There was the chance that Raul would refuse until she wrote down the formula, but she had to play this confidently if she wanted any chance at getting what she wanted.

Clearly he was amused again because laughter danced in his dark eyes as he reclined back on the couch, crossing an ankle over his knee and watching her. She couldn't figure out what he was thinking or if he was going to go along with her demands. He had her trapped out there, he could torture the information out of her if he wanted to. She already knew he was impatient to get the intel he'd bought from the mole, so the chances of torture in her near future were high.

"I'll make the call," he finally announced.

"You will?" she asked, totally surprised. She'd expected a little more resistance.

"The bomb will be gone by tonight. You will start writing out the formula for my scientists after dinner. Dinner is, of course, my treat. I will have my chef prepare us a feast and you will dine with me. After that, you will get to work."

Better than she had been hoping for.

The thought of sharing a meal with this man made her feel nauseous, but at least as soon as he showed her proof that the bomb was gone, she could call in Prey. While she waited for them, she could start writing up something that would pass for the formula while she waited. It would take the scientists too long to figure out she was playing them. By the time they did, Prey would be there, and everyone would be taken into custody.

Possibly herself included.

But at least her family would be safe, and she would make Prey see she never intended to betray them.

"I'll need proof your little mole removed the bomb," she warned.

Raul chuckled like he thought she was the funniest thing he'd ever met, but he nodded. "I'll pass along your instructions." Then he pushed to his feet and stalked toward her, all traces of amusement gone, his gaze now dark, betraying the evil inside him. "But you even think about trying anything, and I can guarantee you won't like the consequences. I've had it with you and your team. I will get that formula, nothing is going to stand in my way. And my men have been waiting a long time to enjoy some fun."

With that warning resting heavily against her, Ella watched Raul walk away and wondered if she'd gotten so deep in this mess that there was no way out.

* * *

FEBRUARY 6TH
    6:05 P.M.

HE'D BEEN BIDING his time.

Waiting for the perfect opportunity to make contact with Ella, and this was it.

If Miguel had accosted her while she was sitting in the lounge room waiting for Raul to show up, he would have tipped his hand. It was pure luck that he hadn't been discovered yet.

After changing into the clothes of the guard whose neck he'd snapped, he'd joined the back of the line of guards escorting Ella to the house. No one had given him a second glance, and the fact that he could converse in Spanish made things much easier. When they'd all arrived at the hidden jungle retreat, he'd merely accepted the orders tossed his way and kept his head down so nobody noticed that he wasn't the dead guard.

From a distance, he'd watched as Ella wasn't taken down to a cell or holding room of some sort, but instead was afforded the luxury of being treated as a guest.

As much as Miguel hated to admit it, it seemed only further evidence that she was there of her own free will. If she was a prisoner like the other members of her team had been, she would be tortured for information, not invited to share a meal with the notorious weapons trafficker.

Torn between anger that the woman would turn on her friends, and a niggling in his gut that he didn't know the whole story, Miguel knew he needed to get some time alone with her where they wouldn't be interrupted so they could talk.

That option had been handed to him practically gift-wrapped when he'd been ordered to take a dress to Ella's room that Raul wanted her to wear when they had dinner. As he headed up the stairs to the room he'd been directed to, he wondered if Ella had done this because she was somehow romantically involved with the weapons dealer. If she wasn't willing to betray her friends for money maybe she was for love.

Or at least what she thought was love, because there was no way that a man like Raul Castillo was capable of an emotion such as love. The man was a psychopath, he just didn't have that in him. Maybe Ella didn't realize that yet, but sooner or later, she would. Whatever she thought was going to happen there, was going to develop between her and Raul, was never going to be a reality.

Things wouldn't go well for her when Raul grew tired of her.

When he reached the third floor and turned down the hall to the right, he was a little surprised to find a guard standing outside Ella's room. When she'd been escorted up there it had looked from where he was that she was just being shown to a room where she could freshen up and get a little rest before dinner. Was the guard there now to keep her safe from any of Raul's men who might try to assault her? Or was the guard there to stop her from getting out?

Miguel wished he knew because it would clue him in as to what side Ella was currently on.

"Bringing her the dress the boss wants her to wear to dinner," he told the guard in Spanish as he approached, holding up the slinky white silk dress.

"Can you watch her room for a while?" the guard asked, pressing a hand to his stomach, and he didn't need to say what he wanted to step away from his post to do.

Fate was practically handing him this opportunity on a silver platter. Without the guard out there, he could take his time to interrogate his pretty little blonde prisoner.

"Sure thing," he agreed, then waited until the guard handed him a key and hurried off down the hall.

So, at least he knew Ella was locked in, he just didn't know whose idea it was.

He was about to find out though.

Opening the door to find the room dark, he noticed the bulge in the middle of the bed and assumed that was Ella. If she was relaxed enough in this house to take a nap, then she couldn't be all that concerned about Raul.

Too late he realized his mistake.

He had underestimated his opponent.

Allowed himself to write her off as not a risk.

A split second before something came swinging toward his head, he noticed the presence that had been behind the door and managed to dodge out of the way.

Apparently, she wasn't going down without a fight.

Ella came at him, swinging what looked like the base of a

lamp, aiming for his head. Miguel had to give it to her, she was giving this everything she had, and she was aiming to eliminate him from the equation, to seriously hurt him, not just give him a little bump.

Did she know it was him?

Would she have attacked any guard who had come in there or did she somehow know he'd followed her there?

No.

There was no way she could know that. She thought he'd fallen for her climbing the tree trick, she would have no reason to suspect that he'd met up with some of Raul's soldiers and come to his house.

Dodging another hit aimed directly at his head, Miguel managed to snag a hold of her wrist and used it to spin her around. Dragging her up against his body, he used his superior size and strength to pin her in place. One arm wrapped across her chest, and his other kept its hold on her wrist so she couldn't try to hit him again with the vase. He had to hand it to her, she'd picked a good weapon. If she'd managed to get in a hit, she could have incapacitated him with a well-placed strike to the head. If she had the stomach for it, she even could have killed him with it, it was a heavy wood, comparable to a baseball bat in weight.

"Stop fighting me, Ella," he whispered in her ear, there was no need to shout it and alert everyone that something was going on.

He could tell the exact second his words penetrated because she stopped fighting.

Still, her breathing was heavy, and she didn't release her grip on her weapon until he exerted just enough pressure on her wrist to make her gasp in pain and drop the lamp.

"Miguel?"

"Thought you got rid of me, honey?" he drawled.

A shudder rippled through her slim body. "I'm so glad you're here."

In his career as a SEAL, he'd rescued plenty of victims. Every single one of them had the same thread of relief and gratefulness, along with a little awe and disbelief in their tone that Ella just had in hers.

"Tell me the truth, Ella. All of it. Now," he added as he pressed on a pressure point on her wrist that he knew would indicate he wasn't messing around. The last thing he wanted was to hurt an innocent woman, but right now, he didn't know for sure that she was innocent.

She whimpered in his hold but didn't try to pull her arm away even though he knew he was causing her pain.

"I want to know everything, Ella. Why you stole the drug, why you're here in Raul's house, and why I brought you a revealing dress he expects you to wear for dinner. I want to know how involved you are. Are you the mole? Did you sell the Reactivator? Were you the one responsible for what happened to Scarlett, Lucy, and Cassie?"

Just like he'd seen a lot of victims, he'd also seen a lot of evil men and women. He knew that they didn't always appear evil until you looked closer. Just because Ella looked all sweet and innocent with her long blonde locks, wide green eyes, and the kind of smile that made you feel like you were being bathed in warm sunlight, didn't mean that she was either sweet or innocent.

So far, her behavior said she was selfish and reckless, determined to get what she wanted without caring about who she hurt in the process. And since one of those people who had gotten hurt was the woman he was sure would one day soon become his sister-in-law, this was personal to him.

Spinning Ella around, he shoved her up against the wall. Using one hand, he pinned both her wrists above her head and caged her in with his body. Towering over her, he didn't try to look less menacing, allowing his height and size to further intimidate his captive little blonde, because he needed to know the truth once and for all.

Leaning in close, he let his lips hover millimeters above hers. Despite everything he knew and all the uncertainties between them, he'd love nothing more than to crush his mouth to hers and kiss her like he'd wanted to ever since he first laid eyes on her. Instead, he whispered a threat he wasn't sure he'd be able to follow through on. "Don't lie to me, Ella. Trust me, you won't like the consequences if you do."

CHAPTER SIX

February 6th
   6:17 P.M.

Right now, Ella didn't even care that the pressure point thing Miguel had done to her arm still had arrows of pain shooting up and down her forearm, or that he was holding her pinned against the wall, or that she was going to have bruises come morning.

Relief.

That was all she felt.

Miguel was there.

She was safe.

There was no way to properly explain the sense of security that seemed to seep down into her until it reached her very soul, but that's how she felt. With Miguel there, it didn't seem to matter that she was still trapped inside the home of a dangerous criminal, she believed that everything was going to be okay.

"Start talking, Ella," Miguel commanded, increasing the

pressure around her wrists until she winced and chewed on her bottom lip to hold in a moan of pain.

She had to make a choice.

Keep her secrets until she knew for sure the bomb was no longer an issue or trust that she was in way over her head and that she needed Miguel.

Considering everything she'd risked so far, it was an easy decision to make.

Trust Miguel.

He was there, he was trained, and she knew he had the skills to keep them both alive. Besides, she was exhausted from carrying around the heavy weight of the lives of her family resting squarely on her shoulders.

"I'll tell you everything," she agreed, more than ready to share her burden.

"I'll know if you lie," Miguel warned, only it was unnecessary, she had no intention of not telling the whole truth.

When he stepped away from her and indicated that she should take a seat on the bed, Ella immediately missed the proximity. She'd hidden the pillows in the bed and drawn the curtains as soon as being locked in there, then grabbed the only weapon she could find and hidden in case she needed to defend herself from an attack. Which she thought she did when the door to her room opened. Once she knew it was Miguel she'd relaxed, allowed herself to feel safe, to know she wasn't going to have to kill to protect herself because Miguel would take care of her.

"Start from the beginning," he ordered as he stood between her and the door with his arms crossed over his broad chest. She wasn't really sure if he was standing there to stop her from making a run for it, or in case one of Raul's guards came into her room. Either way, she wasn't complaining because he was a layer of protection for her regardless of his motivations.

The beginning.

Right.

A good idea, only words seemed to stick in her throat.

You can do this.

You have *to do this.*

If she didn't, this might all have been for nothing, and her family might die anyway.

Drawing in a deep breath, Ella did her best to settle her nerves. Nothing she could say would make her situation better so she may as well just tell Miguel everything and get it over with.

"I'm not the mole," she whispered, hanging her head.

"Eyes on me, Ella," Miguel commanded, but there was no anger in his voice, and she drew strength from that and lifted her head again to meet his gaze.

"I didn't write any emails to Raul Castillo offering him the Reactivator. I would never do that to my friends. I didn't have anything to do with Scarlett getting kidnapped, or the plane crash that almost killed Lucy and Zander, or the bombs." With each word she spoke her confidence grew. It felt so good to say all of this out loud.

"When were you contacted?" Miguel asked, and the fact that he was asking as though he believed her gave her even more confidence.

"The same day that Cassie disarmed the bomb on the cruise ship. I was ambushed at home. Four men. They shoved me into a chair and showed me a video of someone setting a bomb under my parents' house. My sister and her family live there, Miguel. Her youngest is only five months old," her voice hitched, and Miguel grew blurry as tears filled her eyes.

He didn't say anything, just stood there watching her, and she knew he was assessing every word she said, trying to determine if she was telling the truth.

What she really needed now was a little comfort.

Someone to hold her and tell her that everything was going to be okay. Reassure her that the mess the mole had thrown her into wasn't going to keep dragging her down like quicksand.

But she didn't get that.

All she got was a SEAL staring at her, not unkindly, but not with the gentleness she needed right now either.

Dragging in another breath Ella continued, "I was scared, and I fought them, but I was outnumbered and outmatched, and it was hopeless. They held me down and … and … burned the soles of my feet with cigarettes while they gave me instructions. I was told that I had twenty-four hours to be on a plane to Mexico with the vial of the Reactivator or the bomb would be set off, killing my parents, my sister, her husband, and three children. I didn't have a choice," she whispered.

"We always have a choice, Ella."

Anger sparked inside her at the calm way he said that. How dare he belittle her fear for her family and act like she had options when the facts were she hadn't.

"Yeah?" she challenged, shoving to her feet, consequences of disobeying him be damned. "What other choice did I have? The bomb could be set off remotely, which means as soon as the mole got word that I'd told someone, my family would be dead. The mole works at Prey so they have access to our communications. We know Scarlett's phone was bugged which means the mole had the skills to listen in on other devices. Even if they weren't, they were likely watching my parents' house, and as soon as they saw my family being evacuated they would have known I'd talked and set the bomb off anyway, killing not just my family but whoever went there to transport them someplace safe. So tell me, Miguel, what other choice did I have?"

When he said nothing, her anger only grew.

How could he judge her when he would have done the same exact thing she did?

"Are you telling me if it was your family who had been threatened you would have risked their lives?" she asked, cocking a brow, knowing he had no choice but to confirm she was right.

"If it was my family, I would have done whatever it took to protect them, consequences be damned," he acknowledged. "But you took the drug, Ella. You brought it here."

"I didn't," she informed him.

"You're on camera stealing it."

"I took it from the lab, yes. I had to. The mole was likely watching the security footage, so I didn't have a choice, I couldn't risk faking it. But I did not bring it to Mexico."

Arching a brow like he didn't believe he asked, "Then what did I see you hand over to Raul a couple of hours ago?"

"A fake. Something I threw together from whatever we had on hand at the lab. I would *never* risk a man like Raul Castillo getting his hands on the real drug. I rented a storage locker at the airport, the real vial of the drug is there, safe and sound."

Surprise flickered through his dark eyes. "So how did you think this was going to play out? You had to know that once Raul's scientists discovered the drug you brought was a fake he'd torture you for the information."

"I had a plan. The fake vial was just to buy time. I thought I could use it as a bargaining tool to get him to have the mole remove the bomb. Then, once I knew my family was safe, I was going activate a tracker I brought with me so Prey would know where I was. I didn't use a disguise, so I thought you'd already be in Mexico and close by. All I had to do was give him a formula close enough to the real thing to keep the scientists from getting suspicious and buy enough time for Prey to show up."

Maybe it wasn't the best plan ever, but Ella felt it was a solid one, especially given this wasn't what she usually did, and she'd had limited time to come up with it.

"It worked, too. The real drug is safe. I sent a time-delayed email to my team to let them know where it was in case I didn't make it out of this alive. Raul said he's going to get the mole to remove the bomb. And you're here, which means there's a whole team of SEALs nearby, and this time, Raul isn't going to slip through our fingers."

"One little problem with your plan, Ella. You're a wanted fugitive and your parents' house is being watched in case you try to make contact with them. There's no way the mole will risk going in and removing the bomb because there's no chance they can do it without getting caught."

With those words, the bottom fell out of her world.

Everything she'd done had been for nothing.

Her family was going to die anyway.

* * *

February 6ᵀᴴ
6:31 P.M.

He caught her as her knees buckled.

Miguel knew he'd been cruel to deliver the blow the way he had, but he needed to make sure Ella was telling him the truth.

Her reaction pretty much proved that she had.

No way could she possibly fake that kind of terror.

Feeling like a jerk for pushing her when she was clearly teetering on the edge of exhaustion after a two-day-long ordeal, Miguel gathered her into his arms and carried her back to the bed.

Despite her earlier show of spirit, it seemed like all the fight had now drained right out of her.

He didn't like that.

While maybe she could have found a way to alert someone to the fact that she'd been threatened, he could see how she would have felt like she had no other option but to do what she did. And given that she had stashed the drug somewhere in the country, she was one of the people who created it, so it was at least a quarter hers, she hadn't even really committed any crime.

Her plan was insane given her lack of field experience, but he didn't think it could in any way be considered treason.

Setting her on the bed, Miguel kept an arm around her shoulders while he pulled the pillows out from under the covers and propped them against the headboard, leaning Ella back to rest against them. Her eyes were wide and vacant and so very full of fear that he wanted to do whatever it took to soothe it away.

Unfortunately, he couldn't.

Just because he had deliberately delivered the news that her parents' house was being watched in a way he could get her true reaction didn't mean that it wasn't true. Because it was. With people watching the house, there was no way the mole would risk going in and removing it even if Raul did have enough sway over them to get them to do it, and Miguel wasn't sure that he did.

The mole was rogue.

Whatever the initial plan had been, the mole was off on their own tangent now, doing their own thing.

Wanting to snap Ella out of her shock-induced haze, he slid his hands down her calves to her feet and removed her sneakers and socks.

When the shoes hit the floor with a thud, Ella startled.

For a moment, her gaze was blank when she looked at him but then anger and hurt shone through.

"Checking to see if I was lying about them burning me?" she asked, not quite enough heat to her tone, but enough to know she was doing her best to push through her fear and function.

He could lie, tell her he was, but the truth was, he'd always felt like there was more going on than they'd realized. While the others might have believed that she was the mole and had betrayed them all, he'd just known in his gut that it wasn't true. Just because her family didn't know they had been threatened didn't mean they hadn't, and as it turned out, they had in fact been threatened.

Miguel didn't want any more lies between them though. He believed she'd told him the truth, and while there were no guarantees in life, he was going to move forward under the assumption that Ella was no traitor and work with her as a team.

"No, honey, I don't need proof that you weren't lying. I *do* need to see if your feet are healing," he told her gently as he lifted one of her feet. If she'd been in a panic ever since being attacked in her home, trying to come up with a way to protect both her family and the drug, then he very much doubted she'd given herself any first aid.

Add in the fact that she'd been running through the jungle for hours and he shouldn't have been surprised to see the red blistered welts on the soles of her feet.

Sucking in a breath, he looked up to find her watching him with a confused expression. "Honey, how did you walk so far on these?"

Ella shrugged. "Honestly, I wasn't even thinking about them. They stopped hurting almost immediately after they burned me because I was too worried about my family."

That right there told him everything he needed to know.

"Miguel ... is my parents' house really being watched?" she asked, chewing on her bottom lip, from the looks of it trying to hold in her emotions. "You ... you weren't just tricking me? To see if I slipped up?"

Bursting her bubble of denial wasn't fun, but he wasn't going to lie, that wasn't who he was. "I wasn't trying to trick you, Ella. Prey has people watching their house, and yours, and your other siblings, in case you turned up at any one of them."

Her throat moved as she swallowed. "They really believed I was the mole?" she asked in a small voice.

Answering that made his gut churn because he could see the stark pain in her big green eyes. "Things looked bad when you were right there on the security footage taking the drug and then you went right to the airport and got on a plane to Mexico."

Lifting a shaking hand, she brushed at her eyes, catching the couple of stray tears that escaped. "I thought they would give me the benefit of the doubt," she whispered, more to herself it seemed than to him.

"Hey." Setting her feet down, he moved up the bed and nudged her chin with his knuckle so he had her attention. "Everyone is stressed, and your sudden disappearance threw everyone. But deep down, I'm sure they knew you would never betray them like that. Now we'll have proof. The drug where you said it was, the email you scheduled, the bomb under your parents' house. Everything will work out."

"Not if the bomb goes off, I'll have risked everything for nothing."

"I have a plan, Ella. We'll keep your family safe." It was on the tip of his tongue to issue a promise, but he held back. Right now, he couldn't make promises.

"A plan?" she asked, looking at him with such hope, such trust, that it made something shift inside him. When was the last time a woman had looked at him like that? Usually, women saw his body and not much else. They wanted him for sex because he worked hard for his physique, and they loved the whole mysterious SEAL vibe.

Ella seemed to look past that.

Yes, she needed his protection and his help right now, but it was that she looked at him like he held the key to solving all her problems. She had every reason not to trust him since he'd come to Mexico to bring her into custody, and yet it was clear that she did.

"My team is with me. When you did the whole hide in the tree thing I decided to follow you." He winked at her when her cheeks heated to let her know he was teasing. "They were going to wait until I let them know I was ready for them, then we were going to take down you and Raul. But I have a different idea now. I'm going to contact them and tell them to pretend they have you in custody and are bringing you home. That way, the mole should get wind of it, and with you set up to take the fall for them, setting the bomb off would no longer be advantageous for them. In fact, it would be counterproductive."

The plan wasn't foolproof, but it was better than nothing.

It should buy them enough time to keep Ella's family safe while another team came in and they finally caught Raul.

"That could work," Ella said hopefully, some of the fear receding and he felt he could take a full breath again. For some reason, this woman's emotions seemed to be able to leech out of her, into the atmosphere, and then inside him. It was weird and … not completely unpleasant, just nothing like he had ever experienced before.

"It means you staying here and playing this out with Raul until another team comes to help get us out," he cautioned. This plan came with plenty of risks and Ella would be taking the brunt of them.

"You're going to be here, too, right?" she asked anxiously. "You're not leaving me?"

"No, honey, I won't leave you. I'll be here, but I won't be able to make contact with you again. You're going to have to do what you came here to do, pretend you're going to hand over the formula. Pretend you believe him when he gives you what is going to be false information regarding the bomb being disarmed. Go to dinner with him tonight."

Ella gulped when he mentioned that but nodded.

"It also means going ahead knowing the mole will make contact with him at some point to report that you've been caught and taken into custody. Right now, I'm banking on the fact that Raul never bothered contacting the mole about the bomb, but I could be wrong. As soon as they talk it will come out that there are reports you've been captured. Since you can't be in two places at the same time, and Raul knows you're here, he's going to suspect that you're somehow playing him. This plan puts you in more danger than you were already in," he warned.

"But my family will be in a safer position."

"They should be."

"Then I can take whatever the risks to me," Ella said with a determination that would make any SEAL proud.

The problem was, he was starting to wonder if *he* could handle knowing Ella was in such a precarious position.

CHAPTER SEVEN

February 7th
   12:02 A.M.

THIS HAD SOUNDED a whole lot easier to do in theory than it turned out to be in practice.

Ella had assumed the dinner with Raul would be a relatively brief affair. She'd wear the dress he chose for her, something a whole lot more revealing than she was used to but she hadn't made a fuss, just put it on and tried not to think about how it barely covered her backside and was low enough cut that part of her breasts were on display for all to see. She'd sit with him at the table in the grand dining room and eat a meal, doing her best not to worry with each bite that she was being poisoned.

Then that would be that.

He'd send her back up to her room until morning, or perhaps take her straight to a lab and make her get right to work.

Either of those options she could have coped with.

Barely, but knowing she wasn't alone anymore would have given her the strength to do what she needed to do.

Only that wasn't what had happened.

Dinner turned out to be a big affair with a dozen other guests and was still going hours later.

The worst part was that Miguel was nowhere in sight.

She knew he was out there somewhere, watching over her as best he could while still maintaining his cover as one of Raul's guards. Ella hadn't asked how he'd made it onto the estate or how he got the guard's outfit. She didn't want to know the details, and besides, her mind could easily imagine the answer. He'd killed one of them because he'd been following her and wondered if she was going to lead him right to the weapons trafficker.

And she had.

Just not in the way he probably thought she would.

It didn't bother her that he'd killed another man, he was a SEAL, it was part of his job, and besides, the two men he'd killed first had been about to rape her, and whoever he killed to steal their spot on the team was going to wind up saving not just her life but her family's, too.

Ella was glad he was there she just wished he was right beside her instead of off somewhere else.

Maybe if Miguel was right by her side, Raul would stop giving her those heated gazes that made her blood turn to ice. He kept using every excuse to touch her as well and it took all her mental willpower to keep from shying away each time his hand came toward her.

The dealer's touch made her nauseous, but earlier, in the bedroom upstairs, when Miguel had touched her, held her, and gently cleaned the blisters on her feet, it had soothed her racing heartbeat and filled her with calm and confidence.

Now she needed another hit of that secure feeling only Miguel could bring her.

Too bad he wasn't there to give it to her.

Heat flushed her cheeks as she thought about what else she'd love for Miguel to give her. He'd been the star of more than one fantasy over the last several weeks, and if her life hadn't so drastically fallen apart, she might have seen if he could turn all those dreams into reality.

But right now, it was hard enough holding onto some semblance of sanity. She had no leftover energy to imagine sharing a bed with a man like Miguel.

"Ella, darling," Raul drawled, and she couldn't help a small shiver at the way he said her name. There was beginning to be a hint of possessiveness to it, and she had a sinking feeling that she knew what his plans were for her once she gave him the formula he wanted, and it wasn't killing her.

It was something worse.

Because being kept as a toy for a notorious weapons trafficker was a fate worse than death.

"Would you like to dance?" Raul asked.

A no almost came bursting out before she could stop it. Somehow, she managed to keep control of her mouth because turning down a man like Raul at what seemed to be some sort of dinner party even though she had no idea who any of the guests were, was a recipe for disaster. All she needed to do was play the game for a little longer until whoever the new team was who was coming in there to capture Raul arrived.

She could do that.

Maybe.

Hopefully.

Had to.

This wasn't just about her, other people were counting on her. Not just her family, and not just her team, but lots of innocent people would be hurt if Raul continued to stay free, continued dealing in weapons, and selling them to people he knew were going to use them to kill thousands.

Failing here wasn't an option.

"Can I just pop to the bathroom first?" she asked, running the tip of her tongue over her bottom lip and realizing too late her mistake as she watched Raul's hungry gaze follow the movement.

"Be quick," he answered, waving a dismissive hand at her.

Yeah right.

She was going to take as long as she felt she could get away with. Maybe Miguel was close enough that he'd see her slip away and make contact with her. Ella could really do with a little infusion of Miguel's magic right about now. Especially if she was going to have to go back out there and dance with Raul.

Dancing meant letting him touch her.

Intimately.

While wearing this dress that all but left her on display.

Without a major infusion of the calm and confidence Miguel seemed to be able to bring her, she had no idea how she was going to endure that.

It was weird, she thought as she found the downstairs bathroom and pushed inside, drawing in a deep breath as she was enveloped with quiet and privacy, because Miguel had come there intending to take her into custody, and yet, he had believed in her so easily.

Easier it seemed than her own team did.

Pain lanced her chest as she thought of the three women she loved like sisters believing even for one second that she would betray them. Ella felt so conflicted, she knew she'd made herself look guilty, and yet, at the same time, she kept wondering how her team could believe she was guilty. When Scarlett had been set up all of them had known without a sliver of doubt that she was innocent. Why hadn't her friends afforded her the same benefit of the doubt?

Knowing that even if Miguel's plan worked and they made it out of there alive and back home, her life would never be the same again left her feeling empty. She'd been prepared to face prison time if it meant her family were alive, but she'd never truly considered the fact that Prey would believe she was guilty.

Ella was so lost in thought, grieving the loss of the people she considered to be family, that she didn't realize anyone was in the bathroom as she came out of the toilet stall until it was too late.

Until she'd been shoved up against the wall.

A hand clamped over her mouth, muffling her scream as it tried to escape.

It was one of the guards and she didn't even have to look at him to know he was drunk, she could smell the alcohol on his breath as his face loomed above hers.

"Pretty hair," he mumbled as his free hand tangled in her long locks, which she'd left loose hoping she might be able to angle it so it covered her breasts.

Now it was being used against her.

The man tugged hard, making her eyes fill with tears at the stinging on her scalp.

She tried to fight her way out of his grip, but he was so much bigger than her, and he was pinning her in place with his body making it hard for her to find a way to kick out at him.

Still, her fingers clawed at the hand on her mouth, and she wriggled and squiggled to the best of her ability as a meaty hand nudged her thighs apart, heading with precision and purpose right to her panties.

A tearing sound told her her panties had just been ripped,

and then the next thing she knew, a finger was being shoved inside her.

With renewed vigor, she strengthened her efforts to get away.

Already the man was unzipping himself and pulling his erection free from his pants and underwear.

It looked grotesque as he guided it toward her and blind panic had her fighting like a crazy person, anything to stop him putting that thing inside her. His finger was bad enough but the thought of that in her body had her losing control.

Which wound up working in her favor.

Struggling to keep his hold on her mouth and get himself inside her at the same time, the hand on her mouth slipped slightly and she took full advantage.

Sinking her teeth into the tender skin of his palm, she bit down until she tasted blood, then when the hand yanked away, she let out an ear-piercing scream and prayed it was enough to alert anyone nearby that something was wrong.

* * *

FEBRUARY 7TH
   12:26 A.M.

RAGE CLOUDED his vision as he slammed open the door to the bathroom and saw Ella shoved up against the wall with one of the guards pinning her in place.

She was seconds away from being raped and fighting with everything she had to give.

Pride for her warred with his fury toward the man attempting to violate her.

Even if he'd been armed with a weapon he could use

without drawing attention to the situation, Miguel would have wanted to use his bare hands for this. There was a protective and bloodthirsty part of him that wanted to know he'd killed the man trying to take something from Ella she didn't want to give with nothing but what God gave him.

Drunk out of his mind if the smell was anything to go by and preoccupied with his desire to get himself inside the helpless woman at his mercy, the other man didn't even notice Miguel approaching him until his hands were wrapped around his neck.

The guard fought clumsily and uncoordinated, but he fought, even reaching for his weapon at one point. But he was no match for Miguel and the anger raging inside him.

Slowly the man's attempts at fighting for his life dwindled until he was nothing but dead weight. Still, Miguel struggled to unclamp his hands from around the man's neck even though he was dead and no longer a threat.

This man had tried to hurt Ella.

That enraged him in a way he'd never experienced before.

He loved women, he had fun with them, unlike his brother, he didn't go back to the same woman more than once, and it was only ever one night. He'd never felt anything even remotely close to what he already felt for Ella toward any other woman.

She'd been prepared to sacrifice everything for her family.

Including her own life or her freedom.

Even though it terrified her, she had walked into the lion's den with nothing other than hopes and prayers that her plan would work.

Ella reminded him so much of his brother Luis, who bravely took on the role of protector when they were kids. Who had done whatever he had to do to make sure they had food to eat, who had taken beatings to spare him, who had devised a plan—albeit a terrible one—to get them a better life. One that had wound up working just not in the way Luis had thought it would.

His brother was a protector, he was brave, and he did what he had to do without complaining, just like Ella had. Miguel couldn't remember a time when he hadn't looked up to his big brother and hadn't wanted to be just like him. Now he couldn't not look at Ella with an air of awe. Her bravery was impressive, and while he wished she'd found a way to clue in her team so she hadn't walked into this mess alone, he respected that she had prioritized her family over herself, while still remaining true to her Prey people.

Now he'd let her down.

Hadn't been there when she needed him.

Standing there shivering, torn panties hanging tangled around her ankles, the dress he'd had to force himself to let her wear to dinner when all he'd wanted to do was cover her properly so Raul wouldn't be leering at her disheveled, Miguel was confronted with just how badly he'd failed.

"I'm sorry, honey," he murmured as he finally forced his fingers to uncurl and dropped the dead body of the guard at their feet. Taking a tentative step toward her, he lifted a hand, intending to palm her cheek and brush away the black tracks of mascara mixing with her tears and trailing down her cheeks. At the last moment, he dropped his hand to his side. After what she'd almost endured, it was presumptuous to assume she'd want anyone touching her right now.

Ella's gaze was locked on the dead body of her assailant, her chest beginning to rise and fall more sharply as her breathing increased to the point where she was almost hyperventilating.

Knowing he had to calm her before she completely lost

control if he wanted any hope of getting her out of there alive and in one piece, Miguel nudged her chin with a single knuckle, keeping the contact brief, just enough to draw her attention. When she looked away from the body, he offered her what he hoped was an encouraging smile.

"You did good, honey. I'm proud of you, but I need you to hold it together. Can you do that for me?" He knew she could, but at the moment, what he knew didn't matter. Ella had to know she was strong enough to compartmentalize long enough for him to get them out of there. While he could handle the situation with her hysterical it would make it a whole lot harder.

Before his eyes, he watched as she locked her gaze onto his. When she lifted a trembling hand, he had no idea what she intended to do with it until she tentatively rested it on his chest, above his heart, and he realized she was trying to slow her breathing by matching it to his.

The feel of her small hand on his chest, right over his heart, sent his emotions haywire, and since now was not the time to attempt to make sense of them he ignored them all and instead focused on the woman doing her best not to fall apart.

"There you go, honey. That was smart," he encouraged, pressing one of his hands above hers, letting her know with his touch as well as his words that she wasn't alone. He was right there and he wasn't going anywhere.

Bit by bit her breathing slowed. Her unblinking gaze never wavered from his and it took Miguel a moment to realize his thumb was brushing lazy circles across her hand because he was losing himself staring into her deep green eyes.

"Good girl, you've slowed your breathing," he murmured when it was pretty much back to normal. They'd used up as much time as they could. Raul seemed to be developing an obsession with Ella. While Miguel hadn't been able to keep eyes on her every second, he'd seen enough to recognize the way the weapons trafficker looked at her.

Possessively.

The man wasn't going to let Ella go.

The longer they stayed there the more they tempted fate. Raul wasn't going to wait long before sending someone to find Ella and return her to the dining room.

Plus, there was the added concern of the fact that the number of guards at the estate was down by two. Sooner or later, someone was going to find the bodies of the men who had tried to assault Ella in the jungle, and he didn't want to be anywhere near there when that happened, because then Raul would know there was a traitor somewhere.

While he would have liked to be able to hole up there until a team came in to capture Raul, that wasn't a viable option anymore. It wouldn't take long for the guards to realize he was the one who didn't belong there.

Right now, the safest option was to get Ella out of there, find a place to hide in the jungle, and wait for rescue. While Miguel usually liked to be proactive and in the thick of things, the idea of hiding out with Ella wasn't as unappealing as he would have thought.

"You going to be okay?" he asked, already running through their options.

"For now," Ella replied, a shaky nod accompanying the words.

"That's all I need. We have to get out of here."

"I thought the plan was to wait here until help came." Although she said it, he didn't miss the way she shuddered at the thought of staying in Raul's presence. Ella was smart and she had no doubt already picked up on the man's signals toward her.

"If they don't already know guards are missing, it's only a matter of time before they find the bodies and realize one of us isn't who he's supposed to be. I don't want us here when that happens. I'm going to get you to change into the guard's clothes," he said, kicking a foot at the dead man and doing his best to ignore the way her color dropped a couple of shades. "You're small, but so long as we keep moving no one should pay us much attention and notice the size discrepancies. You still have the tracker on you?"

"Yes."

"Good. We're going to climb the back fence and head out into the jungle. The tracker will make it easier for us to be found."

"Okay," Ella quickly agreed, handing him her trust like it was no big deal. And maybe it shouldn't be. After all, he was the expert here, and she was a lab worker, but it felt like something huge.

"Get rid of the dress and pop this on." Miguel reluctantly let go of Ella's hand after giving it a quick squeeze, and then crouched and began to strip the man. He couldn't help but feel as though a clock was rapidly counting down, and he hurried Ella as much as he dared to get her into the guard's clothes.

There was no way the shoes would do her any good, which meant for now, she was stuck with the strappy pair of heels Raul had given her to wear. Not ideal at all for running through the jungle, but he didn't want to waste the time it would take to send her up to her room to get her sneakers.

"The key to fitting in is to act like you belong," he told her as they headed out of the bathroom and toward the nearest exit.

It worked.

Nobody stopped them as they headed outside.

Nobody stopped them as they walked through the gardens.

Nobody stopped them as they reached the fence and started to climb it.

It wasn't until they were halfway up that the first shot was fired.

CHAPTER EIGHT

February 7th
    12:53 A.M.

S<small>OMEONE WAS SHOOTING AT HER.</small>

Someone was shooting at Miguel.

They were being *shot* at.

Panic had her muscles freezing and Ella stopped right at the top of the fence, one leg on either side, unsure what she was supposed to do. She had no weapon, even if she did, she was barely proficient at using it. Scarlett was the expert on their team and Lucy was good, too. Cassie was good only because she was good at everything and not because she particularly liked shooting.

She was the worst.

She hated guns.

Hated the loud bang they made when fired.

It always hurt her ears.

Now there was so much shooting that the bangs all joined

together in one loud explosion of sound, and she cowered, curling in on herself, her panic growing by the second.

What were they going to do?

They were trapped. She was useless. It was Miguel against all of Raul's guards. It was hopeless.

Now that they'd tried escaping, Raul was going to know that she'd gone there with ulterior motives. That meant as soon as his men got their hands on her, she was going to be tortured.

"Ella, come on, honey, you've been so brave, but I need you to hang on a little longer. Can you do that for me?"

Miguel's calm, soothing voice cut through a little of her panic and she forced herself to latch onto it. Just like she'd placed a hand on his chest earlier and used it to mimic his breathing, calming herself and somehow pulling her back from the brink of hysteria, now she allowed his quiet tone to wash over her, cooling the worst of her panic. She had no idea how he was able to still be calm given their near insurmountable odds, but she admired it. If not for him, she'd have been raped several times over already, and now he was the only thing standing between her and death.

"I ... I'm okay," she forced the words out because the last thing she wanted to do was risk the life of the man who was trying to save her. If he needed her to be in control, then she would somehow scrounge up some control.

"I know you are. I know you've got this, you just have to know it, too."

Again, the confidence in his tone managed to infuse just a teeny bit into her. But a teeny bit was all she needed to work with right now.

"I want you to jump down and run," he ordered. "Don't stop. I'll come find you, just get yourself someplace where you can hide. As soon as you get off the fence activate the tracker."

"But what about you?"

"Don't worry about me. Just run and hide. And, Ella." In the dark, she could see the circle of his face peering up at her even if she couldn't make out his eyes. "If you get caught, tell them who I am. That I'm a SEAL, that I was sent here to capture you because you're a wanted traitor. Tell them I took you against your will. That the guard in the bathroom was trying to save you and I killed him and kidnapped you."

Ella gasped and shook her head vehemently against his words. "If I tell them that they'll kill you."

"If you don't they'll torture and kill you. Go. Now."

As badly as she wanted to stay and argue against his words, protest that there was no way she could willingly sign his death warrant, Ella knew that the longer she stayed, the more she was distracting Miguel. The more she distracted him the less chance he had of getting away alive.

With tears tumbling down her cheeks, she dragged her other leg over the fence and avoided looking down. Heights were not her thing, and if she allowed herself to look at the distance between the top of the fence and the ground, and worry about all the injuries she could cause herself landing, then she was never going to be able to jump.

Miguel believes in you.

He needs you.

Don't let him down.

Somehow knowing that their lives were tied together at the moment helped her find the courage to let go.

The fall felt like it went in slow motion, lasting several minutes, but really, she knew it was barely a couple of seconds before her feet hit the ground.

Because she was wearing the world's most impractical pair of escaping shoes, her ankles both gave way beneath her as pain speared up through her feet and into her legs, hips, and torso, and she tumbled sideways.

There was no time to dwell on the pain. Gunshots were still firing at the fence, and she knew without needing to turn her head and look over her shoulder that Miguel was firing back.

Buying her time to get away.

Even at the expense of his own life.

Tears continued to fall down her cheeks as she took off into the jungle. The shoes were utterly useless, doing more harm than good, so she paused just long enough to kick them off before she kept running. The blisters littering her soles protested, but in reality, her feet weren't any worse off without the shoes. They'd cause their own blisters and do little to protect her from the sticks, roots, rocks, and other debris that littered the ground. Besides, wearing them while running through the jungle would almost guarantee a broken ankle.

Gunshots began to fade. The jungle was relatively quiet at this time of night, and for a second, she wished for the too-loud bangs of the guns being fired because at least that meant she wasn't alone.

Now she was.

The silence was too loud.

Too terrifying.

She felt trapped all over again, only this time in a different way than being locked in Raul's house.

"The tracker, activate the tracker," she told herself aloud just to break the crushing silence.

Her fingers fumbled as she found the tracker she'd hidden in a cute tiara ring she always wore. It looked too small to fit a tracker, and since it was a simple piece of jewelry, she'd hoped that Raul's men wouldn't remove it if they decided to search her.

With the tracker activated, she spun in a slow circle.

What should she do now?

Keep running?

Wait for Miguel?

What if he never came?

What if he was already dead?

Don't be dead.

Please, don't be dead.

"Told you to hide, honey."

The voice startled a squawk out of her, and she spun around to see Miguel standing right behind her. How had he done that? How had he snuck right up behind her without her even realizing it? Probably the same way he'd tricked her when she thought she lost him by hiding in the tree and never noticed that he was following her the entire time.

Ignoring the reprimand in his voice, Ella just threw herself at him, wrapping her arms around his neck and her legs around his waist and clinging to him. He was alive. The relief at knowing he'd escaped, too, was almost overwhelming, and not just because she needed him to get her out of there alive.

Because he'd been kind to her when he hadn't had to. He'd killed for her on two occasions. He'd been willing to sacrifice his life to give her a chance.

"You're alive," she whispered, burying her face against his neck.

Slowly, his arms came up to hold her, and he gave her a tight squeeze. "Course. Wasn't going to leave you alone out here," he said, tone light-hearted, but she could feel the tension in his body.

That wasn't all she could feel.

This position was more intimate than she'd realized when she threw herself at him. In the moment, all she cared about was holding onto the man who would have made the ultimate sacrifice for her without giving it a second thought. Now that she was in his arms, she could feel the hardening ridge of an erection nestled right against the part of her that had been violated earlier.

A wave of panic at the thought of anyone touching her there ever again was chased away by a wave of desire for this man and this man only. Another wave of panic followed in its wake as she remembered the feel of the guard's finger forcing its way inside her, and she quickly pushed at Miguel's shoulders, needing to not be touched right now.

Like he seemed so good at reading her, he set her on her feet and even took a step back to give her space.

"Sorry," she murmured, completely mortified. Ella wasn't even sure what she was apologizing for. For almost getting him killed? For implying he was like the man who would have raped her? For throwing herself at him? For reacting to his touch?

"Hey, you don't have anything to be sorry about, you've had a hell of a last couple of days," Miguel spoke in that soothing tone that actually seemed to work at calming her nerves.

Just as she was about to thank him for what he'd done in the bathroom and just now at the fence, he stiffened and spun around.

A second too late.

Another bang.

Another gunshot.

This one must have hit its target if the grunt of pain from Miguel was anything to go by.

Something dark and deadly stirred inside her.

Someone had hurt Miguel.

The man who had risked so much for her, who had believed in her even when the people who knew her best hadn't.

A growl that kind of sounded more like a baby lion than

the king of the jungle rumbled out of her, and she threw herself at the man emerging from the trees.

Caught by surprise, she managed to knock him down, and the next thing she knew they were rolling down a decline in a tangle of limbs.

Ella lost count of how many times her body slammed into things, and by the time she and the man landed with a splash in a river, she was dangerously close to losing consciousness.

* * *

FEBRUARY 7TH
    1:13 A.M.

PAIN RADIATED down from his shoulder.

Damn it.

He'd allowed himself a moment of distraction and it had gotten him shot.

Miguel cursed his own stupidity. It was his feelings for Ella that had done it. When she'd thrown herself into his arms, everything other than the feel of her against his body had fled from his mind.

Like the open book that she was, he'd felt the myriad of emotions flash through her. Desire had warred with fear, and with it had come rising panic. Even though she'd been the one to initiate contact, she'd quickly needed distance and he'd given it to her. While he would have loved to hold her, soothe her fears, reassure her that she was safe and that he'd never hurt her, he'd given her what she needed and set her down.

The mumbled apology almost had him rethinking that decision.

He would never disrespect a woman by touching her

when she indicated she wanted space, but the urge to hold her and make her take the apology back, force her to accept she had nothing to be sorry for, was almost more than he could stand.

Soothing her was a need.

When she was upset, he felt unsettled in the strangest of ways.

Now knowing that Ella was in trouble again had panic settling in his gut.

Because he'd been more focused on soothing Ella, he hadn't noticed someone sneaking up behind them until it was too late to do anything about it.

Ignoring the burn in his shoulder, he flexed his fingers. They all moved on command, and while it hurt, he was pretty sure the wound was nothing more than a flesh one. Nothing that would inhibit him from doing what he needed to do.

His little lioness had thrown herself at the man who had shot him with the most adorable roar he'd ever heard. Even as he wanted to spank her cute little butt for doing something as crazy as tackling an armed man, Miguel couldn't deny that he also felt a whole lot of pride.

As scared as she was, as rough as the last couple of days had been for her, she hadn't hesitated to put herself in the line of fire to protect him.

Protect *him*.

The only person other than his team who had ever done that for him was his brother.

Now, a woman who stirred up feelings he was determined to do his best to ignore was in danger, and his chest felt so tight he had to actually rub at it to try to alleviate the sensation.

Unprepared for the tiny warrior to attack, the man who'd shot him had lost his balance when Ella's body collided with his own and they'd both gone down a small hill. Scooping up the guard's weapon, which he must have dropped before he fell, Miguel started down the decline.

It was fairly sharp, and it was easy to make out the trail the two bodies had taken even in the dark. There were enough obstacles along the way that by the time he reached the bottom and found a fast-flowing river, he was genuinely concerned about whether or not Ella had been conscious when she'd gone in the water.

Scanning the river, searching for signs of Ella, when he saw none, he started jogging along the bank in the direction the current would have taken her.

Aside from whatever injuries she may have sustained in the fall, she was also there with a man who wouldn't hesitate to kill her, or at least incapacitate her and take her back to Raul.

Even if she survived this dip in the river, Raul now knew something was wrong. Luckily, Miguel had been able to kill the guards shooting at them, but that was only because there were just a few of them. Even with the four he'd killed before jumping the fence and going after Ella, there were still at least twenty men on the estate.

Enough to outnumber them.

Enough that if they were surrounded, he might not be able to protect Ella.

Shoving away those fears for the moment he stopped when he spotted something that looked like it could be a body.

While he wasn't yet allowing himself to consider the possibility that Ella could have drowned, if she had her body would still float to the surface. The river was wide, and he was too far away from the body to see if it was a man or a woman, but he wasn't going to risk not checking it out because there was a fifty-fifty chance that if it was a person that it was Ella.

Wading into the cold water, Miguel had never been more thankful in his life that he'd decided to become a SEAL. In high school, he'd warred with himself about whether he wanted to be a SEAL like his big brother or try for Delta Force. In the end, following in the footsteps of the brother he adored had won out.

Because of that decision, the water had become like a second home to him.

The fast-moving current was no match for his skills, and he made quick work of closing the distance between him and the body shape he'd seen. The closer he got, the more he realized it was indeed a person, and from the way they were thrashing about they were alive.

They were also too small to be the guard.

"Ella," he called out.

Struggling in the water, she managed to turn until she was looking at him. "Miguel!" she said with a sob, and he could hear the stark relief in her voice.

"Hold on," he urged as he quickened his strokes to get to her faster.

"I … I can't … I'm not … I can swim but … never in a river … not even the ocean … always in a pool," Ella babbled as her clumsy movements barely kept her afloat.

"I'm almost to you," he assured her, trying to shove as much confidence into his tone as he could manage so he could soothe her.

She was drowning, just because her head was currently above the water didn't change that fact, and drowning people panicked. Totally understandable, but the calmer he could keep her the better chance she'd have of keeping her head up until he got to her.

Ella let out a startled squawk and then she was gone.

Disappeared beneath the surface.

Unsure whether her own fear had taken her under, if a predator had latched onto her, or if the guard she had attacked had gotten a hold of her, Miguel didn't hesitate to draw his weapon.

Whatever it was it wasn't going to take Ella from him.

Diving under the water, he aimed right for the spot Ella had gone under and swam with everything he had to give.

When his hand connected with something, he grabbed onto it. It was too dark down there to see anything, but from the way it grabbed onto him, he assumed it was Ella. Pulling her up to the surface with him, he held onto her with one hand while searching her body for whatever had almost stolen her from him.

It wasn't a predator.

Wasn't the guard.

The offender was nothing more than a branch that had bumped into her leg and gotten caught up in her too-long pants.

"Calm down, honey," he soothed as she scrambled to wrap her body around his. As much as he liked the feel of her in his arms, he needed those arms and his legs to swim them back out of the water.

"I thought I was going to drown," she whimpered, pressing closer, her movements growing sluggish.

Concerned about her growing lack of strength, Miguel disentangled her arms from around his neck and eased her onto her back. Then he wrapped one arm around her chest, and allowed the current to do half the work as he angled himself for the bank and swam them back to land.

It didn't take long, and as soon as his feet hit the ground, he swung her up into his arms and quickly got them out of the water. Finding a fairly clear patch of grass, he quickly laid Ella out and began to run his hands up and down her body.

From the small gasps as he went, he knew she had to be covered in bumps and bruises, but other than the small flinches, she didn't scream or try to pull away from him, so he determined there were likely no broken bones. Wishing he had more gear on him so he could properly check her out, his fingers cradled her head as he ran his thumbs over her face checking for injuries that could account for her sudden lack of energy.

There was a bump on her forehead, and she winced as his thumbs brushed over it.

"Miguel?" she asked, voice slurring, "I … I think I'm going to pass out."

No sooner had she said the words than she did just that.

CHAPTER NINE

February 7th
   1:40 A.M.

PANIC.

That was the first conscious thought Ella was aware of.

As quickly as it came, it passed as she felt the strong arms wrapped around her and the sense of fear was chased away by a sense of security.

"Miguel?" Even half out of it as she was, Ella knew there was only one thing that gave her that feeling of safety and that one thing was the tall, dark, and handsome SEAL who had saved her life on more than one occasion.

"You back with me, honey?" he asked.

Was she?

Maybe.

Kind of.

Okay, the more thoughts that slipped into her mind the more awake she felt. Even though it might be nice to stay tucked away in a little cocoon where she didn't have to acknowledge what was happening to her, she couldn't do that.

Not here, not now.

Just because Miguel had pulled her out of the river, where she had truly believed she was going to drown, didn't mean that they were safe. They couldn't be all that far away from Raul's place, which meant his men would still be out in the jungle searching for them. Hunting them.

If ever there was a time where she had to pull it together and be strong, this was it.

Miguel was counting on her, and she didn't want to let him down.

"Are you okay?" she asked, remembering that he'd been shot before she'd tackled that man and sent them careening down the hill and into the water. "You were hurt."

A surprised chuckle rumbled through the chest she was tucked against, and she lifted her head from a surprisingly comfortable shoulder to find him looking down at her. In the dark, it was hard to see much, to make out his expression, but she could feel his dark eyes on her, and they felt like they were probing her very soul.

"I'm fine," he said, brushing off her concern.

"But you were shot," she persisted. She knew he had been, remembered his grunt of pain, yet he'd swum through the river like it was nothing, and now he was carrying her. That couldn't be good for him.

"A flesh wound, nothing serious."

"Did you check?"

"No time for that, you were gone," he said simply, and she smiled as something warm unfurled low in her belly. She liked the way he said that, liked knowing that he was protective of her. What she didn't like was knowing he was hurt and hadn't taken care of his injury.

"Put me down," she said, lightly pushing at his shoulders. She was reasonably sure she could stay upright on her feet.

For a second his hold on her tightened, and she got the feeling he didn't like the idea of not holding her any more than she liked the idea of no longer being in his arms. Then he carefully lowered one arm until her feet touched the ground. The other arm he kept around her waist for a moment longer while he waited to see if she could stand without support.

Only when he was sure she could did he take a step back.

Ella wanted to protest the distance between them even if it was only a foot, but she knew that was silly. Just because Miguel had saved her and just because he believed in her didn't change the fact that he'd come to Mexico to arrest her and once he handed her over to Prey, or an agency, or whoever was going to want her when they got home, he'd disappear, and she'd likely never see him again. His brother might be dating her friend, but right now, Ella didn't know where things stood between her and her team. There was every chance those bridges had been burned too badly to repair, and they would not be part of her life going forward either.

"You hit your head," Miguel said. A fingertip feathered across a lump on her forehead, and light as the contact was, she soaked it up. "Not sure if you have a concussion or you just passed out from exhaustion. Maybe a little of both."

"Where did you get shot?"

"Shoulder. But it's just a flesh wound, El."

Maybe.

But she found herself consumed with the need to check.

"I know it's dark, but can I check?" she asked uncertainly, so very aware of the fact that he was there because it was his job, because even if she wasn't going to jail, she had important knowledge of a wanted weapons trafficker. Just because she got all warm and tingly every time he touched her didn't mean that he felt the same way.

"You can check," he agreed, the husky quality to his voice making her shiver in a way that had nothing to do with her soaked clothes and wet hair.

"Your left shoulder?" she asked, noting the slightly stiff way he held that side of his body.

"Yeah."

Her hands trembled as she stepped closer and reached up to probe the area. She quickly found the wound, it was low on his shoulder, the fact that he'd sensed the guard's presence a split second before the man fired his weapon likely meant the bullet hadn't plowed through his body and instead grazed along his skin.

He was right, it was just a flesh wound, he was going to be fine.

Still, tears burned the backs of her eyes.

Miguel had been shot because of her.

Because she'd distracted him when he should have been focused on his job.

"I'm sorry," she whispered, standing on tiptoe to touch a kiss just beneath the gash.

A shudder rippled through the large body beside her, and when he spoke there was emotion she couldn't quite name in his voice. "You don't have to apologize, Ella. It wasn't your fault."

Some of the tears building leaked out and she wished she could stop crying. It made her feel weak, but she couldn't seem to stop herself. Weariness seemed to steal whatever strength she'd managed to recover, and she swayed and braced her hands on Miguel's chest.

"Of course it is. This is all my fault. I panicked, and I honestly didn't see a way where I could contact anyone at Prey without possibly alerting the mole. I love my family, they're everything to me, and I couldn't risk them. I'm sorry," she whispered again. While she knew in her heart she'd made the best choices she could with the situation she'd been thrust into, she still understood she'd created one giant mess that wasn't going to be easy to clean up.

"Hey." Turning, Miguel hooked an arm around her waist, lifting her off her feet so they were eye to eye. "You did what you had to do while still protecting your team and the drug. I respect that. Do I hate that you got so close to Raul? Yes. Hell, yes. Absolutely. But you had a plan that you thought through, were prepared to see through, and were prepared to risk your life to do. I respect that, Ella. And so will your team once they get their heads on straight."

Maybe they would.

Maybe they'd regret suspecting her, believing she could betray them, but she was pretty sure the damage was already done. How could she trust them going forward?

Call her naïve, but she honestly hadn't thought they would doubt her. Not deep down. She had just assumed they would believe she knew what she was doing and that whatever she was doing was in their best interest.

"Your team, they headed home, pretending they had me in custody?" she asked.

"They did."

"My family ... do you think the mole is still watching them?"

"Probably is. But I don't think they're going to do anything stupid. Besides, I think there might have been a little "incident" on their street that necessitated evacuating the whole block."

That coaxed a smile out of her. Whatever had happened to have the street evacuated she had a feeling that Miguel had something to do with it. A big something. He'd managed to get her family to a safe place where they were no longer in danger. "You got them out for me. Thank you."

"You're welcome."

The urge to kiss him was strong. Heat was building between them, and she didn't think it was them sharing body heat. It was something deeper. There was a thread of something there, she could feel it. The problem was, she didn't know much about Miguel but what she did know was that they wanted different things out of life. He wanted casual and she wanted serious when it came to the opposite sex. And even if he didn't, she had a huge mess to clean up when she got home. Her future was uncertain and she was in no place to start anything up with anyone.

"You shouldn't thank me too soon," Miguel said, a light teasing tone to his voice now that made her smile again.

"Yeah? Why not?"

"Because you need rest and the best place for us to hide out is one you're not going to like."

"Why? Where is it?" she asked suspiciously.

"Up there." He tilted his head up to look at a huge tree beside them.

"Up a tree?" she groaned.

"Yep. After seeing your tree climbing skills earlier, I thought it was the perfect place." He chuckled and she swatted at his shoulder.

"You were watching me, so you know I did a terrible job. I was shaky and almost fell a dozen times."

"Two dozen," he corrected. "I was counting."

"I don't like heights, and I'm not very outdoorsy," she huffed, defending herself.

"But you did it anyway," Miguel said, more seriously now. "Because you're brave, Ella. You do the things that scare you."

Ella pondered those words as she followed Miguel to the tree and copied his movements as they worked their way higher and higher. She didn't feel brave, but she agreed she did the things that scared her because she'd had no choice.

When she came to Mexico, she had been prepared to suffer whatever consequences she had to to ensure her family was safe. Now it sounded like they were out of danger so it was time to face those consequences.

Was she brave enough to do that?

* * *

FEBRUARY 8 TH
   12:00 A.M.

IT WAS time and he should be a whole lot happier to get out of Mexico than he was.

Miguel wanted to get Ella safe, wanted to make sure her name was cleared, and wanted her to be able to move forward with her life. He'd lost his comms somewhere along the way, maybe while he was in the river searching for Ella, so he wasn't able to check in with his team anymore.

Before they'd left the country pretending to have Ella with them, he'd asked them to fake an arrest or something in her parents' street. A hostage situation or something that could believably be passed off so the mole wouldn't be suspicious and set off the bomb. It was a big ask but Eagle Oswald owed Ella for being quick thinking enough to get the Reactivator someplace safe and walking into the lion's den to get the notorious dealer off their backs once and for all. He had no doubt that Eagle could pull off something that would get her family safe.

While he hadn't been able to communicate with his team since they left the country, the distance too big for their comms units to work, he knew that Eagle would have prioritized getting Ella's family out of that house. The man took good care of his people, and even though Prey had doubted Ella, Miguel hadn't spoken to the CEO, so he didn't know if that included Eagle.

Somehow, he couldn't see the former SEAL doubting Ella.

How anyone could was beyond him.

Yet he'd been the only one who hadn't readily believed the worst of her, and he knew that was hurting her deeply.

She was too sweet for her own good, that was the problem. Because she wouldn't have doubted her friends if their positions had been reversed meant that she was genuinely surprised to learn they hadn't afforded her the same courtesy.

He was worried about how she was going to handle things when she got home. Was she going to feel alone and abandoned? She didn't have the support of the people who should have been there for her, and while she'd have her family this was all classified information that she wouldn't be able to share with them.

Who was going to be there for her?

To support her and make sure she was okay?

And why did he feel the need to stay by her side? Protecting her from the people she should have been able to trust just like he'd protected her from Raul's men.

Maybe it was for the best that he wouldn't see her again once they got home. When he was with her, he wanted things he knew he could never have. There was no way he was going to risk tainting Ella and her life with the darkness that ran through his veins.

Best to get her away from him as quickly as possible, she'd been through enough and she didn't need his family demons getting their tentacles into her.

"You ready to go?" he asked, nudging the woman curled up against his side.

"Do we have to?"

Knowing her fear of heights made her anxious about climbing down the tree, he ruffled her hair. They'd grown close over the last twenty-four hours, between bouts of sleep Ella had shared bits and pieces about her life and he'd done the same. While he was sure they were both selective about what they'd shared, he could feel a bond forming and solidifying.

If he didn't get away from Ella soon, he might do something stupid.

Like take her to bed.

Like sleep beside her.

Like cook her breakfast in the morning and ask her for a repeat.

Something he never did.

Something he'd never wanted to do.

"Come on now, where's that lioness who launched herself at an armed man?" he teased.

"She disappears when she's forced to confront her fear of heights," Ella replied.

"You can do it. You've already been up and down this tree three times now," he reminded her. They'd taken a couple of bathroom breaks, but other than that he'd wanted to keep her up and out of the way because they both knew that Raul's men would still be hunting them. The guard who had shot him had gotten away. Sure, there was a chance he'd drowned, but there was also a chance that he'd made his way back to the house and told everyone that Ella had attacked him.

His plan to make Ella seem like she was still on Raul's side if she was captured again, that he'd taken her against her will, was useless now.

She'd tried to save his life, there was no way she would have done that if he'd kidnapped her.

That meant he couldn't allow her to fall into Raul's hands. The man was already more obsessed with her than he would have liked, and the last thing he wanted was to allow Ella to be kept as some sort of perverted sex toy for a weapon's dealer who would wind up killing her when he got bored.

"You'd think it would get easier each time," Ella complained as she started to climb down after him.

Doing this in the dark made it harder on her, but he hadn't wanted them to move while it was light out. This made it easier for them to move without being spotted and he was going to play this as safe as he could because Ella was his priority.

The other team coming in to extract them and hopefully bring Raul into custody would be there, somewhere close by. All he needed to do was get Ella to the exfil spot and then it would be as good as over. Although he doubted that Raul was still close by, the man usually fled when it looked like he might get caught, which meant the threat to Ella and her team wouldn't be completely gone, but at least she'd be back home where someone could keep her safe.

Not him.

The longer he spent around her the more he was tempted to give in to the need to touch, taste, and risk everything to have her, even just for one night.

"I don't think I'm ever going up in a tree again for as long as I live," Ella said when their feet finally touched the ground.

There was relief in her tone.

Relief he hated he was about to wipe away.

"Go back up the tree, Ella," he said, voice low so it didn't carry. They weren't alone anymore. Someone was coming. Not whichever team was coming to extract them, because they would know he was there and have let him know it was them.

That meant it had to be Raul's men.

"Is someone there?" Ella asked in a scared whisper.

"Yes. Now, go. Get up there. Don't come down unless I tell you to. I mean it, Ella," he added. "No more heroics. I'm here to rescue you, not the other way around."

"You were here to arrest me," she muttered under her breath, but she began to climb the tree she'd only just gotten out of.

With Ella out of the way, Miguel faded into the trees, moving so he was behind the man he had sensed approaching their hiding spot.

Thankfully the man was alone and didn't appear to know he wasn't alone.

Palming the handle of the knife he'd taken from the guard in the bathroom, he pounced on the man, burying the blade in his neck.

A panicked gurgle was all the man gave as he tried desperately to slow the flood of blood as he sank to the ground.

Just as Miguel was going to return to Ella, tell her to hurry back down so they could get away from there and to the exfil location, he spotted another man. Once again, he circled around until he was behind the other man, before striking. Another well placed blade to the neck left another body bleeding out on the jungle floor.

Two dead but there would be more.

Raul wasn't the kind of man who just gave up.

Not when he'd spent a month trying to get his hands on this drug. It was about principles. He wasn't going to miss out on something he wanted, wasn't going to lose, and definitely wasn't going to be bested by four women.

Before returning to the tree, he spotted another three

men approaching him. There was no way he could take them out silently. If he used his weapons, he risked bringing in every other guard anywhere nearby, and if he thought he was outnumbered three to one he wouldn't like the odds when it was five to one, or ten to one, or worse.

At least Ella wasn't with him.

If the guard she'd attacked had made it back to the house, maybe he hadn't hung around long enough to watch as Miguel pulled her out of the water.

Could he use that to his advantage?

Allowing himself to be captured could buy time for the team coming in to find and rescue Ella. She still had the tracker which meant they'd find her, and if Raul believed that he and Ella had been separated then they wouldn't need to search this area to see if she was nearby.

They'd just take him in and leave her behind, giving her a fighting chance at surviving.

CHAPTER TEN

February 8th
   12:17 A.M.

ELLA WAS TORN.

Part of her wanted to hide where she was at least relatively safe. At least safe for being stuck in the middle of the Mexican jungle, up a tree, with men with guns hunting them. The other part of her felt it was cowardly to hide and leave Miguel to fight for their lives alone. Especially since he was only there because of her.

These last twenty-four hours had actually been nice, and it was only because of the company.

Miguel had held her while she slept, making her feel secure in the knowledge she wasn't going to fall out of the tree while asleep. When she was awake, he talked with her, sharing pieces of his life so she didn't lose her mind to the terror of being up in a tree so far off the ground with no choice but to endure something she hated.

She'd known it was because of her they were hiding out

there. Because she was weak and exhausted and needed the rest. Because she wasn't going to be any help as they made their way through the jungle.

As badly as she wanted to get to the exfil spot and get out of Mexico, there was also sadness at leaving Miguel behind. Just because he hadn't said the words didn't mean she wasn't well aware of what was going to happen. Once he handed her off, he'd be gone, and she was going to miss him.

The fear she felt for him now, knowing he was down there, doing anything he had to to keep the men away from her, was almost more than she could handle. How would she deal with it if he was killed because of her?

That would have hurt enough twenty-four hours ago when they were shot at as they escaped. But now, after they'd bonded and gotten to know each other better, see each other as real people and not just the SEAL who was saving her, and the woman he'd come to arrest, it would make the loss so much deeper.

Which was silly because she still didn't really know him.

She just felt him.

Like an imprint on her soul or something.

Likely it wasn't as romantic as she was making it out to be. He'd saved her life on several occasions now, of course she was going to feel an attachment to him. This was not an everyday occurrence for her, while for him saving victims was what he did for a living.

Only this time *she* was the one who needed saving, and it felt wrong just to sit there and let him risk his life for her.

The other team would come, she knew they would. While she was hazy on the details, hadn't felt the need to push because Miguel would have it under control, and she couldn't handle another responsibility right now, she knew that the plan had been for them to meet at the extraction point. If she and Miguel didn't show up on time, she knew the team would follow the tracker until they found her.

But if she waited it could be too late for Miguel.

How far away were they from the exfil site?

How long had it been since Miguel left her?

How long would the team wait before coming looking for them?

So many questions and for each one that popped into her head and had no answer, her anxiety began to mount. She wanted to go home, hug her family, and forget all of this had happened. If there was one thing she had learned over the last few days, it was that she did not do well in a high-stress situation.

Too much anxiety.

It wound around her like a tangle of vines, squeezing her until she felt like there was nothing left, like she was just an empty bag of skin and bones, and anxiety and nothing else. It consumed her, overwhelmed her, and she wondered how she ever thought she could pull this off.

"Come back, Miguel. Please," she whispered aloud, praying that he might hear her and suddenly appear out of thin air like he'd done when they escaped.

Only he didn't come.

The only thing to meet her murmured words was silence.

Silence she was beginning to hate.

She'd never really thought about just how scary silence could be. With three sisters their house had never been silent when she was growing up. Add in that all six people who lived in the house were musicians, and more often than not, at least one person was rehearsing. Even at night she usually played music in the background because it helped her sleep better. When working at the lab, if she wasn't talking to one of her friends, she usually had her earbuds in and music playing.

Now the silence was freaking her out.

She didn't like it at all.

Yet when a sharp whistle suddenly cut through the air she yelped and almost fell right out of the tree.

Even though she wasn't a field operative, she knew how military people worked and spent time around them every day. They had a whole series of whistles and sounds that they could use to communicate, and she would bet her life on the fact that that particular whistle was meant to alert Miguel that whoever was coming was not a threat to him.

Only Miguel wasn't there right now and she didn't know what she was supposed to do.

It had to be the team coming in to get them, but what if she was wrong? What if it was Raul's men trying to trick her?

Miguel should be back by now, Ella knew that. That he wasn't meant only one thing. He was in trouble. He'd either been caught or killed. If he'd been caught, why hadn't one of Raul's men come looking for her?

Surely they knew she was with him.

Unless …

No.

He wouldn't do that.

But she knew that was a lie. He *would* do that. Miguel would make any sacrifice to get her out of there, it was just the way he was wired.

Another whistle had her losing her grip on the branch she was clinging to, and Ella only just managed to regain a hold of it before she fell. If Miguel had done what she feared he had, then she had no choice but to call out and hope this was the good guys and not the bad ones. He had sacrificed for her, and she wasn't going to let it be in vain.

"H-hello?" she called out, voice shaking despite her efforts to sound strong and sure of herself.

"Ella?"

She knew that voice. It belonged to Blake "Rocco" Wise, the leader of a SEAL team who had been working with Prey to find the mole, the weapon's dealer, and keep the Reactivator safe. They'd played a part in saving Scarlett, Lucy, and Cassie, and now they'd come for her, too.

"I'm up here," she called back.

"Can you get down?" Rocco asked.

"Yeah." She hated it but she could do it. She had to do it because she needed to get to them and tell them they had to go and find Miguel before it was too late.

Quicker than she had any other time, Ella scampered down the tree, her fear for Miguel overriding her fear of heights. By the time she reached the ground she was breathing hard, and the sight of the six large men dressed in combat gear did nothing to soothe her.

Unlike Miguel who could soothe her just by being there.

"Miguel, I think he might have let himself be captured to draw Raul's men away from me," she blurted out without preamble. "We have to go and find him."

"Not our orders," Rocco informed her.

"But Miguel is in trouble," she insisted. If they wanted to put her in handcuffs, then so be it. She had no idea what intel Miguel had been able to share with his team, so she didn't know if they knew the drug was safe, or if they had it if she was still considered a traitor. Right now, she didn't care either. Miguel was what was important.

"And we'll go for him as soon as we get you safe," Decker "Gumby" Kincade assured her, not unkindly, but also in a voice that told her their minds were made up.

Well, she was going to change their minds.

Nothing was making her leave behind a man who had saved her over and over again.

"No. Miguel needs us. We were coming to meet you, but Miguel saw or heard someone, or however you guys do that superpower sensing someone's presence thing. He went to take care of it, but he should have been back already. Something's wrong. I know it is, and I won't leave him behind. He saved me, he believed in me, I won't go without him."

Before anyone could say anything else, a gunshot sounded, and without thinking about what she was doing, Ella was running toward the sound, positive that Miguel had just been shot.

* * *

FEBRUARY 8ᵀᴴ
12:58 A.M.

THE BULLET STRUCK the ground millimeters from where he was down on his knees, surrounded by a dozen of Raul's men.

Even though dirt kicked up as the bullet flew off close enough to hit him that he could have sworn he felt the heat of it, Miguel didn't flinch.

Wouldn't flinch.

So long as the men had their attention focused on him, they couldn't be searching for Ella.

The exfil time was zero thirty, and they'd been less than a mile from the prearranged meeting point. The team coming in for them would wait a short time before moving in to follow the tracker's location. By now Ella should be safe with them. That's all he cared about.

They'd come back for him, Miguel had no doubt about that, and he also rated his chances of being alive when they did as fairly high. Sure, he'd likely be sporting a few new bruises, and maybe even a bullet hole or two, but Raul's men would want to torture him for Ella's location so they couldn't kill him right away. And he could withstand hours and hours of torture without cracking.

Especially if he knew that his little brave lioness was safe.

"You killed the missing guards, the ones we found in the jungle," the man who seemed to be the leader said, still keeping the weapon he'd just fired trained on Miguel.

"Hey, not my fault they were thinking with the wrong head," he shrugged. In addition to being on his knees surrounded by a dozen armed men, his arms were tied behind his back and he'd been stripped of his weapons. These men thought it gave them the upper hand, but so long as Ella was nowhere near there, Miguel firmly believed the ball was actually in his court.

"You are American," the leader spat at him.

"I am. I'm here to capture Ella Whitlock." Even though he doubted it was going to do any good he would stick with his plan to pretend he'd taken her against her will. While he was sure she was safe now, he'd rather add a second layer of protection just in case it was needed.

"The boss is not happy that you took her," the other man informed him. "He has taken a liking to her."

"Raul has to know it's not reciprocated. Ella said she came because her family was threatened. She fought hard when I told her I was taking her with me. Said she couldn't leave because your boss was threatening to blow up her family if she didn't give him what he wanted. What he'd been trying to get for over a month now," he added with a mocking smirk.

The fist that came flying toward him, connecting with his jaw, was not unexpected. He took the blow, the jolt of pain, and relished the fact that he was the one being hit and not Ella. The thought of anyone putting their hands on her, causing her pain, made him want to burn the entire world to the ground.

"She will tell the boss what he wants to know," the leader

sneered. "And then, if he wants to keep her as his pet, she will learn to obey and follow his commands. She is nothing. You are nothing. Your country is nothing. You are not in control here. You do not have the power."

"I do," Raul Castillo said as he strode out of the trees. "Now I believe you stole something from me and I want it back. Now."

Miguel merely met and held the weapons dealer's gaze.

Just because Raul was accustomed to throwing around his money and power and getting what he wanted didn't mean he was going to get it this time.

In fact, what the trafficker wanted the most was already out of his reach.

Ella was safe and protected, away from a man who wanted to treat her like a possession instead of a human being.

"I have ways of making people talk," Raul threatened like Miguel cared.

"So I've heard. Only I don't think it's yielded any results," he taunted.

Even in the dull light of the guards' flashlights, Miguel could see the rage brimming in Raul's dark eyes. "I know you took her. I know she wouldn't have risked her family's lives to go with you. I know you have her stashed out here somewhere. You pulled her out of the river, my man saw you, but he was on the other side and couldn't get to you. She's out here somewhere and if you don't produce her then you won't like the consequences."

To highlight his words one of Raul's men pulled out a vial that Miguel was sure was filled with the arousal drug the man had already tried using on Scarlett, Lucy, and Cassie without result. If he had to take a hit of the drug he'd do it. Didn't mean he was going to give up the fact that Ella had already been rescued. And the whole time all he'd be thinking was how glad he was that he was the one suffering the effects of it and not Ella.

"I've yet to see how this works on a man, it should be interesting," Raul said, watching with glee as the man closest to Miguel delivered a blow to his stomach, shoving the air from his lungs and making him sag to the ground, while another approached with the drug.

Even though he wasn't fighting back the men got in a few more blows before the one with the syringe knelt beside him.

Just as the needle was about to prick his skin, the man holding it suddenly dropped as a shot tore through the night.

Chaos ensued.

Bullets were fired.

Men screamed as they were hit.

Bodies dropped.

Miguel rolled to the side, slamming his bound wrists against his backside to break the zip ties, his gaze searching for Raul. The man wasn't getting away again. For whatever reason, the team who were supposed to be getting Ella out of there were saving his behind, and while he was grateful, he'd rather know Ella was safe.

To keep her safe Raul had to die.

Simple as that.

Catching sight of the man darting away like the coward that he was, Miguel jumped to his feet and took off after him.

"No. You don't get to run away."

The voice had him freezing.

It was Ella's voice and coming from just up ahead of him.

Why was she there?

Why wasn't she safe?

"What are you going to do to stop me?" Raul sneered, and Miguel about had a heart attack.

The last thing he wanted was Ella anywhere near that man.

117

But as he kept moving forward, he saw that not only was she near him, but she was holding a gun on the weapons trafficker.

It wasn't even shaking.

The look in her eyes was something he hadn't seen on her before. It was a mixture of fear and determination. She wasn't going to let the man who had caused her and her team so much suffering get away alive, even if she had to be the one to pull the trigger.

"It's over, Raul," he said, trying to move slowly to get between his girl and the dealer. While he was so proud of Ella for what she wanted to do, he didn't want her to actually have to do it. Whether the man deserved it or not, taking a life would change something in her, something she'd never be able to undo.

Ella's gaze flicked to him, and he could see relief in it.

Knowing that she cared about what happened to him touched a place inside him that had been hardened by the neglect of his biological parents. Knowing that she was likely the reason the SEAL team had just saved him an unpleasant few hours with a rock-hard erection and no way to get off softened that place of abandonment every child who'd had parents who abused them had inside them.

"It's not over," Raul announced before underestimating his opponent and rushing Ella, likely intending to take the weapon from her then use it to kill her.

But Ella was strong.

Stronger than Raul understood, stronger even than Miguel gave her credit for.

Because she fired.

Over and over again until the weapon was empty, and the body of the man who had slipped through their fingers more times than he liked to admit, lay riddled with bullets at her feet.

Still, she pulled the trigger, her eyes wide with shock, even as her body stood tall and straight, confident that it had done the right thing.

"You did it, honey," Miguel murmured as he edged closer, wishing he had been able to take this burden from her before she saddled it to herself for life.

She made no protest as he slipped the weapon out of her hands, then folded her into an embrace, crushing her against him. They clung to one another, needing to hold each other as confirmation they were both alive and in one piece.

As her fingers curled into his shirt, fisting in the material, her wet face nuzzled against his chest, Miguel realized that she wasn't the only one who had saddled herself with something she'd never be able to shake off there in the Mexican jungle.

He had, too.

Because wanted or not, this woman had wriggled her way under his skin and he had no idea what he was going to do about it.

CHAPTER ELEVEN

February 8th
   4:38 P.M.

IF SHE THOUGHT she was exhausted in Mexico it was nothing to how Ella felt in this moment.

Completely wiped out.

Empty.

Like there was nothing left for her to give.

Just the thought of having to catch a cab or an Uber back to her house, cook herself some dinner—even ordering dinner—cleaning herself up, and falling into bed was more than she could handle.

Everything was too much.

She was overwhelmed to the absolute extreme.

"So I can go?" she asked Eagle and another man from some agency only he hadn't specified which one in particular. Even though the first words out of Eagle's mouth when their plane landed at Prey's private airfield, and she was transported back to the office where he was waiting for her

121

were that she was not under arrest, she hadn't quite believed it.

Answering every question she was asked—the same ones over and over again until she was precariously close to screaming or bursting into tears—as honestly as possible, giving as much detail as she could remember, it had all felt pointless. Ella had been convinced that at the end they were going to change their minds, snap handcuffs on her and drag her away, locking her up in some tiny cell in some remote location and she'd never see the light of day again.

Eagle's blue eyes met hers, open and honest, inviting her to search them and confirm her fears were for nothing. "Ella, you are not under arrest. Everything you said checked out. The vial of the Reactivator was in the locker at the airport, it's already been tested. The bomb was found under your parents' house. You have the wounds to prove you were threatened into doing what you did. I can't say I'm not disappointed I don't have an emergency system in place that can be used in the event of a situation like this and you felt you had to go it alone, but that failing is mine, not yours."

Tears welled in her eyes at her boss' kind words, for his understanding, for his willingness to believe her, and for having everything corroborated so someone couldn't twist things against her.

"Thank you," she whispered.

"For what it's worth, Ella. I never believed you were guilty," Eagle said. When she studied his gaze, she found it sincere and there was not a single thread of dishonesty in his tone either.

"Thank you," she whispered again, knowing how lucky she would have been to have Eagle on her side if things hadn't turned out the way they had and she'd been arrested. He would have fought for her.

Unlike…

It hurt to think, but she'd seen the way Fox and the guys wouldn't meet her gaze directly. They hadn't believed in her, and it hurt more than she could express, more than she ever would have thought.

"Go home and rest, we'll have people watching over you. Raul Castillo might be dead, but the mole is still out there," Eagle said. The pride in his voice as he mentioned the dead weapons trafficker managed to drag a small smile out of her. If nothing else, her ordeal had wound up taking out a wanted dealer and that was definitely something.

Wearily, she pushed to her feet and opened the interview room door, kind of surprised to find it wasn't locked.

More surprised to see who was lounging against the wall in the hall.

"Miguel? What are you doing here?" she asked. She would have thought after his debriefing he would have left, never giving her a second thought. Instead, he'd stayed, which somehow made things a little better.

Okay, maybe more than a little.

It helped to know she wasn't completely alone. She had Eagle and she had Miguel. Only two people, but way better than zero.

"Checking to make sure you're okay," he said, straightening and taking a step toward her. He stopped just shy of touching her and Ella found herself almost overwhelmed by the need to throw herself into his arms.

What she wouldn't give to soak up a little of his soothing calm right now. It was just that she no longer knew where she stood with him. They were back home, his job was over, and he had no obligation to stick around, and yet he had and that left her feeling so confused.

Maybe she would have outright asked, too tired to play any sort of games, and with no mental energy to figure this man out, but then she caught sight of more people coming down the hall and immediately stiffened.

Her team.

With their partners.

Panic fluttered to life inside her. She wasn't ready to see them yet. Might never be ready. Perhaps she was being overly sensitive, after all, she knew what she was making things look like when she took the drug, but she felt what she felt. It was that they just believed she was a traitor so easily. She'd expected better from them, more, expected what she would have given in their place.

Noticing her panic, Miguel looked over his shoulder, and when he saw who was coming, he shifted slightly so he was between her and her team. His protectiveness eased a little of her fear and she could just kiss him for being so in tune with her feelings and actually caring enough to do something about it.

"Ella? We were hoping we could talk to you?" Lucy asked, sounding uncharacteristically uncertain.

There was no way she was ready for that. Whether she was being overly sensitive or not, right now, she could barely stand to look at these three women, let alone talk to them. Her emotions were way too raw, and she didn't want to fall apart, or have the energy for it at the moment.

Later.

When she'd had time to process everything that had happened.

"Please," Scarlett added when she didn't answer. "We know you must be tired, so we won't take up much of your time."

"We shouldn't have doubted you," Cassie blurted out, tears shining in her eyes.

"No, you shouldn't have," she agreed softly.

"You took the Reactivator on camera," Tate said, and she

winced at the hard tone of his voice. It was clear while maybe her friends felt bad about doubting her their men didn't. Even if she could move past their lack of faith in her, how could she ever work with them again when their partners obviously didn't like her? There was no way she was petty enough to make them choose between the loves of their lives and her, so it left them at an impasse.

"Because if I didn't make it look believable my family, including my five-month-old nephew, would have been blown up. I arranged for emails to be sent to let you know where it was in the event I didn't make it home," she explained wearily, wondering if there would ever be a time when she didn't have to defend herself.

"You didn't call," Scarlett said, sounding hurt, but if their positions were reversed Scarlett would have protected her family however she had to as well.

"Couldn't risk it knowing the mole could have tapped phones and be listening. Whether you agree with my decisions or not, I did the best I could to protect my family and the Reactivator at the same time, whatever the consequences to myself."

"Your friends would have been there for you," Luis lectured like she was some stupid kid. "Do you have any idea how upsetting it was for them?"

"Back the hell off, man," Miguel growled, and she rested a palm on his forearm to calm him—although she appreciated him being the only one on her side—and stepped around him, no longer willing to hide behind him. She'd made her choices and done what she had to do, she didn't need to be ashamed of that.

"Actually, yeah I do," she said calmly. "I remember when we were faced with "proof" that Scarlett was a traitor, and I never once believed it. Not for a single second. I was on the phone with the rest of you when Lucy's plane went down, and I remember the terror I felt. Same fear as when I got the call that the lab had been blown up with Cassie inside. Never once did I doubt any of you, it never even entered my mind. I was just scared for my friends, the people I loved and considered family. If you can't understand why I would feel upset about not getting that same love and support, then I don't think there's anything to talk about. I'm going home."

"I'll drive you," Miguel immediately offered.

Managing a smile for him, Ella shook her head. "Thank you, but I think I need a little time on my own to come to terms with the last few days and think about my future."

"Ella, you aren't thinking of quitting Prey are you?" Cassie asked, sounding aghast.

Not willing to get into any discussions tonight, not before she'd had time to think, Ella ignored the question. Instead, she stood on tiptoe and touched a kiss to Miguel's cheek. "Thank you for saving me. Over and over again. Thank you for giving me the benefit of the doubt even though you didn't know me. And thank you for being here for me tonight, it made me feel a little less alone."

With that, she turned and walked away, feeling very much like she was leaving Prey and her team behind for good.

* * *

FEBRUARY 8TH
   5:01 P.M.

"WE MESSED UP," Lucy said as Ella disappeared around a corner.

"You think?" Miguel snarled, whirling around to face the three women who should have had Ella's back no matter what. It didn't matter if they'd learned the mole was a woman. Didn't matter if Ella was seen on camera leaving the lab with the Reactivator. Didn't matter if she hopped on a plane to Mexico. She'd earned the benefit of the doubt by being a contributing member of Athena Team and a friend to all three of them.

Why was he the only one who'd had doubts?

He didn't even know Ella, yet he'd felt like something wasn't adding up. If he could see that, why couldn't the people who knew her the best?

All you needed to do was look at all the pieces and you'd see that, at the very least, they were worth looking into before jumping to conclusions.

Yet nobody who claimed to care about Ella had bothered to do that, and for some reason, it made him irrationally angry.

"Ease up, little brother," Luis warned.

Usually, Miguel would defer to his brother. They might both be in their thirties, but Luis had been more of a parent to him than a brother for the first decade of his life, so he was more than just a big brother.

But not this time.

Ella needed somebody on her side, and it looked like he was the only one who wanted the job.

"This wasn't easy on Scarlett, Lucy, and Cassie," Zander said quietly. Of all six who had accosted Ella outside the room she'd been interrogated in, he'd been the one to throw off the least number of antagonistic vibes. That was the only reason Miguel could keep his voice relatively calm even though he was seething on the inside.

"Wasn't easy on Ella either," he reminded them. "She was the one who had her family threatened. She was the one who willingly walked into danger because it was the only way to protect those she loved. She was the one who still had the wherewithal despite her fear to make sure she also protected the drug. Flat out, no lies, no sugarcoating things, Ella deserved better than what she got from you."

"The evidence—" Tate started, but Miguel wasn't having excuses, wasn't interested in them, the only thing he was interested in right now was Ella.

"Don't make excuses," he said, cutting off the other man.

"He's right," Lucy agreed. "We're the ones who messed up, not Ella. What she said was true, she never doubted anything, and we let her down when we didn't at least fight for her. We know her, she's a sweet person, hardworking and dedicated. There's no way she would ever betray us and we should have known that."

Slightly mollified by the fact that at least one of them was willing to acknowledge their mistakes, Miguel nodded. "You have no idea what she went through in Mexico. What she risked to try to end this for all of you."

Scarlett paled. "Did Raul ... use the drug on her?"

"No. He tried to use it on me, but Rocco's team showed up before he could. Raul was going to keep Ella for himself," he informed them. While he didn't necessarily feel good about sharing this with them, it wasn't like everything that had happened to her wasn't already in her statement.

Cassie gasped. "He ... he was going to keep her? Like a ... a ... pet?"

"Like as his own personal sex slave," Miguel replied, seeing no reason to mince words. If these women who should have had faith in their friend wanted to tear her down, they should know exactly what she had been facing in her attempts to protect everyone and everything except herself.

Another gasp fell from Cassie's lips, and Luis wrapped an arm around her pulling her close and touching a kiss to her temple. "But she's okay, princess. He didn't get to keep her, and she killed him."

As his brother said the words, Miguel could see the full meaning of what he'd just spoken sunk in because Luis went pale. For the first time, it looked like his brother was seeing this whole mess from someone other than the woman he was falling in love with's point of view.

From Ella's point of view.

It was all well and good to say she should have told someone about the threat to her family, but there was a credible threat to security and if she tipped the mole off to the fact that she had no intention of following through with the orders she'd been given her family would be killed.

There was no choice.

She'd done what she had to do, and he had no intention of standing by and allowing her to be torn to shreds over it.

If she didn't want him with her right now, and he would gladly have driven her home, been a friend, given her a shoulder to cry on if she needed it or someone she could rage at about the unfairness of it all, then he would at least stay there and defend her. It just sucked that she needed defending to people who should have known better.

"We messed up," Luis said, echoing Lucy's earlier words.

"You did and you hurt her a lot," Miguel agreed, focusing on the three women. Tate and Luis had known Ella only a month, so their not believing in her was more rational. Zander had known her for a few years since he wasn't just Lucy's boyfriend but Scarlett's twin brother, but he knew the man hadn't known any of his sister's teammates very well, so again it wasn't him not believing in her that had upset Ella.

Scarlett, Lucy, and Cassie were the ones who should have known better. They were the ones who had broken Ella's heart.

While he hadn't known Ella long, he was protective of her, he liked her, they'd bonded, and if he wasn't afraid of what might happen to him in the future if he could no longer control his inner demons then he might even have been tempted to throw away his usual one and done policy and ask her out on a real date.

Just because he couldn't do that didn't mean he couldn't give her this. Make sure her friends knew how badly they'd messed up. It wasn't much, but at least Ella would know she wasn't alone in this.

"Do you think we can fix it?" Scarlett asked him, and he knew then that they really got how badly their unwillingness to extend Ella the benefit of the doubt until they knew more had damaged their relationship with her. They were the ones who knew her, they should know whether or not they had a shot at repairing things, yet they were looking to him.

Miguel couldn't deny that gave him a little caveman kind of rush because it almost made it seem like Ella was his. He knew she wasn't and knew she never could be. Yet there was something between them, and it had only grown in the hours they'd spent together in Mexico, and in the hours it had taken to get back home when Ella had been unwilling to allow him out of her sight, needing his presence to reassure herself she was safe.

Not that he'd been complaining.

He'd needed her close to reassure himself that she was safe.

But the facts right now were that Ella was hurting, she felt alone, the people who should have had her back hadn't and he honestly had no idea if they'd be able to mend fences enough to get their friendships back to what they'd been before.

"I don't know," he answered.

"Can you talk to her for us?" Cassie asked. "She seems to trust you and you're the one who saved her. I think she'd listen to you. If you just tell her how sorry we are and how much we'd like to tell her that in person then she might listen."

Honestly, if it wasn't what Ella one hundred percent wanted, then he wouldn't do it. She was his priority. She was the one who had been wronged, and if she wasn't ready to talk to her friends then he wouldn't try to pressure her. Ella deserved to have someone putting her first and that's what he intended to do.

"I'm sorry I can't agree to that," he replied. "I don't mean to be harsh, but you guys made your bed and now you have to lie in it. I hope for all your sakes, that you can work things out, Ella loves her job, and she loves you guys, and I don't want her to lose that. But right now, she's traumatized and she's hurting, and she needs someone in her corner."

"That someone is you?" Luis asked, his gaze a whole lot more probing than Miguel would have liked because he knew he could never hide anything from his big brother.

Aiming for nonchalance, Miguel shrugged. "For now. Yeah. Ella needs a friend and has me. When she's ready I'll encourage her to reach out, but I'm not making any promises. Ella lost her control when her family was threatened, I won't take it from her again."

With that, he turned and headed for the lifts, refusing to allow himself to consider the whispering thought at the back of his mind, that he wanted to be more than Ella's friend.

There was no way he could risk hurting her by being more.

CHAPTER TWELVE

February 8th
5:44 P.M.

EMPTY.

Her house felt too empty.

Ella gazed around at the airy, open space. It was a huge family room that had sealed the deal when she'd been looking at properties to buy. There was a kitchen on one side with a big table then the other side of the room had an enormous fireplace and enough space for three big, comfortable sofas. Doors led out onto an enormous deck and into a pretty yard, a nice mix of trees, plants, flowers, and a grassy lawn.

When she'd bought the house, it was with a family in mind. She'd been able to picture kids running in and out through those doors on a warm summer's day, and a husband grilling on the deck.

Slowly, over time, those dreams had drifted into the background, and now there she was, almost thirty, alone, not even a boyfriend, not even a prospect of a boyfriend. If that wasn't bad enough, now she felt like she might lose the job she loved and the team she considered family.

Going back to Prey, working every day with Scarlett, Lucy, and Cassie, with Fox and the rest of the guys seemed impossible. How could she face them knowing what they'd thought of her? How could she ever trust them again? How could she have ever believed with the actions she'd chosen that they would ever think anything but that she was guilty?

Maybe that was the real problem. She was as frustrated with herself for being so naïve as she was with everybody else.

Loneliness was like an ache in her chest, and as she wandered aimlessly through the living room and flopped down onto one of the sofas, she wished she'd taken Miguel up on his offer to drive her home.

Out of everyone, he seemed to be the only person who believed in her. Well, Miguel and Eagle. It did mean a lot to her that her boss had believed in her innocence, especially given that there had been a mole at Prey before and all the evidence pointed to her, but it wasn't enough to ease the hurt of knowing her friends had thought the worst of her.

It wasn't that she didn't understand why they'd thought it. She got it, she truly did. Evidence suggested it was her and she'd had to make it look believable if she didn't want to get her family blown up, but they hadn't even given her the benefit of the doubt.

She had to get over it, Ella knew that, too.

But how?

How was she supposed to forget they had believed she would betray them all and go back to work like nothing had happened?

What she needed was to stop thinking about it for a while.

To stop thinking about all of it.

The mole, the Reactivator, the threats, what had almost happened in the jungle. What would have happened in the jungle if Miguel hadn't been there. Maybe if she could just block it all out of her head, she could get a few moments peace.

Peace was what she needed, and some real rest. She should probably eat something, too, only the thought of food made her nauseous. It was still early but the idea of a hot shower and bed was appealing. There had been no real rest for her since those men forced their way inside her house, which meant she was definitely running on fumes.

Only as appealing as bed sounded in some ways, in others, it left her feeling swamped with loneliness all over again.

Tears were pricking the backs of her eyes when her phone began to chirp.

As much as she wanted to leave it and spend a little time wallowing in misery before she formed a plan for what her life was going to look like moving forward, when she saw her mom's picture on the screen, she knew she had to answer. They didn't know anything about her being accused of being a traitor and rushing off to Mexico in an attempt to save their lives, and they never would.

Most of her job was classified and her family was used to her not talking about it, but this was one time she desperately needed someone to talk to. It was so tempting to just unload everything on them, knowing with absolute certainty that they would offer her the support she needed.

But she couldn't do that.

So instead, Ella wiped her eyes to ensure there were no giveaways to the tears that wanted to fall free, and pasted on a smile as she scooped up her phone.

"Hey, Mom," she said in as bright a voice as she could

muster as she answered the call. "What's going on?" Since there was no way she should have known about the fake siege in her parents' street that had allowed Prey to get them out of the house without raising suspicions, she couldn't ask about it even though she needed the reassurance of hearing they were okay even if they didn't know just how close to death they'd come.

"You won't believe it, Ella-boo," her mom said, an excited smile on her face.

"Won't believe what, Mom?" she asked, playing along even though she knew where this was heading.

"We had the most surreal experience the other night. There was a criminal holed up in a house right down the block from us," her mom exclaimed.

"A criminal? How do you know?" Even though she couldn't talk about what had really happened it helped just hearing her mom's voice and knowing that while she might be traumatized by this whole ordeal, they didn't even know there was an ordeal.

"Because a whole bunch of cops came to the door and told us we had to leave, that there was a wanted criminal in a house a few doors down, that he was holed up in there with hostages and they weren't sure what he was going to do so they were evacuating everyone. We had to get into a big, black car, and cop cars were everywhere in the street. They took us to a hotel and made sure we were settled, then a few hours later we were told it was all safe to return home."

"You make it sound like quite the adventure." Ella wished she felt the same about the whole thing, only from her point of view it had been nothing close to a fun adventure.

"Well, I guess it was," Mom said with a chuckle. "No one was hurt, the man was arrested, and Rachel and Sarah thought the whole thing was a lot of fun. The hotel had a pool and they got to swim even though it was the middle of the night. The only ones who didn't think it was exciting were your sister, because she'd just worked a double shift and gotten into bed, and the baby, who did not appreciate the change in his routine."

At least they were all still alive.

There would always be time to sleep, but if she hadn't made the choices she had, she and her other two sisters might be planning seven funerals right now, including picking out three small white coffins.

Whatever it cost her, Ella knew she had done the right thing.

The same exact thing any of the other women on Athena Team would have done if their situations were reversed. The same exact thing anyone else at Prey would have done. They would have put their own life on the line in an instant, without a second thought, if it meant protecting their families. So why was she the one being vilified for doing it?

"How are Elsbeth and the baby now?" she asked, wishing she could go over there and hug everyone to reassure herself they were okay. Only there was no way she could lie to her family in person. Pretending she was fine on the phone was one thing, but in person, she'd give herself away in seconds.

"Oh, they're fine, sweetie, all fine. We all are. It was a shock at first, and definitely exciting, it gave me a little taste of your life. I know you mostly work in a lab, but you travel a bit. I know you were out of the country when this happened because I wanted to call you, but your boss told me you were unavailable. I don't know the things you've seen, or the things you've had to do, my sweet little Ella-boo, but I know how proud of you I am."

Her mom's words soothed the rough edges of her pain at being let down by the people she loved. If her mom knew that she'd put herself in a precarious situation where she'd almost been raped, almost been kept as a sex slave for a notorious weapons trafficker, and had to kill said trafficker then her mom would take back those words and probably replace them with a you're crazy.

No.

There was no way her mom couldn't be proud of her even if she'd chosen a very different life path than the rest of her family.

The truth of what happened was on the tip of her tongue, about to burst out because Ella couldn't hold it in any longer, when two little faces appeared on the screen behind their grandmother.

"Auntie Ella!" six-year-old Rachel enthused.

"It's Auntie Boo," four-year-old Sarah protested, loving the nickname Ella had had since she was a baby and preferring it to Ella's actual name.

Seeing the two little girls she adored didn't soothe her like it usually did. Instead, tonight it just made her feel that much more lonely. She didn't have kids, didn't have a husband, didn't even have a boyfriend, and while usually that was okay, tonight when she was already feeling adrift in the big, wide world, all it did was make the ache in her heart grow.

* * *

FEBRUARY 8TH
6:56 P.M.

COMING HERE COULDN'T BE CONSIDERED a good idea.

Nor could it be considered to be in anyone's best interests.

Not his and certainly not Ella's.

Yet Miguel parked his car on the street outside the pretty

family home that seemed too large for a single person and, at the same time, absolutely what he could picture someone like Ella living in.

He didn't just park his car. He climbed out of it and walked down the stone path through her front yard and up her porch steps.

Even though he had pretended to his brother and Ella's friends that all he felt for her was compassion and all he was aiming for was being her friend, that felt like a lie when he was standing in front of her front door. It felt like more even though it shouldn't.

For either of their sakes.

Being there could be a mistake. Ella had asked for time alone to process, and while he didn't want to disrespect her wishes, he couldn't help but feel that what she really needed right now was to *not* be alone. When she'd been threatened the mole's access to Prey had meant she had to fight alone. He needed her to know that she had someone at her back.

After he checked on her, if she still said she wanted him to go, then he would. Miguel had no intention of forcing himself on her. There was no possible way he could have gone home without knowing for certain that Ella was hanging in there.

So, to that end, he knocked on her door and waited.

While he wouldn't have been surprised if she'd gotten home, eaten, taken a steaming hot bath or shower, and fallen into bed, there were lights on—upstairs and downstairs—so he knew she was still up.

What was in question was whether or not she would open up and let him in.

Turned out he didn't need to worry about it. The door swung open, and she stood there looking small and lost. Her long blonde locks were twisted into a messy bun on the top of her head, she was wearing leggings and one of those huge, oversized hoodie blanket things that was white with pretty pink, yellow, green, and blue butterflies on it. Her feet were bare, and a rush of protectiveness hit him as he remembered the burns and blisters that littered the soles of her feet.

She shouldn't be standing on them.

She shouldn't be there alone.

Someone should be with her. Taking care of her. Making sure she was doing okay physically, psychologically, and emotionally. Or at the very least that she was hanging in there because there was no way she could be okay after everything she'd been through. One of those things on their own was enough to tear apart a person's psyche, let alone the blow after blow that had battered Ella.

"Hey, honey, how you doing?" he asked, trying to keep his tone gentle but not patronizing. Because despite everything she had been through, Ella was still standing, she had managed to withstand all those blows and come out the other end. While she might not realize it yet, she was strong, and he found himself not wanting to leave until he knew she was aware that she could make it through this ordeal and come out the other side.

Ella shrugged, and he was pretty sure she was going to reiterate her need for time alone, but then she turned and disappeared inside her house, leaving the door open behind her.

Taking that as an invitation, Miguel stepped inside her home and locked up before heading down the hall the way Ella had gone. He found her in a huge family room at the back of the house, curled up on the sofa in front of the fireplace. With her legs tucked underneath her hoodie, and her face scrubbed free of makeup, she looked so young and vulnerable, and he felt an unfamiliar ache in his chest.

He and Luis had been messed up by their childhood only in very different ways. Luis had kept his distance from women, only allowing himself casual encounters because of one bad decision he'd made at the tender age of eleven that had almost gotten Miguel killed and them both arrested. On the other hand, he had kept things casual with women because he was more like their addict mother than he cared to admit. It was one thing to date around, have sex, a good time with no strings attached, but risking falling for someone and repeating his parents' mistakes was something he had vowed never to do.

Which meant never allowing things to get serious. Women were for fun, he was respectful with them, always made sure they enjoyed themselves and knew the score up front, but never once had even a hint of a feeling beyond fun possessed him.

Ever.

Certainly never anything like this overwhelming protectiveness he felt when it came to Ella.

Shaking off the feeling, he crossed the room and dropped onto the sofa beside her. "Let me check out your feet," he said, needing to do something so he didn't feel so helpless. Apparently, there was a flip side to protectiveness, and it was helplessness. He needed to fix this for Ella somehow, and since he couldn't it left him feeling edgy and uncomfortable.

"You don't have to," she protested but didn't stop him when he reached out and snagged her ankles, twisting her so she was facing sideways on the couch and resting her legs on his thighs so he could check out the soles of her feet.

The blisters looked painful, and a couple were red and puffy like infection might be attempting to set in.

Good.

That was something he could fix.

"I don't like the look of a couple of these," he told her. "You got any antibiotic cream?"

"There's some in the bathroom cabinet," she replied, a little of the weariness in her eyes wiped away by curiosity.

"You have to try to stay off them if you want them to heal," he reprimanded, knowing she'd really had no opportunity to do that. It was himself he was frustrated with. He'd known he shouldn't have let her come home alone, he should have insisted on taking her. If she'd needed to be by herself, he could have stayed in a different room, or even in his car in her driveway, anything so she knew she wasn't alone anymore.

Heading up the stairs, he located the master bedroom and was unsurprised to see the huge canopy bed littered with frilly pink and white pillows, the overstuffed armchair in the corner, and the little knickknacks on top of the nightstands and dresser. There were photos on the walls, and he knew when he saw all the happy family snaps of Ella with her parents, siblings, and nieces and nephews, that he was right about her.

She was everything he wasn't.

She was sweet, and light, and wanted the whole fairytale romance. He was darkness that could destroy her if he let himself.

Something he couldn't afford to do.

Protectiveness and friendship were all he could offer.

Nothing more.

Locating the antibiotic cream in her bathroom cabinet, he headed back downstairs to find Ella right where he'd left her on the couch. There was something in her eyes he couldn't let himself acknowledge as she watched him sit down beside her and lift her legs again, so they rested on his thighs.

When he began to rub the cream onto all the blisters, Ella sank back against the cushions with a small sigh, and he knew he'd made the right choice in going there instead of heading home. He'd told Luis and the others that he'd support Ella and be the friend she needed when she felt betrayed by everyone she knew. Miguel was still determined to do it, but he realized with each passing second that it was going to be a whole lot harder than he had thought it would be.

How was he supposed to spend time around Ella and not fall for her?

It wasn't something he could allow to happen.

Never could he allow himself to forget that his mother's blood ran through his veins. There was only so much his foster parents could do and while they had been everything he could have hoped for in parents, it hadn't been enough to undo biology.

Addiction had come for him.

What had started as just smoking a little pot with his friends in high school had spiraled out of control. It had taken everything he had to pull himself out of that hole, to get clean, to get his cravings under control.

There was no way he could risk ever dragging anyone else down with him if the addiction he managed to keep on a tight leash of control should one day snap.

Especially not a woman like Ella.

CHAPTER THIRTEEN

February 8th
   7:12 P.M.

ALLOWING Miguel to touch her didn't seem wise.

Especially since Ella knew what kind of man he was and the kind of relationships he had with women.

Crushing on him for the last couple of weeks, there was a reason why she hadn't approached him that went beyond the terrible timing and her fear for her friends and the drug they had created together.

They were too different.

She wanted marriage and a family, Miguel wanted fun and no commitments.

Neither of them was right, and neither was wrong, they just didn't want the same things. Ella knew she was vulnerable right now, with too many emotions and no appropriate outlet. Allowing a man who had saved her life, who had believed in her, who had come to check on her even though he barely knew her, to touch her and comfort her, was asking to get her heart broken.

The problem with believing in dreams coming true was that you looked for those answers everywhere.

Only this time, she already knew that Miguel was *not* the answer.

Still, even knowing that, she craved more of his touch as his hands worked their way up her calves, massaging the weary muscles and drawing a small content sigh from her lips.

It felt so good to have someone there taking care of her.

She hadn't really wanted to be alone, she just didn't have anywhere to turn. With her family unaware of all that had happened, and the distance between her and her friends, there was no one else.

Until there was.

Until this man showed up seemingly determined to stand by her side.

"Here, sit up. Let me do your shoulders," Miguel's voice rumbled as his large hands circled her wrists and tugged her up.

Shifting her so she was perched on the edge of the couch between his spread knees, he began to work out the kinks in her neck and shoulders. Each firm stroke of his fingers eased some of the tension, released another string tying the heavy burdens to her back, and strengthened the connection she felt toward the man who had shown her kindness even when he had no reason to believe in her.

When his hands finally dropped, Ella mewed a protest, making Miguel chuckle.

"Why don't you head up and take a nice hot shower? I'll make you something to eat, and then you can head to bed."

"Come with me." The words tumbled from her lips before

she could stop them, but even once they were out there Ella felt no desire to pull them back.

"Upstairs?"

"In the shower," she clarified, willing him to understand without her having to say it so blatantly.

This wasn't her. She didn't use sex as a Band-Aid for her problems. Yet she had never wanted a man more than she wanted the one staring at her like she'd suddenly grown an extra head. It was a craving that ran deep, he was the only one who had believed in her, and he'd saved her over and over again.

She needed him.

Needed him to help her forget for just a little while all that had happened to her.

"Ella, honey, we can't. Not after what you've been through. I'm not going to take advantage of you," Miguel said gently.

"It's not taking advantage if it's what I want," she assured him.

Sex didn't have to be a big deal. Just because for her it was usually a way to express intimacy with the person she had feelings for didn't mean it always had to be that way. It could be just sex. It could just be about her and Miguel, here tonight, no worries about the future, no plans, no strings, nothing.

Just the two of them.

Just a human connection when she felt so very isolated and alone.

Just a moment to forget the horrors that had infiltrated her mind and were seeping down into her soul, infecting it with a disease she would never be able to completely recover from.

"I don't mean to sound condescending, honey, but I don't

think you're in a position to be making choices about anything big right now, and sex is a big decision."

With his thoughtful words and determination to still look out for her, even if it meant turning down sex because he wanted to do the right thing, it was only making her want him more.

Was it so wrong of her to need just a tiny break from the disastrous mess her life had become?

If it was only about forgetting then she might feel bad for trying to use Miguel, but it ran deeper than that. She didn't want sex with a random man, she wanted it with someone she trusted, someone who made her feel like she wasn't completely alone.

She wanted sex with Miguel.

"Please don't make me beg," she whispered, averting her gaze because she knew if she spotted an ounce of rejection, it would break her.

"How about a compromise?"

That sounded too close to rejection for Ella's liking.

Fingers caressed her cheek before gently grasping her chin and angling her head so she was looking over her shoulder with no choice but to meet Miguel's dark eyes.

"I like sex, Ella. I like no strings attached sex which I think is what you're trying to offer me here, but I don't think it's what you like. I don't want to be something you regret in the morning. Especially when you feel like you don't have anyone on your side right now, and I think you trust me to be there for you."

"I do," she whispered, unable to break eye contact now it had been established. Something about this man drew her in like a moth to the flame. Ella knew she was going to wind up getting burned yet she couldn't seem to stop herself.

"Then we compromise. You let me make you feel good if you're certain that's what you want but no sex."

If she couldn't feel the bulge in his pants, then she might have thought he wasn't interested in her, but that clearly wasn't the case. He was attracted to her, and she hoped he was just trying to be noble and there was nothing more to it.

"Are you only agreeing to touch me because you feel sorry for me?" she asked. Normally, Ella wouldn't be so forward. She wasn't shy but wasn't overly confident in herself either.

"Hell no," he said vehemently. "I feel bad for everything you had to go through and for what would have happened if I hadn't found you in the jungle. But I don't pity you. You're too strong to deserve anyone's pity."

"I don't feel strong, Miguel," she said softly. "I feel ... empty. Take me upstairs and make me feel something else, please. I need you."

Something sparked in his eyes.

Something that looked a lot like disappointment and shame.

But he hid it quickly, and then the next thing Ella knew she was being swept up into a strong pair of arms. Despite having seen this man in action, seen him kill, seen him take blow after blow, she found a softness to him that she liked even more than his strength.

In her bathroom, Miguel set her on her feet. After pressing a tender kiss to her forehead—a kiss that almost brought her to her knees because it was every bit the sweetness and connectedness she needed right now—he grabbed the hem of her Oodie and pulled it over her head.

Next, he grabbed the waistband of her leggings and panties and eased them down her legs. When she stepped out of them, she was left completely naked before him and the embarrassment she thought she should feel was absent. All she felt around Miguel was comfortable.

Fingers fumbling in her hair, he was able to untie the

band holding her hair in a bun and it tumbled free, hanging around her shoulders in long, blonde locks.

"Much better," he murmured as he ran his fingers through her hair and then framed her face, his palms warn and rough against her cheeks. "Almost as beautiful as you are strong," Miguel said with a wink before leaning in to brush his lips across hers.

Then he was gone, opening the glass door to her walk-in shower and leaning over to turn on the faucets before stripping out of his clothes, leaving him gloriously naked. She'd seen men who looked like him before, worked with a whole bunch of them, but usually when she dated it tended to be fellow musicians. It never worked out because, in the end, they wound up jealous of her talent even though she gave only a handful of concerts a year and her music wasn't the center of her life.

Seeing Miguel now, his wide chest, his chiseled abs, the bulging muscles of his arms, it was like looking at one of those marble statues sprung to life. Most impressive was his length that stood rock hard and at attention.

It was so irresistible that when Miguel reached her for and guided her into the now steamy shower, Ella couldn't resist stroking her fingertips along it.

"Babe," Miguel groaned, making her grin as the nightmare of the last few days slipped out of her mind.

"What?" she asked innocently, stepping under the spray.

"This is about you. Me touching you, no sex."

"I can touch you, too, that isn't sex," she sassed back, feeling strong and powerful in this moment with this gorgeous man beside her. She knew what he'd been about to sacrifice for her, knew what effects the drug Raul Castillo wanted to give him would have, and she wanted to show how much she appreciated everything he'd done for her.

Besides, he was the one who'd made the no sex rule, not her.

She was all for as much touching, as much pleasure as they could give one another before the clock struck twelve, and like Cinderella, she had to go back to her regular life and face all her problems all over again.

"You're all sugar on the outside and spice on the inside, aren't you?" he teased as he reached for the shower massager. Just the sight of it in his hand, as he fiddled with the settings, had her bud beginning to throb in anticipation.

It had been a while since she'd had a boyfriend, almost a year, and while she wasn't averse to a little solo play, she rarely had time. It had probably been six months since her last orgasm and her body felt like it was wound up so tightly it wasn't going to take much to make her snap.

"Come here," Miguel ordered, positioned her under the spray so her palms were pressed against the tiles, then nudged her legs apart so he could drag a fingertip along her center.

When that same finger circled her entrance before slipping inside, Ella moaned, greedily pushing her hips back to seek more.

Miguel just chuckled and stroked deep, managing to angle things just right so he brushed across the spot inside her that made a tingle ripple out across her body. Then he was crowding against her back shifting the shower head so the water pulsed against her bundle of nerves as another finger joined the first inside her.

Pressed as he was against her, Ella could feel the hard ridge of his erection, and as pleasure began to build inside her she reached back and grasped his length. His giving her something and her not being able to return the favor felt wrong, it felt too much like using him. This man might be little more than a stranger, but he felt like something else, something more.

There was a connection there, it was the only way to explain how he'd been able to look past everything screaming she was guilty to see something else was going on. It was the only way to explain how she felt comfortable and at ease with him, even after what she'd been through.

"You don't have to, El," he whispered in her ear.

"I want to," she assured him, warmth settling in her chest at his constant need to ensure she was all right. She wasn't, but in this moment, with him, there in her shower, she was.

With each stroke of her hand up and down his length, and each thrust of his fingers as he pumped them in and out of her, the pleasure inside her grew. Bigger and stronger, it filled her until she felt so close to bursting that she whimpered, needing something to push her over the edge.

When lips pressed a kiss to the curve of her neck, Ella shattered.

The unrelenting pounding of the water against her bud seemed to make her orgasm last forever and she clung to this beautiful moment, treasuring it, wanting it to never end.

A grunt from behind her told her that Miguel had also come, and she felt the stickiness of his release on her hand. She wanted to take that release, absorb it, make it part of her, and use it somehow to make Miguel stay.

Because one thing she was certain of in the giant storm of uncertainness her life had become was that Miguel wasn't sticking around. It was a silly thing to be worried about, given everything else she had on her plate, but the idea of Miguel leaving made her feel almost sick with loneliness.

FEBRUARY 9TH

5:33 A.M.

SOMETHING WARM TICKLED HIS SKIN, stirring him from sleep.

Miguel blinked open heavy eyes, not immediately real-izing where he was.

Years in the military meant he usually woke up instantly and completely. If you were in the field even losing a couple of seconds could mean the difference between life and death, so you learned pretty quickly to snap from sleep mode to awake mode in the blink of an eye.

Thankfully, this morning it didn't matter that his brain woke groggily, taking a moment to put all the pieces together because he was curled up in Ella's bed.

In Ella's bed.

Shock had him jerking sideways, rolling to his feet, and staring down at the woman still sleeping, tucked beneath the blankets.

What was he doing falling asleep with Ella in his arms?

That was not the way to keep distance between them. Being her friend didn't mean he had to climb into bed with her.

Only...

She'd asked him to.

Seemed he was powerless to say no when it came to this woman.

Getting in the shower with her was a crazy move when he wanted to stop himself from getting emotionally invested. Attraction was one thing, it was okay for his body to crave her, to want to sink inside her, feel her come around him, and touch and taste every inch of her delectable body. It was even okay to want to be her friend, to make sure she was okay, to be there for her, and offer her the support she needed when she felt adrift and alone.

But making out with her in the shower was only going to make him crave her more.

Still, when she'd looked up at him with her big green eyes, every drop of pain she was feeling shining brightly, and asked if he pitied her, he'd felt this awful clawing feeling in his gut. A need he couldn't even begin to explain.

Ella was hurting and he had to make it stop.

That was all he'd been able to register.

So he'd soothed her fears, telling her quite honestly that he didn't pity her. His only reservations were that she would regret it in the morning and the thought of her resenting him didn't sit well with him.

His other reservation was that he was already getting more invested than he should.

It was too late to worry about that now, though.

He'd touched her, made her come all over his fingers, felt her hands on him.

Not that he'd stopped there.

After the shower, he'd dried her off, helped her get dressed then carried her back downstairs to feed her. Carrying her had just been so she didn't have to walk on her feet when he knew they had to be bothering her. Definitely not because he just liked the feel of her slim body in his arms.

Definitely not.

At least if he was lying to himself.

When he'd made sure she'd eaten a decent meal he had intended to leave so she could get some rest. People were watching her house so he knew she was safe and if he stayed any longer he knew it would be even harder to walk away from her once the mole was caught and she was able to find her footing again.

Then she'd asked him to hold her while she fell asleep.

She'd looked so sweet, so innocent, so unsure of herself. He could tell it had taken all the courage she had left to ask.

It was hard to ask for help when you needed it, and he respected that she'd twice been able to ask him to give her what she needed.

He'd been helpless to say no.

His intention had been to lay there until she fell asleep and then slip out of the bed and spend the rest of the night in her spare room or on the couch in her living room.

Only as soon as he had her in his arms, he'd been unable to move, and he must have wound up falling asleep holding her. There was just something about this woman he couldn't seem to walk away from. She was strong and determined, she cared about the people she loved, she was loyal and intelligent, and sweet and innocent even despite the world she knew existed through her work at Prey.

Ella Whitlock was the whole package, only he wasn't looking for a package to keep.

If Miguel thought there was any way he could keep things casual with Ella, maybe even hook up with her a few times without feelings getting in the way then he'd go for it.

That could never happen though.

He was already catching feelings.

Feelings he couldn't afford himself.

Not if he wanted to protect Ella and keep her safe.

And he did. There was no way he would allow his personal demons to infect someone so sweet and pure. Someone who had already been through so much and had even more she would have to deal with once the full impact of everything that had happened sunk in.

Maybe if she hadn't traipsed off to Mexico, ready to sacrifice herself to save everyone else, he might have given in to the attraction he had been sure wasn't one-sided, but not now.

Now Ella needed him to be strong.

Needed him to keep things in perspective.

Hurting her was out of the question, and if he allowed himself to get in any deeper, he risked falling for her for real. Allowing those feelings he was already catching to develop into something he wouldn't be able to ignore.

If that happened and he and Ella fell for one another, and he lost the tight grip he retained on his addiction, he would drag her down with him. Knowing he had destroyed something so bright and good would also destroy him, and he'd tumble further and further down into the addiction hole until he was in so deep that he'd never be able to climb out again.

"I'm sorry, honey," he whispered as he reached out to brush a stray lock of hair off her cheek. Her hair felt like silk, and her cheek like the softest satin. Staying there would be so easy, allowing himself to fall for her would be much easier than he thought it would be.

All his life he'd found it easy to maintain an emotional distance between women that weren't part of his family.

Until one woman stood before him in the jungle, shaking and crying, lying to him to get away because even though she'd come mere seconds away from being raped she was determined to follow through with her plans.

"Miguel?" Ella asked, voice husky with sleep as she blinked and shifted so she was looking up at him.

This was it.

Time to break his own heart to protect a woman he'd never expected to fall for. But he was falling, and this was the only way to protect Ella. Given enough time, he'd wind up hurting her, he was sure of it, positive that sooner or later genetics would catch up with him and he'd wind up like the deadbeat dad who abandoned him or the druggie mom who lived only for her addiction and not her two little boys.

"Sorry, El, I have to go," he said softly. Miguel wasn't a monster, he knew that Ella was floundering right now, felt all alone, and he had no intention of telling her he would be there for her only to then bail.

He'd be there. He'd just have to do it more carefully.

No more shower playtimes, no more coming over and hanging out for hours, and definitely no more climbing beneath the covers and holding her in his arms all night long while he slept the sleep of the dead.

"You're leaving?" The vulnerability in her voice about undid him. Had him rethinking everything, doubting himself.

Only there was no room for doubts.

Just facts.

Facts were, he came from two parents who were addicts. Facts were, he'd had his own battle with addiction. Facts were, it was a daily battle for him to keep those urges under control. Facts were, he worried constantly that something might happen to send the house of cards he had so carefully constructed from falling down around him.

If his life fell apart and he was the only one impacted he could deal with that, but not if he took Ella down with him.

"Yeah, honey, got to go catch up with my team."

Giving him a tremulous smile, she nodded. "I appreciate you coming over last night, Miguel. I appreciate ... everything. The shower, the food, you taking care of me, holding me even though I know you weren't real comfortable getting into bed with me."

That she didn't beg him to stay even though she obviously wanted him to was just another reason for him to like her.

Another reason for him to have to get out of there.

Ella was too perfect, he couldn't be the one to corrupt her.

"I put my number in your phone last night, call or text if you need anything. I mean it, Ella, I'll drop everything and come right over." Not an exaggeration. Just because he couldn't let things develop more than they already had didn't mean he wasn't all in when it came to supporting Ella through this mess the mole had thrust her into.

When she shot him a brilliant smile, Miguel was struck by the thought that he was already fighting a losing battle.

He was falling for this woman, and if he couldn't stop it from happening then he could be the straw that broke the camel's back and wind up being the cause of Ella's life imploding.

CHAPTER FOURTEEN

February 9th
11:28 A.M.

THIS SUCKED BUT it was the right thing to do.

Ella knew that Miguel had told her she shouldn't make any big life decisions until the dust settled a little and she was able to think more clearly, but the bottom line was, she just couldn't see herself not coming to this same conclusion a week, a month, or a year down the track.

It was what had to happen.

Didn't mean she was happy about it or that there weren't about a million doubts running rampant through her mind right now.

As she parked her car at Prey's office building, she wished Miguel was there with her. This would be so much easier if she felt like she had someone on her side.

While he might not have outright said the words at her place this morning, she knew what he'd been feeling and thinking and what his plans were for the future.

Those plans didn't include her.

He'd made her a promise to be there for her while she healed, and Ella one hundred percent believed he was going to follow through with that. If she texted, he'd answer. If she called, he'd come. If she needed him, he'd be there.

For now.

Until he knew she'd found her footing again.

Then he'd be gone.

While she wanted to hold onto him, keep him close, she appreciated him trying to keep a little distance between them. Looking out for her again. Because the truth was, she wasn't emotionally or psychologically okay, and if she wasn't careful then these tiny little feelings she was developing would quickly bloom into something more.

Something that would only wind up getting her hurt.

Last night was a one-off. Once she'd taken that first step, asked him to go upstairs with her to the shower, she'd made herself a promise. For one night, she was going to ask for what she needed, take anything he was willing to offer her, and pretend that maybe Miguel could be hers to keep.

If he hadn't had to leave so early, Ella prayed she would have had the strength to stick to that plan. They wanted different things, they couldn't work long term, that was something she had to keep at the forefront of her mind so she didn't allow those teeny feelings to grow.

Still, what she wouldn't give to have him there by her side as she climbed out of her car and squared her shoulders.

Just as she reached the door to the building, her phone beeped with a text, and when she fished it out of her purse she saw Miguel's name. In the few hours since he'd left her house, they'd texted at least a couple of dozen times, and every time he sent her a message she smiled, a tiny ray of warmth and light hitting her bruised and battered soul.

So much for keeping things in perspective and remembering that Miguel wasn't looking for anything serious and she wanted the whole white picket fence fairytale. Again, she was grateful that he seemed to be able to keep a level head because she certainly couldn't. Although knowing he was doing what was best for both of them when she couldn't quite manage it only made her fall for him more.

MIGUEL
> You weren't supposed to be making
> any rash big life decisions

DESPITE THE CLEAR reprimand in the words, Ella's smile only widened.

It felt so nice to have someone looking out for her even if the only thing they were giving her was friendship. It was what she needed, and she was going to grab onto it with both hands and hold on. Hopefully, she could even convince Miguel to remain her friend even after things calmed down and she felt more stable and secure.

Ella
> How do you even know what I'm doing?

MIGUEL
> Eyes everywhere, honey
> You best remember that

. . .

His words warmed her again, and Ella typed out a quick response as she strolled into the building that had been such a big part of her life these last several years.

> Ella
> By eyes everywhere I assume you mean
> you're texting with the guys following me

Miguel
I don't give away my secrets 😉
Seriously though, want me to come
right to Prey?
Can be there in 30

She did.

But she also knew that part of healing was going to be learning to stand on her own two feet and handle her life without a crutch.

> Ella
> Thank you but I got this
> Maybe if you're not busy we
> could do dinner tonight?
> Just take out or something easy

Standing on her own two feet or not, this was a big step, and even though she knew she wasn't going to change her mind, it would still help to have a little company tonight because this was the end of an era and it hurt to be closing this door.

MIGUEL
    Are you sure about this?

Ella
Yes

MIGUEL
    I'll be round at seven
    Text me your favorite pizza toppings later
    Good luck

LUCK WASN'T GOING to make this any easier, but Miguel's support did. Knowing she'd get to see him later helped even more. Before tonight she was going to make sure she had herself in check. There could be no more making out, no more falling asleep in his arms, but she could still enjoy his company and soak up some of that strength he seemed to have an endless supply of.

The foyer was quiet. Dora Hibbert, the receptionist, wasn't at the front desk, but since she hadn't yet handed in her letter of resignation and key cards she didn't need to be buzzed into the secure side of the building.

Sadness seemed to echo around her as she walked through the halls for the last time. There were so many happy memories there. Not just of spending time with her team, but memories of happy moments with the former

SEALs who ran the West Coast office of Prey, and with the women of Artemis Team who had all recently found love and peace after the man who had caused them so much pain had finally been caught.

Walking away was going to be harder than she imagined, even with the pain of knowing that they had all let her down softening the blow.

With a heavy heart, she knocked on the open door of Fox's office and took a step inside. Since Fox had been the leader of the SEAL team, he was the unofficial top dog of the West Coast office even though technically all six guys had the same position.

When his dark eyes met hers, she saw the pain and guilt there. Felt it filling the room. It was so potent that for a moment, Ella second-guessed herself. If the guys felt bad about letting her down, could she find a way to get past it and stay at Prey?

No.

Don't back out now.

You just feel bad because you hate when others are upset.

This time you have to do what's best for you.

Her mental pep talk did the trick. Reminded her of her own needs. She'd only been home a day, there had been zero time for her to even begin processing the fact that she had almost been raped several times, or that she'd killed Raul Castillo before he could keep her locked away as his own personal toy.

When that happened, she wouldn't have the mental energy it would take to figure out a way forward with the people she had considered a family.

Fox's gaze moved to the envelope in her hand and if she'd thought the level of guilt in the room was strong before, it crescendoed until it was almost overwhelming. Again, her resolve wavered but she quickly strengthened it before she could say something stupid like she was making a mistake.

"Don't do this, please," Fox said, the usual confidence in his tone lacking.

"I have to," she whispered, crossing the room on shaky legs to set the envelope on his desk.

"We messed up. Big time."

Ella nodded, fighting back tears. It helped a little to know he wasn't pretending otherwise but it didn't erase the gaping hole in her chest at knowing her people had so quickly believed she would betray them all.

"I messed up. I'm the one who should have known better, I'm the one everyone looks to for leadership. If I'd believed in you the way Eagle did, the others would have as well."

"I know I set it up to make it look believable, but for some reason, I thought only the mole would think I really stole the drug. That was silly of me."

Scraping his hands down his face Fox sighed. A deep, sorrowful sound that made her want to say something to make things better for him.

But what was there to say?

There was no going back. What was done was done. They all had to start finding a way to move forward.

"I'm sorry, Ella. I did the one thing no team is supposed to ever do. I left a man behind. I left you behind. I let the stress of the last month make me forget the last several years. I have no right to ask for your forgiveness, or to ask you for a second chance. To ask you to reconsider resigning and stay here, give us a chance to prove to you that we can earn back your trust."

Fox rounded the table, stood beside her, and waited until she finally lifted her head to look up at him. There was no doubt that his remorse was genuine, Ella just wasn't sure it changed anything.

"I shouldn't, but I'm going to," he told her. "I won't leave a teammate behind again. I'm not giving up on you. None of us are."

With a nod toward his office door, Ella turned to see everyone else flooding into the room. These people used to be her family, now they were ... she wasn't even sure. All she knew was that the mole had managed to blow up her life and she wasn't sure she'd ever be able to remove enough rubble to go back to being the person she was before.

* * *

FEBRUARY 9TH
11:39 A.M.

NO SOONER HAD Miguel set his phone down than the door to his apartment opened and his big brother came strolling in.

"I think it's about time I returned the favor," Luis said as he headed for the fridge and helped himself to a can of soda.

"Return the favor?" Miguel asked, his mind still stuck on Ella and his internal debate on whether he should hop in his car and head straight for Prey.

Just because she said she had this didn't mean she couldn't use some support right now.

As soon as he got a text from the guys Eagle had assigned to watch Ella, letting him know that she had gotten into her car and was heading for Prey, he knew what she was doing. There was only one reason he could think of that she would be going there now when she was hurting from their betrayal.

That was to hand in her resignation.

They'd talked about her not making any life-altering decisions right now. It was never a good idea to do so right on the heels of trauma. You couldn't be in the right frame of mind to ensure you were making an informed decision and not reacting to the emotions raging inside you.

Which was exactly what Ella was doing.

Did he blame her for wanting to cut ties with Prey?

No.

Did he think it was the right thing for her?

He wasn't sure of the answer to that.

While he understood where Prey had been coming from, the evidence had indeed pointed to Ella being the mole they had been searching for the past month, Miguel could also understand where Ella was coming from. If his team had been so quick to believe the worst of him, even if there was evidence supporting that decision, it would have damaged his trust in them to the point where he might have made the same decision Ella had.

"Hey, lover boy."

Fingers snapped in front of his face and Miguel blinked, then swatted away his brother's hand.

Even though there was only two years between them in age, Luis had always very much been more of a parent to him than a brother. Especially for the first decade of their lives. When you grew up with an absent dad and a mom who was in and out of toxic relationships while always being true to her greatest love, her addictions to drugs and alcohol, then you bonded with your siblings.

Especially when they looked out for you the way Luis always had for him.

From stealing food so they didn't starve to coming up with a plan only an eleven-year-old could think would work, his brother had been there for him. That plan of Luis' to join a gang to get them money so they could have a better life had wound up working in their favor just not in the way his pre-teen mind had thought.

After their first job for the gang, to gain entry to a store the gang intended to rob, got them caught in a shootout that had almost taken Miguel's life, they'd wound up being fostered by the kind of parents kids like them could only dream about. Parents who were still part of their lives today. Well, their dad was since their mom had passed away a little while back. But there were also four foster siblings and their families, and he treasured every one of those relationships because he still remembered what it felt like to be forgotten and unwanted.

Miguel still carried around a heavy load of shame for knowing he had almost wasted the life his brother had managed to get for them by turning to the very same vice that had haunted their biological mom.

"Lover boy?" he repeated. "I think that's a little extreme considering I'm not in love with anyone."

"Not yet," Luis said, lounging back against the counter.

"Not ever," Miguel amended. Just like Luis had reasons for keeping his distance from anyone who might get close enough to hurt him by becoming a responsibility, he had his own reasons for doing the same.

They were just reasons Luis was unaware of.

Luis had enlisted right after graduating high school, he hadn't been around when Miguel fought his battle with addiction. Shame had him keeping that secret from the person he admired most in the world. Luis had sacrificed so much for him, and he didn't want to see the disappointment in his brother's eyes.

"I seem to remember about a week ago someone showing up at my place and telling me that I deserved to be happy and that I should give things with Cassie a chance," Luis said.

Shrugging, Miguel grabbed a soda and dropped into one of the chairs at his kitchen table. Sure, he'd gone to his brother's place to make sure Luis wasn't going to waste the once-in-a-lifetime opportunity to find your other half, but Luis and Cassie's situation was nothing like his and Ella's.

"Not the same thing, bro."

"Don't see what's different about it," Luis insisted as he took the chair opposite. "You like Ella, I know you do, and I'm guessing she likes you, too. It certainly seemed like she did when we saw you two together yesterday."

"I'm being her friend."

"Doesn't change what I just said. You like her, Miguel. I know you, I can tell. I get why you might not want to make a move now given what she's just been through, but when things settle down, you should ask her out."

"Not going to happen."

"Why not?"

Because Ella was too special to risk.

Because even though his addictions were under control now, it didn't mean they always would be.

Because the world was an unpredictable place, and he couldn't guarantee that he wouldn't wind up hurting Ella.

"Something else is going on," Luis said, eyeing him carefully. "You're keeping something from me. What is it, Miguel?"

Just because they'd gotten a foster family when they were nine and eleven, well over two decades ago, didn't mean that Luis had ever stopped completely acting like a second dad. Even though his brother sometimes kept him at arm's length didn't mean he didn't treasure the relationship they shared. They'd lived through hell together and had been all each other had, that kind of bond would never disappear.

The last thing he wanted was to taint that bond. For Luis to know how badly he'd messed up, and how much he feared messing up again.

"I'm your big brother, there isn't anything you can't tell me."

"Yeah, there is," Miguel whispered tiredly. Carrying this secret around had weighed on him. As much as he'd had all the support he needed from his foster parents and siblings, he'd wanted his brother's support, too. Just not enough to risk Luis being disappointed in him.

"What's going on?" Luis demanded, a thread of worry in his voice.

"I don't keep things casual with women for the fun of it," he admitted, it was time to clear the air. Whatever happened, happened. But he didn't want secrets between him and his brother any longer. "Well, it is fun, and I enjoy women, but there's a reason I haven't had a serious relationship and never intend to. I'm an addict, Luis."

His brother's brow furrowed. "I don't understand. What do you mean?"

"When you went off to the military I messed up. Big time. I thought it was no big deal, that I could be cool, smoke a little weed, and fit in with the guys. Only it turned out to be a big deal. A huge deal. Weed quickly spiraled into harder drugs, and before I knew it, I couldn't go a day without getting high."

"But you joined the military, too. You're a SEAL. No way you can hide that kind of addiction."

"Couldn't hide it from Mom and Dad either. They realized pretty quickly what was going on. Insisted I go to rehab. Got me counseling and gave me everything I needed to get clean. I haven't touched anything since I was seventeen. Don't even drink because I don't trust myself not to fall down a rabbit hole. You getting it, big brother? I can't be in a relationship whether I want to be or not. I can't risk turning out like Mom. Can't risk something happening to cause me to lose my control. Can't risk hurting someone innocent like Mom hurt us."

Instead of the disappointment he expected to see in his

brother's eyes, the judgment, there was only compassion and love.

Enough of it to have him getting choked up.

"Miguel, you aren't Mom. I don't know who she was before the drugs got her, what she was like, who was in her corner. But I do know you. I know you're strong enough to have kicked an addiction that she never could. I know you're strong enough to keep it under control for almost fifteen years. I know you're strong enough to care about others and put their needs above yours. I know that you would never hurt anyone and that if you stumbled, you would do whatever was necessary to right yourself so you didn't cause your own life or anyone else's to crumble around you."

His brother might believe those things, they might even be true, the problem was, Miguel didn't and had no idea how to even go about beginning to believe they might possibly be true.

CHAPTER FIFTEEN

February 9th
  11:57 A.M.

THEY WERE ALL THERE.

All of them.

Not just her team and the Prey guys, but all the guys' wives and kids as well. Which was kind of a dirty trick because they all knew she loved those children and would do anything for them. There was no real need for them to be there, they'd had nothing to do with the whole mess. The oldest of them was Spider and his wife Abigail's seven-year-old son RJ, the youngest King and his wife Faith's two-year-old daughter Indigo, they were all too young to even understand. The wives had nothing to do with it either. She had no idea if they'd also believed the worst of her, but if she knew the guys, and she did, they wouldn't have told their wives what was going on until they had her in custody, so there was a good chance they'd been none the wiser until she got home from Mexico.

While it definitely wasn't uncommon for the wives or kids to hang out in the Prey building, Ella knew why they were all there today.

To reinforce the idea that Prey was a family.

She certainly wasn't naïve enough to believe that families never hurt one another, that they didn't mess up, that sometimes they didn't even do the unforgivable. It was just that knowing that in theory and living it in practice really were very different things.

It wasn't even the forgiving that was making this so hard. Truth was, with enough time Ella was sure she could forgive every single one of these people, after all, she loved them like family.

Trust was the issue.

How could she ever trust them again?

And if she couldn't trust them, how could she work with them?

Prey Security's strength was that Eagle Oswald had worked hard to make the company one great big family. A lot of the teams had known each other before joining Prey, some had even been teams in the military first. There was camaraderie there, bonds had been formed, and there wasn't anything you wouldn't do for one of these men or women or the people who were important to them.

Which was why this all hurt so much.

She'd given that kind of support but hadn't received it in return.

That's why she had to leave.

"Every single one of us let you down, Ella," Fox spoke. "No one is denying that, we're all owning our mistakes."

That was evident from the expressions on everyone's faces. Even the kids, young as they were, seemed to sense that something big was going on, their little faces were somber, missing their usual brightness.

"We all suspected that this was what you were going to do, and Eagle and I talked it through. He won't accept your resignation," Fox informed her.

Ella's mouth dropped open in shock.

Eagle couldn't just decide not to let her leave.

If he wouldn't accept a resignation, she'd just quit.

One side of Fox's mouth quirked up into a smile. "I can see your brain running a mile a minute. Eagle said he won't let you leave Prey, but if you decide you can't stay here and work with us, you'll have a job at Prey's main office."

Surprise—and an unexpected dose of gratefulness—swamped her. That could be the answer she was looking for. The last thing she wanted to do was leave Prey. They were the best of the best, a wonderful company to work for, and not just because of the pay and benefits.

It was that whole family thing again. Eagle had believed in her, and she would feel comfortable working for him directly or being assigned to another team, or another job in the East Coast office.

Fox's smile turned sad. "I can see you like that idea. None of us want you to leave, Ella. Not a single person. I asked Eagle for a compromise."

"Compromise?" she asked, somewhat suspiciously. Why did there always have to be a catch?

"It's not the worst thing in the world," Fox assured her. "At least I don't think it is. I'd like you to give us a month."

"A month?"

"To make things up to you, rebuild some trust, see if there's a way we can keep you here where you belong. If at the end of a month, you still feel like you can't work here, then Eagle will transfer you."

Could she do that?

Stay there a month and give it an honest try at making things work?

It sounded like a lifetime, but in reality it was only thirty days. In the scheme of things it wasn't that big an ask, especially if she knew she had an out at the end, a safe place to go where she could still do what she loved with the people she loved. Picking up her entire life and moving it across the country would be hard, especially leaving behind her family, but it wasn't like she'd never see them again and it would be nice to have a fresh start.

"One month, then if I want to leave I can?" she confirmed.

"One month," Fox agreed. "But I hope you can give us a real chance, Ella. We want to make this up to you, show you that we know how badly we messed up, and that it won't happen again. No excuses, but I think the stress of the last month has worn us all down and we just snapped in the worst possible way."

"You deserve better than that," Night spoke up.

"You deserved the benefit of the doubt," Chaos added.

"We know you, know you're not the kind of person who would ever betray the people you care about," Spider said.

"If nothing else, we should have known the only reason you would sneak the Reactivator out of here was because you'd been threatened," King told her.

Everyone was keeping a respectful distance, giving her space. In the end, the first person to approach her was Shark. Of all the former SEALs who now ran this office, Shark was by far the scariest of them. At least he had been. Before she met him, before he met his now wife Claire and fell in love, Shark had gotten his nickname because of the blank look behind his dark eyes. She hadn't known that man, but even now, with as madly in love with his wife as he was, with his twin four-year-old daughters having him wrapped around their cute little fingers, she still saw glimpses of who he had been before.

Now he stood before her, his expression serious. "Human

beings make mistakes, Ella. Not to downplay us not believing in you like we should have. It was a mistake, a big one. I know a little something about making mistakes. I made a huge one walking away from my woman." Shark glanced over his shoulder to where Claire stood smiling at him, each of her hands holding one of their twin daughters. "I'm thankful every day that she was able to forgive my stupidity and build a life with me."

"Your life is here, Ella," Cassie said, rushing forward. "Please give us this chance."

"I know it's unfair to ask so much of you when you're hurting," Lucy added, also stepping forward. "But we're a team—"

"A family," Scarlett inserted, coming to join them.

"And we've all been through so much," Lucy continued. "I know how much I need you guys, and I know deep down you need us, too, even though we hurt you and you're angry with us."

One thing her mom had always taught her was not to hold onto grudges. Even when someone legitimately did something to hurt you, maybe even on purpose with the express intention of causing you pain, when you clung to those feelings it was like consuming acid that would slowly eat away at you.

Over the years, Ella had tried to follow that advice. If people hurt her, she always made sure she forgave, never held onto things, and never let them fester. This was the first time she'd ever had to work at it though.

Nothing this big had ever happened to her before and it was throwing her through a loop.

Still, everyone was being honest, acknowledging that they messed up, asking for an opportunity to make things right, and it felt like if she didn't give it then she would be letting them down like they'd let them down.

Worse, it felt like she would be letting herself down.

The last thing she wanted was to be consumed by anger, especially not when she already had so much to deal with.

When she looked at herself in the mirror, she wanted to like the person she saw looking back at her. After all, in life the most important relationship you had was with yourself, because you were stuck with yourself every second of every day from the moment you were born until you took your final breath.

If she wanted to be able to find peace, find her footing again, and move forward, she had to find a way to move past her hurt and feelings of betrayal.

Especially given that the mole was still out there and standing together with the people she considered family at her back they had a better chance of finding them and eliminating them once and for all.

Because if they couldn't then she could lose everything, including her life.

* * *

FEBRUARY 9TH
    8:28 P.M.

FOR SOME REASON, it felt weird walking up to Ella's front door tonight.

It was late, much later than he'd told her he'd be there, but according to Luis, who had gotten a text from Cassie, Ella's attempt to hand in her resignation had wound up backfiring on her. Everyone had gathered, her whole Prey family, and announced their determination to earn back her trust and show her that she was family, and they didn't want to lose her.

Even though Luis had invited him to attend the Prey party Miguel had declined.

They weren't his family, he wasn't part of them, and at the back of his mind was a lingering fear that he didn't want to acknowledge.

Maybe Ella didn't need him now that she was making up with her people.

He'd told her he would be there for her as long as she needed him, that he would be a friend she could count on. Even after allowing himself a tiny taste of what life with Ella could be like if he could get past his fears and ask her out on a date, he'd determined to just be her friend, to keep himself in tighter check and not allow another slip-up.

It would be easier for them if Ella had the support of her team back and no longer had a use for him. Then he could just slip away and banish all thoughts of her from his mind because his craving for her was growing, and he didn't know how much longer he could spend time around her and not do something stupid like confess he wanted her and damn the consequences.

But he couldn't do that.

Not when the consequences could be so severe.

Having lived the life of an abused and neglected child who came in a distant ... nothing ... compared to his mom's habits there was no way he would ever risk putting someone in the position of being on the receiving end of his addiction.

Taking that first step with Ella, admitting he liked her, was attracted to her, and interested in her seemed innocent enough. But one date would lead to another and then another. All too easily, he could see himself becoming addicted, and once he was, he'd ask her to marry him. Obsessed as he was, there was no way he'd be able to keep his hands off her and soon they'd have a house full of kids.

What happened when something knocked his perfect world out of sync?

How would he cope?

Could he guarantee that if something awful happened, he wouldn't go running back to the cold comfort of drugs?

Until he could, he had no business getting involved with anyone.

And he certainly had no business standing on Ella's doorstep.

Yet there he was.

Couldn't seem to stay away from her.

Since she'd partied at Prey, he hadn't brought pizza around like they'd discussed. He'd also been so afraid that she'd tell him thanks for being there for her, but she didn't need him anymore that he'd given her the impression without outright lying that his team was working on something and kept his phone on silent.

She'd gotten the hint and not texted, leaving him feeling … lost.

Which was why he was there when he should be at home doing his best to forget about sea-green eyes, silky blonde locks, about sweet determination, and more courage than he could ever hope to have.

All he was going to do was check on her.

That was it.

Nothing more.

No showers.

No cooking for her.

No falling asleep holding her.

Just a quick hi and make sure all was okay. Then he'd say goodnight and head back to his place. Honestly, it was crazy he was even there. If he needed to check on her, all he had to do was call or text, he was sure she'd answer.

Yet it wasn't enough.

Miguel kept finding himself consumed with a need to see Ella. To hear her voice. To touch her. Just being in her presence filled him with this soothing warmth he couldn't seem to get enough of.

Nervous butterflies fluttered in his stomach as he knocked on the door. It wasn't since middle school that he'd felt anything like that. The first time you asked a girl out, even if you had only just turned thirteen, and the date was nothing more than hanging out after school, it was a nerve-wracking experience.

This, on the other hand, should not be.

There was not going to be any asking out, no dating, no falling in love, no marriage, no kids, no future.

No anything.

After waiting a full minute without getting any response, a tingle of unease wiped away the butterflies.

Ella was home, he knew that because the men watching her had texted to tell him. The car parked across the street confirmed that she'd also been watched since she got there. Nothing should have happened to her, she should be safe in her own home, and yet …

Scarlett had been kidnapped from her house.

Only a month ago this entire ordeal for Athena Team had begun when Scarlett was snatched from her bed in the middle of the night and spirited away to Mexico where Raul Castillo had attempted to torture the formula for the drug out of her.

Was it really outside the realm of possibility to believe that the mole couldn't get to Ella even if she was being watched?

No, it wasn't.

Not wanting to alert anyone else yet, because Miguel was all too aware of the fact that he was more than likely overreacting, he picked the lock and slipped inside Ella's house.

There was every chance she was just sleeping, or maybe taking a bath, but until he saw her with his own two eyes, nothing was going to calm his racing heart or remove the knot of fear constricting his chest.

With his hand hovering above his weapon, he moved through the house. It was quiet and dark like nobody was home, but Ella wouldn't pretend to come there only to sneak away. Why would she? She wasn't a prisoner. If she wanted to go somewhere then she could, there was no need for theatrics.

He was halfway up the stairs before he heard it.

The soft sounds of music.

Amazing music.

Since he knew Ella had been a child music prodigy before she'd decided to take a different road in life, he knew it was her playing.

Knowing she could play, knowing she must have been good to be performing to sold-out audiences before she hit the first grade, knowing that she was good enough to still put on concerts even though it wasn't her primary job, couldn't have prepared him for this.

Feeling like he was being pulled in by a siren playing classical music on a cello, Miguel climbed the rest of the stairs and followed the strains of music coming from one of the spare bedrooms.

The door was open, and when he stopped outside it the sight before him took his breath away.

Ella sat on a chair, her hair hanging down her back, catching the light from the moon that shone through the open window and shimmering like threads of spun gold. With her eyes closed and her head tipped back she was lost to the music she was making. Dressed in a pair of leggings and a tank top that molded to her beautiful breasts and accentuated her arms as they weaved the bow and made magic happen.

He had no idea how long he stood there watching her, listening to her, completely and utterly enthralled.

This was amazing. Ella was out of this world good at what she did, and even knowing the good she did at Prey and what a valuable member of the team she was, he wondered how she could have given up doing this for anything else.

Watching her, it was more than obvious that her gift wasn't just being able to play with proficiency it was being able to play with her soul. You didn't just hear what she was playing you felt it. Each note hit felt like it was speaking directly with the deepest parts of you, talking in a language you didn't even know existed.

How did the woman get to be even more amazing?

After seeing firsthand her determination to save her family and protect her drug in Mexico, Miguel hadn't thought it was possible to think more highly of her. But then she'd killed Raul Castillo herself, been brave enough to ask him for the things she needed, and forgiving enough to give her team another chance.

Now she was there bewitching him with the most perfect melodies and he had no idea how he was supposed to keep pretending he could handle just being her friend. Reminding himself that keeping some emotional distance was the only way to ensure that Ella was able to keep making beautiful music like this, touching hearts and souls, was only going to work for so long before he cracked and did something he shouldn't.

CHAPTER SIXTEEN

February 9th
   8:42 P.M.

PANIC BUBBLED to life inside her when she realized someone was standing in the doorway to her music room.

Then disappeared as quickly as it came.

Miguel.

It was only Miguel.

Ella's fingers quickly recaptured the tune she'd faltered with when she realized she was no longer alone. Something about the expression on Miguel's face urged her to keep playing.

That smile, it was … magical.

Rapt.

Almost awe-struck.

It wasn't like Ella needed to constantly have her ego massaged, she knew she'd been born with a gift, that she could have made music a career, and that even though she had chosen not to, she was still able to play in front of sold-out audiences a handful of times a year. With her gift, she was able to keep her skills at the same level that someone who practiced hours a day every day had even though she usually practiced only a couple of times a week.

But these last few days she'd been doubting everything about herself. Had she made the right choice by not telling anyone at Prey about the threats so she didn't risk the mole getting wind of the fact she had no intention of handing over the Reactivator? Was there another road she could have taken that, at the time, she hadn't been able to see? Was she overreacting to what she perceived as betrayal by the people she trusted?

Was she crazy to keep thinking about Miguel even though she knew if she allowed herself to develop feelings she would wind up with a broken heart?

And why did none of it mean anything in this moment when their eyes connected, and they seemed to speak the language of music in a conversation that wasn't spoken aloud?

"That was beautiful," Miguel murmured when the last notes had died away leaving them in silence.

Ella felt her cheeks flush with heat at his praise. "Thank you. It was Antonio Vivaldi's The Four Seasons. Technically, it's a solo violin piece, but I love it, and I play it on the cello sometimes when I just want to relax and unwind. I love the way he used music to represent so many things from nature. Singing birds, buzzing flies, flowing creeks, warm winter fires, it's so well done, so beautiful, I just ..."

"Love it," Miguel finished for her, and Ella nodded.

"Baroque music is my favorite. Vivaldi, Bach, Handel."

"The Messiah guy?"

"Yep. I love that piece, it's another of my favorites."

"Do you miss it? Playing every day? I can't imagine that

with your workload at Prey you get to play as much as you want to."

"I don't," she agreed as she stood and began to pack away her cello into its case. "When I was younger, I used to play six instruments professionally—in concert—and another dozen just for fun. When I decided to go to college and study chemistry and forensics, I had to give up everything but the cello. It's my favorite, and I couldn't imagine not having it be part of my life so it stayed even when I had to give up the others."

"I bet you could pick up any one of those instruments and blow my mind away playing them."

Her blush deepened at Miguel's compliment. "I could probably still play them, but I'm not up to performance level in them anymore. Takes all the time I have to just keep up my skills enough on the cello to be able to perform the occasional concert."

"Your worst is still going to be better than everyone else's best."

"That's sweet of you to say but not actually true," she told him with a grin as she closed the music book she'd been using and returned it to the shelves to join the others.

"I don't make the rules, honey," Miguel teased, making her laugh.

It felt nice to be able to relax, and she wished he hadn't pulled out of having dinner with her tonight. If she had to guess, it was because he was already wondering how he could extract himself from her life, and if she made up with the people at Prey then he could back away from her with zero guilt.

Pure speculation on her part, but she got the feeling that Miguel's playboy reputation had a basis in something that had happened to him. Keeping things casual with women was a way to protect his heart, she just wished she knew what he was afraid of so she could help him work through it.

Bad idea or not, she was already developing feelings for him.

Crazy since she'd only met him a month ago and spent only the last few days of that month having any real contact with him. But the time they'd spent together was intense. He'd saved her on multiple occasions, been prepared to be tortured for her, and been the only one on her side.

How could she not develop feelings?

Despite his reputation, she couldn't help but think her feelings weren't completely one-sided. That maybe he might have some for her, too. It was the way he looked at her, the way he touched her so gently, the way he was so protective, and seemed to be able to make her feel like she was being taken care of while simultaneously like she was strong enough to take care of herself if he wasn't there to do it.

Too bad it didn't look like he was going to do anything about it.

Yet ...

He *was* there.

Even though he'd told her he had something on with his team tonight and couldn't make dinner, he'd still come by.

After hanging with the Prey people all afternoon, she'd come home feeling like things weren't completely hopeless when it came to them, that maybe those relationships could be salvaged if she gave it a little time. But as soon as she'd walked back into her home, she'd been hit by that wave of loneliness again.

There had been only one person she'd wanted to call.

Just one.

Miguel Aguilar.

Not her family, not her friends, just him.

She'd gone so far as to bring up his name on her phone, but her finger had hovered above the call option, unable to make herself do it because of fear of rejection. If she told

Miguel that she had feelings for him that were more than just wanting to be his friend, she knew what would happen.

He'd vanish from her life like a puff of smoke.

"Ella?" Miguel stood before her and she realized she'd been standing stock still, lost in thought, trapped in an internal battle of wanting to ask Miguel for more while also attempting to be content with what he was comfortable offering.

"Mmm?" When he was standing close enough, she could feel the heat pouring off his body and engulfing her in a heady brew of comfort, strength, and arousal it was hard to concentrate on anything other than that she craved more. More of his presence, more of his touch, more kisses, more pleasure, more everything.

"Are you okay?"

Lifting her head to meet his gaze, she saw the same things she felt reflected back at her. Miguel might not like it, but he craved her, too. How badly she wished he would give in to his desire, pick her up, carry her to her bed, make sweet love to her, and then hold her all night while she slept.

In his presence, she didn't care about the short time they'd known each other, or the intensity of her feelings. She didn't care about anything other than him and her, the two of them, together.

When his palm cradled her cheek, she released a soft sigh, nuzzling into his hand. Was she okay? No, of course not. Would she be? Yeah. One day at least.

"I have an appointment tomorrow with a therapist," she admitted, a little conflicted on how she felt about that. On the one hand, she knew she needed it, on the other, it would feel weird talking to a stranger about things they couldn't understand. Not that it was a complete stranger. Piper Hamilton-Eden was Prey's on-staff psychiatrist who was flying out there to stay for the next few weeks so she could

189

counsel not just Ella but all of Athena Team. Of course, she knew what Piper had been through, and the woman was married to Antonio "Arrow" Eden from Prey's Alpha Team, if anyone could help, it was certainly Piper.

"You feeling okay about it?"

"Kind of. I know it will help."

"I'm sure it will," he agreed. "You have anyone to take you?"

"Take me? Umm … no. I was going to drive myself."

"I'll drive you."

It didn't sound like an offer, it sounded more like an order, like he had already decided that was what was going to happen.

This man.

He made her feel like he saw her as someone who could be more than a friend, and yet he also seemed to make it clear that friendship was all he was offering. All he would ever be offering. Then he went and did something like this, offering to be there for her when they both knew she would likely wind up needing some support.

How was she supposed to figure out if she had a chance with him when he kept sending her these mixed signals?

* * *

FEBRUARY 10ᵀᴴ
2:37 P.M.

IT FELT like ants were crawling all over his skin.

Not a sensation he should be having when all he was doing was sitting in his car outside a small house where Prey's on-staff psychiatrist, Piper, her husband Arrow, and their baby daughter Dana were staying for the next month while they stayed in San Diego so Piper could help Athena Team.

Only Ella wasn't in his line of sight.

For some reason that was beginning to cause issues for him.

Truth was, even though Miguel was convinced it was for the best he just couldn't seem to maintain any distance between them.

He wanted to be around her.

Simple as that.

When he was with Ella, he felt this peace take up residence inside his soul. It calmed him in a way nothing else ever had.

Being that he was nine when he almost died, and he and Luis went into foster care he had limited memories of his life before. Enough to remember how bad it had been. The drugs, the hunger, the men parading in and out of their house at all hours of the day and night. He remembered the beatings his brother had gotten trying to protect him and even the couple he'd received himself.

But there was a distance there. For half of his childhood, he'd lived a good life. A happy life. More importantly, a safe life. Things had been good with their foster family and he'd known what it was like to be loved, supported, and receive appropriate discipline handed out in a caring manner.

Never had he known peace like this though.

In fact, he hadn't even known that peace like this existed. Was this what it was like for Luis when he realized he was falling for Cassie? Had he felt this deep belief that as long as he was with her everything was going to be okay?

The relief he felt sharing the secret of his teenage addiction with the big brother he idolized had been unexpected. There had been no disgust or disappointment in Luis' eyes and now he wished that he'd told his brother a long time ago.

When he was with Ella, he felt like he would always be able to keep those addictive traits under control. How could he not when he had the best motivation in the world to seek help immediately if he felt like he was going to slip up?

It was in the moments when they weren't together that the doubts slid in.

What ifs.

A million of them.

Running rampant through his mind because he wasn't with Ella, and he couldn't ensure she was safe.

Miguel was well aware he was allowing Ella to become an addiction. Far too quickly. They'd met only just over a month ago, and in that time, they'd exchanged only a handful of words until four days ago when his team had been tasked with going to Mexico and retrieving a suspected traitor.

It shouldn't be possible to be falling this fast.

And yet it was.

Because he was falling.

Faster than the speed of light.

What happened when he hit the ground?

Could he get everything he had wanted since he was a small boy looking at the other children at school, knowing they went home to a normal life, to normal parents, that they got to be happy? He'd wanted that happiness, too. Craved it. Wanted to one day be just like them, just like their parents, just like the people he saw on the streets going about their lives.

Of all the women he'd been with not a single one of them had stirred up feelings.

None of them had made him question his future and the vow he'd made to himself.

Only Ella.

She made him want to throw caution to the wind and jump in with both feet. She gave him confidence he'd never felt before that he had what it took to keep his addictions under control, or at the very least recognize if he couldn't and do something about it.

Yet, as he looked at the house she'd entered almost an hour ago an icy dread filled him as he forced himself to remember that there were no guarantees in life.

If he let himself fall all the way for her, he really could destroy her.

Was it worth the risk?

That was what it really boiled down to. Was having Ella worth risking the possibility that one day he might hurt her?

There was no easy answer to that question. None he could come up with now at least. The only way to know for sure was to take that plunge, and as badly as he wanted to jump all in he couldn't. The fear was too strong, the doubts too controlling. Maybe in time he'd be able to think with a clearer head.

He had time.

Wasn't like Ella was asking for a marriage proposal.

In fact, he could tell she was being as careful as he was to keep things just friendship even though when he gazed into her eyes, he couldn't not feel how much she wanted to ask for more.

But she had a lot on her plate, a relationship—especially with someone like him—wasn't what she needed right now. Time. That's what she needed, what he needed, too. Then, hopefully with time, all the answers he sought would become clear.

Straightening abruptly when he saw someone meandering in front of the rental Piper and Arrow were staying in, something about it, about them, put Miguel on edge.

The person didn't have a dog with them, and they weren't dressed in the kind of clothes one usually wore when they went out for a jog. They weren't dressed for the weather either, wearing black pants and a white blouse.

From the size and shape of them Miguel knew it was a woman.

The mole at Prey was a woman.

Was it possible …?

After initially making a list of three people they thought could likely be the mole, Prey had cleared two of them and one had been found to be set up. After that, they'd gone back to the drawing board, gone through every single person who had ever worked at the company, from the cleaning crew up. They weren't doing things by halves, but the reality was, it just took time to go through dozens of people looking for any evidence that they might betray the company and try to steal a drug that was worth millions.

It helped now to know that they were looking for a woman, but that still left a lot of people, and it had only been just over a month since this whole mess started. Even working on it around the clock, Prey hadn't been able to zero in on any one particular current or past employee.

Now someone dressed in work clothes was standing outside a house where his woman was. His woman who had just been threatened into putting her life on the line and almost losing everything.

Anger took hold inside him.

This could be nothing—just a neighbor or local out for an early afternoon stroll—or it could be the answers they'd been looking for.

Shoving open his door he climbed out, doing his best not to draw attention to himself. Lucky for him, the figure in front of the rental house didn't seem to realize they were being watched. Either they were completely innocent and had nothing to do with the mess at Prey or they were cocky enough to believe they were going to remain on top forever.

They weren't.

All it would take was one little slip-up, and the precarious house of cards they'd built would come tumbling down around them.

He couldn't wait for that day.

Just because the future for him and Ella was uncertain didn't mean he didn't want the absolute best for her. That started with the target on her back being removed so she was free to heal without having to worry at the same time about her life and safety.

While he wanted to streak across the street and barrel into the person still standing there watching the house, Miguel forced himself to move slowly. If this was just some innocent person, the last thing he wanted to do was knock them to the ground and bind their wrists.

Just as he was about to come up behind them, close enough he could get a look at their face and see if he recognized it, the person startled. Knowing that his presence had been detected, he picked up his pace.

"Hey, I need to talk to you," he called out.

But the person took off at top speed. Confident he could outrun whoever this was, innocent or not—and the running clearly made them look guilty—he followed. Only instead of running straight down the street the person veered to the left. The house four down from the one where Ella was had a broken wooden fence, and the woman headed for it.

Her much smaller body was able to wriggle its way between two of the palings, disappearing just as he reached out to grab hold of them, his fingers instead snapping together around nothing but air.

Nuh-uh.

No way.

If the mole wanted a chase, he'd give her one.

This person didn't get to just slip away.

Not when Ella's life was hanging in the balance. So long as the mole roamed free, she would never be safe, never be able to find peace or move on.

Grabbing hold of the top of the fence, Miguel heaved himself up and over it. He wasn't giving up until he had the mole in custody and knew his girl was safe.

CHAPTER SEVENTEEN

February 10th
   2:55 P.M.

HOW HAD an hour flown by already?

Felt like only a couple of minutes ago she had assured Miguel that he could wait in the car, that she could do this on her own, and nervously knocked on the little house's front door.

From the second Ella met Piper face to face, she knew that this would help. There was just something about the woman's warm, compassionate brown eyes that told her everything was going to be okay.

It was more than just knowing what Piper had been through at the hands of an obsessive stalker who blamed her for losing his job at Prey. It was a deep feeling of being understood. Not only had Piper lived through a horrific ordeal, but that ordeal had also started with an obsession, the same way this mess with her and her team had.

In the entire history of Prey there had only ever been

three times the company had hired someone who turned out to be unstable and evil. Once was before her time and had almost wound up costing Fox the woman he loved. Once was with Piper and the man who blamed her for getting him fired. And the third time was the mole now determined to get their hands on the Reactivator.

How could she not feel a connection to this woman?

"Thank you, Piper, for not just letting me talk but for sharing with me, too," she said as they walked side by side toward the front door.

"You don't have to thank me for that, Ella. That's part of how I work. I share because I know how important it is that nobody should feel alone. If talking about what happened to me helps someone else, then I do it. It's not fun, but I care about every single person at Prey. Genuinely care about you all. Whatever your role at the company, you help make the world a better place and that means I'll give you all one hundred percent."

"You couldn't not," Arrow said, appearing in the living room door with his six-month-old daughter nestled in his arms.

"Thank you for bringing your family all the way over here for us," Ella said to the man who hadn't hesitated to hop on a plane with his wife and baby daughter because she needed help.

Arrow smiled at her. "We've all been there, Ella. All been in that place where we need help. There's no way I'd deny anyone that help, especially since my wife is the best," he teased Piper who blushed and waved her hand like it was nothing, but her eyes lit up anyway.

"I don't know about being the best, but I do know I'll give you my best, Ella. All I ask is that you give me your best in return."

"I will," she said solemnly. And it was true. Her life felt

like it was spinning out of control, and she had no idea how to right it again, but she knew she was going to try. With everything she had to give. "I better get going."

"Yeah, put that hulk out there out of his misery," Arrow said, turning teasing eyes in her direction.

Like Piper, she blushed. Miguel had come there for her, it was his idea to bring her, and even though she'd assured him it wasn't necessary, he'd decided to stay and wait until she was done rather than going somewhere for an hour and returning to pick her up.

"Miguel is one of the good ones," Piper assured her as she opened the front door.

"He is," she agreed. That didn't mean she had a shot with him.

"Same time tomorrow," Piper reminded her.

"I'm ... actually looking forward to it," she admitted.

"Talking to a shrink isn't as bad as it's made out to be," Piper said with a chuckle.

Wasn't that the truth. Or maybe it was just that Piper didn't make you feel like you were talking to a shrink just chatting with a friend.

Saying her goodbyes she hurried across the street to Miguel's truck and found him sitting in the driver's seat, sweaty and glowering.

"What's wrong?" she asked immediately, his angry energy soaking into her the moment she slipped into her seat.

"Someone was watching the house."

When her hands shook at his words, Miguel reached over, grabbed her seatbelt, and did it up for her. "Watching the house? Watching me?"

"Given they ran when I approached, I'm going to guess watching you," he replied, starting the engine.

Icy dread filled her.

What would have happened if Miguel hadn't brought her this afternoon?

Had the mole been lying in wait for her to leave on her own before making a move?

"Hey, I got you, honey. That woman is not getting to you," Miguel vowed.

"It was a woman? For sure?" Given what Cassie had been told when Raul Castillo had abducted her, they knew the mole was a woman, so knowing it was a woman watching her today reinforced the idea that it could be the mole.

"For sure. She ran, got through the fence. By the time I got over it she'd disappeared. I looked around for as long as I could, but I wanted to be here when you came out just in case she had something planned and doubled back."

Regardless of the vibes he put off, Miguel had been putting her first every step of the way. "Thank you," she whispered, reaching out to grab his hand and clutching onto it like it was her lifeline.

"Any time, honey," he said, his eyes softening when he looked at her.

They lapsed into silence as Miguel drove her back to her place. A million thoughts tumbled together in her head. How close she could have come to being taken if that's what the mole had been there waiting to do left her feeling scared, but she was also still riding the high of her session with Piper.

There were no guarantees in life.

That was becoming clearer and clearer to her.

Not even your next breath of air was guaranteed.

If you didn't reach out and take what you wanted, there might never be another chance.

That thought was the most prevalent in her mind as she and Miguel walked up her front path thirty minutes later.

Whatever was going to happen with Miguel, whether they'd ever get a chance to explore this thing brewing between them, she didn't want him to walk away without her getting to have him just one time.

One time to remember, to look back on if he walked away from her.

If it wasn't what he wanted then she'd understand, she wouldn't push, and she wouldn't ask for more than he was willing to give. But you never knew unless you went for it.

As soon as Miguel locked the door behind them, Ella reached for his shoulders, tugging on them until she could press her lips to his. For a second, he stood there unmoving. She'd caught him off-guard, and she could guess that he was warring with himself about how he should best respond.

Just as she thought he was going to push her away, a growl rumbled through him, and one of his arms snaked around her waist, pulling her possessively up against his rock-hard body. His tongue nudged against her lips, and when she opened them, it swept inside her mouth, a little precursor to what she hoped would happen in the next few minutes.

Her body was a needy, throbbing mess. Sex had always been fun, and she'd been lucky enough to be with partners who cared about her pleasure. But never before had she felt this burning need. It pulsed through her veins, consuming her with each beat of her heart.

They were both breathing hard when Miguel finally pulled back enough that he could look down at her. His dark eyes were stormy with emotion and Ella wished she could soothe it away for him.

"Ella, I can't ... I'm not ... I want you ... want this ... but I can't make any promises about the future."

Those words buried themselves deeply in her heart. It wasn't fair to want him to make promises and yet she couldn't deny she wanted him to.

One day at a time.

Seize the moment.

Don't have regrets.

Regardless of whether or not she'd love a promise to explore this thing between them, Ella knew that if she let this opportunity pass her by then she would wind up regretting it. For now, she had to focus on just this, not on what could or couldn't be in the future.

"Okay," she agreed, shoving away the pain in her heart. If this was meant to be, it would work its way out eventually, and if it wasn't then she'd patch her heart back together again.

"Are you sure?" he asked, studying her eyes, searching for the truth.

"I'm sure that I want you. Here. Now. I don't want soft and sweet, I just want raw and passionate. I want to feel you inside me, I want to be consumed by you. I don't want anything between us. I'm on birth control and I'm clean. If you're okay with it we don't need a condom. I just need you, Miguel. I need you," she said again, allowing a little of the vulnerability she felt beneath her desire to shine through.

"I'm here, honey. I'm right here. I've never gone bare before, but with you ... with you I can't think of anything that feels more right."

With those words, his hands gripped the hem of her sweater, and in one smooth move, he tugged it up and over her head, tossing it onto the floor. His own sweater fell next, and then before she knew it, both their jeans and underwear lay at their feet and they were standing before each other completely naked.

"So beautiful," Miguel murmured as he reached out and tweaked one of her nipples.

"You're pretty handsome yourself," she whispered back, tracing her fingertips along the ridges of each defined muscle on his sculpted chest and abdomen.

Her hand drifted lower, trailed along the hard length standing ready and at attention. At her soft touch, it jerked and she smiled, liking the powerful feeling she got from knowing with one little touch she could affect this man so much.

"Nuh-uh, honey, no touching," Miguel said as his hand circled her wrist, tugging it away so she could no longer stroke his erection. "Not if you don't want this to be over real quick."

Even though she'd asked for hard and passionate and not soft and sweet, Miguel somehow managed to give her both as he lifted her, encouraging her to wrap her legs around his waist as he ground her center into his hard ridge.

Her head fell back on a moan at the contact.

The friction felt amazing, and she could already feel the heat in her veins turn into fire.

"I could get lost in you," Miguel whispered against her lips.

"I am getting lost in you," she murmured back.

Another growl rumbled through him and then his hands were on her hips. "Are you wet for me, Ella?"

"Yes," she said, squirming as he pulled her slightly away from his length, taking away the beautiful friction she got every time she rolled her hips against him.

"So wet, aren't you, honey, so ready for this," he purred, moving her hips until his tip nudged against her entrance. Even though she tried to shift, to take him deeper, he held firm and chuckled when she mewed a protest.

"Please," she begged needily.

"Please what, honey?" he teased, moving her hips just a tiny bit closer so another inch slipped inside her.

"Please, I need you, want you inside me. Oh ..." she moaned when she was rewarded by a hard thrust that buried him deep inside her. So deep that she knew she would forever feel the remnants of this moment. This moment when nothing else mattered but them, but this, but being there together, sharing something bigger than either of them could name.

"Like this, honey?" he asked as he began to thrust into her.

"Mmm," she moaned. "So good."

"Perfection," he agreed. "Is my girl going to come for me like a good girl?" he asked as one of his hands moved to touch her aching bud while his other kneaded her backside.

Why did those words make her insides flip?

Being called a good girl was a massive turn-on.

"Hmm, honey? You going to come for me?" Miguel asked as the fingers working her bundle of nerves began to press harder and faster.

"Yes," she gasped as sensations prickled to life inside her.

His mouth closed over one of her breasts, and once again, her head tipped back as the fire inside her licked at every nerve ending, setting them all alight so that when she came it was going to be in a fiery inferno.

Each thrust, each swirl of his tongue, each stroke of his fingers worked her higher until she was sure she was seconds away from combusting.

Then his teeth scraped over her pebbled nipple, and his voice rumbled on the sensitive bud as he gave her an order her body couldn't refuse.

"Come for me, Ella. Come now. Show me what a good girl you are."

Just like that he set her on fire.

A powerful orgasm roared through her, scorching her very soul with its power and leaving her a shuddering, shaking mess as she felt Miguel spill his own release inside her.

In one simple moment, he had ruined her for all other men.

This was the only one she wanted.

She just didn't know if he would let her keep him.

* * *

WHY WAS it so easy to believe that everything could turn out all right when he had this woman in his arms?

What was it about her that stilled everything inside him?

"Miguel?" Ella asked, turning her head so that her chin was propped up on his chest and she looked up at him. They were still in bed, he hadn't even put up a protest when Ella asked him if he'd stay the night and hold her while she slept. Given that she'd had a couple of nightmares, he was glad he hadn't let his fears get the best of him so that he was there to soothe her as she trembled and cried.

When he woke a couple of hours ago, the urge to tuck tail and run had been there, but he hadn't given into it. With no idea what the future held, he wanted to make the most of the opportunities to touch and hold her while they were there.

In a blink of an eye, he could lose this and he wasn't ready to face that possibility yet.

For now, he just wanted to be there, support this brave woman, and give her the strength and comfort she needed. For now, that had to be enough. He could worry about everything else later.

"Yeah, honey?" His hand trailed absently up and down the length of her spine, maybe more in a gesture to soothe himself than her.

"Can I ask you something?"

Even though his stomach dropped at the question he nodded. "Yeah, you can ask me anything you want."

And he'd answer it.

Whatever she wanted to know he couldn't help but feel like she had earned the right to an honest answer.

"I know that I probably shouldn't ask, you've already done more for me than you had to. You saved me, and you've been here for me. I was just wondering … is there a reason that you … keep things casual with women?"

Without her having to say the words aloud Miguel knew what she was really asking.

Was there a reason he didn't want to give them a chance?

If he hadn't just confessed his secrets to Luis, he might have been tempted to hold back now. To tell her that it really wasn't any of her business. But for some strange reason, it didn't seem all that daunting to tell Ella the truth. Besides, it affected her too since it was those fears that prevented him from asking her out.

"Do you know much about Luis and my history?" he asked.

"No. I don't know much about him at all other than Cassie has fallen head over heels for him." There was a wistfulness to her tone that he wished he had the ability—or the courage—to smooth away. If he just believed that he had what it took to keep his dark urges under control then he could.

But he wasn't sure if he could.

Wasn't sure that he wasn't making her his latest addiction.

That would be the ultimate irony. If he finally found a woman he wanted so badly to stay clean and sober for, only to have her become his obsession and that be the thing that wound up destroying them both.

"Our childhood wasn't a good one. Dad bailed and left our mom alone with two little kids and addictions she couldn't—or didn't want to—get a handle on. Any money she got went on drugs and booze. Usually, we went through dumpsters searching for food so we didn't starve and stole a little on occasion. There was a parade of boyfriends in and out of the house, all were addicts, and some were violent. Mostly they pounded on Luis, he was older and tried to shield me as best as a little boy could."

There would never be a day that went by when he wasn't grateful for everything his brother had done for him. He'd always wanted to prove himself to Luis and be just like him. Following him into the SEALs had been a no-brainer, but could he follow his big brother into the land of love and relationships?

"I'm so sorry," Ella said, her fingertips tracing small circles on his pecs.

"When I was nine and Luis was eleven, he decided that if we joined a local gang we'd be able to get money and get a better life for ourselves. Made sense in his eleven-year-old head. Since we were so little the gang decided to use us as a lure to break into a couple of businesses, thinking they'd open up for two kids who needed help. It worked. Only the business they hit up the owners fought back. There was a shootout, cops came, and I was critically injured."

One of Ella's fingers moved to his neck and trailed along the pale, silvery scar there. "This?"

"Yeah. I almost bled out, people died, when the cops realized how young Luis and I were CPS got involved. We were removed from our mom's custody and put in foster care. We really lucked out there. Wound up with a former military family, they had four biological kids but wanted to help some kids in need. I consider them my family, more so than the people who created me. They've been there for me through everything since I was nine years old." Miguel paused to drag in a long breath. It was now or never. "Including through my own addictions."

For a second Ella stilled, but then she snuggled closer, plastering herself against his side, and her fingers resumed tracing circles on his pecs. "Drugs or alcohol?"

"Drugs. I started out just thinking I was cool and fitting in, smoking a little weed. Then my DNA took over. I almost threw away everything that I'd been given, the second chance at life, a real shot at a future. Before I knew what had happened, it was spiraling out of control. I was lucky my parents noticed and didn't hesitate to do something about it. They put me in rehab, and I worked the program hard. I didn't want them to be disappointed in me. Didn't want my brother to be disappointed in me. I got clean and haven't taken anything since, alcohol included, because I don't trust myself."

They lay there in silence for a few minutes. Ella didn't pull away, even though she had every reason to put a little distance between them.

It was one thing for her to be interested in him when she didn't know that he was an addict who could blow up her life at a moment's notice, it was another now that she knew the truth.

Only she didn't move.

Didn't stop touching him.

Her expressive eyes remained warm and open, full of care and compassion.

Each thump of his heart seemed to echo through his body. Was this something Ella thought she could handle? Being an addict was a lifelong problem, it wasn't just going to magically go away, he would always have to be careful when stressors arose that he handled them in an appropriate manner. It was a lot for anyone to take on, especially a woman who had just lived through her own hell.

"Why don't you trust yourself?" Ella finally asked.

Not the question he'd been expecting.

And not one he was sure he knew an answer to.

"Hard to trust yourself when you know how addiction destroyed your parents and almost took you down with it," he finally said. "I never want to put an innocent person in the position that Luis and I were in. I couldn't do that to someone."

"You seem pretty aware of your issues, and it seems to me you have all the motivation in the world to keep yourself clean. What would you do if it felt like you were slipping?"

A much easier question to answer. "Book myself straight into rehab."

Ella smiled like that was exactly what she had expected him to say. Then she rested her cheek on his chest and snuggled closer against his side. "Seems to me you already have a plan in place if the worst were to happen. If there's one thing I've learned from this whole thing with the mole, it's that you can do everything right and things still don't work out. You can't control that. You can't control anything. Nothing that happens around you. The good or the bad. The only thing you have any control over whatsoever is yourself."

"And what if you lose that control over yourself?"

"Then you do whatever you have to in order to get it back. Doesn't make it easy, but nothing in life is easy. I might not know you well, Miguel, but I know you're a good guy. I know you save the world, I know you've saved me. I know what you were prepared to go through to give me a chance at being safe. I know that you have people in your life you care about, your brother, your family, your team. I know you would protect those people any way you had to. I know that you're strong and brave. I know that you can do anything you put your mind to, including having a future and keeping your addictions under control. The thing is, though, it doesn't matter what I know. It only matters what you know. I just hope you can figure it out so you can have the future you deserve."

All this time he'd been so focused on any potential partner's future and what they deserved that he hadn't given much thought to himself.

Was Ella right?

Did he deserve a future, too?

Could he find happiness with a woman, have a family of his own, and manage to keep his addictions in check as he weathered the storms life would inevitably throw his way?

Or was that nothing more than a dream that would forever remain out of reach?

CHAPTER EIGHTEEN

February 11th
8:08 A.M.

THIS LITTLE TASTE of domestic bliss was enough to have her craving more.

After Miguel had told her about his childhood and his fears for his future, they'd made love once in the bed, and then again in the shower. Now they were downstairs in her kitchen cooking breakfast.

Nothing fancy, just making a little French toast. They didn't talk much as they bustled about the kitchen, yet they seemed so in sync with one another it was hard not to want more of this. Mornings where they barely had a chance to talk as they both hurried about grabbing bowls of cereal and heading off to start their days. And mornings where they could take their time, make something special, just enjoy being together and soaking up the little moments.

"Syrup?" Miguel asked.

JANE BLYTHE

"Are you kidding? Of *course* I want maple syrup on my French toast," she informed him.

Chuckling, he grabbed the syrup and set it on the table as she scooped the bread out of the frying pan and divided it up between the two plates. There was already coffee and juice on the table, and she'd cut up some fruit to go on the French toast as well.

Before she could pick up the plates, Miguel nudged her out of the way, shooing her toward the table, then grabbed both of their plates and set them on the placemats. While she'd been cooking, he'd somehow managed to find a couple of candles and set them up on the table and her heart melted at the sight.

Her guy might be unsure about reaching out and taking what he wanted, but he was so sweet and he did the nicest things for her. Ella understood where he was coming from, why he would have the fears he did, and she would do her best not to add any more pressure to him in addition to the pressure he was heaping on himself.

If this is going to work out then it will.

Those were the words she kept whispering to herself. They were true and she was doing her best to believe in them. Just because she wanted Miguel, and just because he wanted her in return, didn't mean they were supposed to be together. There were no guarantees in life, she knew that, had said it to Miguel just a little while ago, and you couldn't fight against fate.

She just hoped with everything she had that this time fate was on her side.

"What are your plans for the day?" she asked as she took a bite of the fluffy toast, letting it melt on her tongue.

"What are your plans for the day?" Miguel shot back, catching her by surprise.

"Umm, well, I guess going into Prey for a while this

morning. I promised to give things an honest try and I intend to do that. I guess we'll go through files again, see if we can match up the description you gave of the woman you saw yesterday with one of our current or former employees. Then I'm seeing Piper again at two. After that, I'll probably just come home and hang out. Why?"

"Because you can consider me your shadow until the mole is in custody."

Even as his words warmed her there was an ominous ending to the sentence. The words he hadn't said affected her just as deeply as the ones he had.

Once the mole was found, Miguel could vanish from her life as quickly as he entered it.

It hurt to think about that, so Ella quickly shoved the thoughts away. They didn't fit in with her live life in the moment plan.

"My shadow, huh?"

"Yep. If the mole is following you around, then they're not getting to you. If they try they'll have to get through me."

"You know I've been thinking," she said slowly. "It seems like this isn't just business. At least on the mole's part. It was for Raul Castillo. He just wanted the drug and didn't want to give up on getting it, he didn't want to be bested by a bunch of girls he couldn't coerce into doing what he wanted. But it feels different with the mole."

"How so?"

"Well, they didn't have to get Scarlett kidnapped and tortured. They couldn't get to the vial without us, and we were careful to protect the formula. The mole sold the drug to Raul, or at least sold the ability to get the drug, but they took it so much further than that. I mean, someone sold out Zander because he and Lucy were kidnapped by his enemies, not Raul and the mole. Someone knew about him and used it almost as a way to punish Lucy. Then with Cassie, they used her fingerprints to program into the bomb on the ship. The only way for it to be disarmed was with her, which meant she had no choice but to head right into danger. That wasn't really productive in terms of getting the formula. In fact, none of the bombs were. Sure the email said it was as motivation, but it really seemed like it was more punishment."

But why would someone who worked for Prey want to punish them?

Athena Team wasn't a field team, they were lab workers, scientists.

Someone seemed to have a grudge against them specifically, and she was starting to wonder if maybe the Reactivator was just a secondary motivator. Like maybe the idea of selling it to a notorious weapons dealer wasn't so much about the money as it was just a way to make her and her team suffer.

If that was the case, then it changed things. Definitely changed how they should look at the files. All along they'd been looking for someone who might have a need for money as the primary motivator. What if they swapped that around? What if the money was just an extra benefit but the real goal was to destroy Athena Team?

"Whoever it was really doubled down after you guys started falling in love," Miguel said slowly.

"That's true," she agreed. Things had continued to escalate after Scarlett had fallen for Tate, then Lucy for Zander, Cassie for Luis, and now her for Miguel. Just because of all four of them she was the only one whose future with the man she wanted was up in the air didn't change the fact that she had fallen.

What did that mean?

It had to mean something.

Didn't it?

Or was she just clutching at straws here?

A month of living on edge had made them all desperate for any kind of answers, but looking for things where there was nothing wasn't going to help.

Somehow, she had to cling to a little logic.

Was there someone at Prey who might have already disliked Athena Team but then had cause to take that dislike to a new level when they all started falling in love?

Something was prickling the back of her mind only she couldn't quite figure out what it was.

Falling in love changes everything. Changes you.

Those words whispered through her head only she couldn't remember where she'd heard them before or who had said them.

"Ella, you got an idea?"

"Maybe. I ... I'm not sure ... I have this feeling like I'm close to figuring everything out, but I can't quite get there," she said, frustrated with herself. There was a lot riding on this. They *had* to figure out the mole's identity. If they didn't then this would never be over, and she didn't want to keep living her life this way, constantly looking over her shoulder and expecting the worst.

"You'll get there," Miguel said confidently.

"What you said before, about them doubling down, it made me think of something I just can't remember the details."

"Stop pushing yourself, let it happen, the more pressure you put on your shoulders, the harder it will be to get there. Just relax. Take a deep breath. Let go of everything else. Just be."

Allowing his words to settle over her like a weighted blanket, smoothing out all her anxieties, Ella did as he instructed, drew in a slow breath, and then just let go. Let everything fall away. If the answers were inside her head, they'd come to her.

215

Love was a crazy thing. Possibly both the best and worst things in the world. It could build you up but it could also tear you down. It picked you up like a tornado and tossed you about until you had no idea what direction you were facing.

It also made people do crazy things.

What wouldn't *I do for love?*

Those words echoed through her mind, and when she stopped and held onto them, let them shimmer into focus a face came along with them.

One she knew.

One she had trusted.

One that Prey had already looked into and discarded as a possible suspect.

Snapping her gaze to Miguel's, she reached out blindly, only feeling grounded when he clasped her hand and gave it a gentle squeeze.

"I know who it is."

* * *

February 11TH
9:04 A.M.

One hour had changed everything.

Ella's house was bursting at the seams with people. There were no more chairs left, people lounged against the walls and sat on the floor. The atmosphere in the room was off the charts with excitement. After over a month of sitting around twiddling their thumbs, playing defensive as they tried to cut off the mole's attacks without ever being able to get on the offensive, the tide had turned.

Prey was in control now.

And it was all thanks to his girl.

She was the one who finally solved the mystery of the mole's true identity, and apparently, according to her, it was all because of something he had said. Miguel was more than happy to hand over all credit to where it belonged though, and that was squarely on Ella's shoulders. He might have said something that got her thinking, but she was the one who had managed to put all the pieces together and come up with an answer.

"Okay, we're going to hand this over to Ella," Fox announced, and the excited murmuring calmed down as Ella stood in front of her Prey family.

It was obvious she was nervous, the way she swayed slightly from foot to foot gave her away. As did the way she held her hands joined together so tightly that even from there he could see that her knuckles were blanched white.

When her gaze roamed the room and settled on him, Miguel gave her an encouraging smile. She had this. She was the one who put it all together, she deserved this moment to stand proudly before her family and tell them what she had deduced. Then together, they would all come up with a plan that would take the mole down once and for all.

"Well," Ella began, clearing her throat, then visibly pulling herself together. "It was something Miguel said to me this morning while we were eating breakfast. Something about love and it triggered a memory of a conversation I had. The conversation was with Dora Hibbert."

Gasps echoed around the room and over a dozen shocked faces stared back at Ella.

After she'd managed to figure everything out, they immediately called Prey. Given that the mole had an in, they hadn't wanted to discuss on the phone what she'd figured out. So all she'd done was ask if Fox could come over because she wanted to discuss the terms of her staying for the next month. Of course, he'd figured out that it was more than that, but she hadn't said the name aloud until he was standing there in her living room.

Now that news had been shared with everyone else, even Miguel—who knew nothing about the ins and outs of Prey and their workplace—could see how shocked everyone was.

"I thought we cleared her," Spider said.

"We did," Fox agreed. "She didn't need the money, and she'd been at Prey for years. We even managed to clear her husband's name when there was some shady stuff going down with his Green Beret team."

"So what changed?" Night asked.

"For one, Ella figured out a few suspicious things, and two, when I went looking for her this morning she was nowhere to be seen. Hasn't been back to the office since lunchtime yesterday," Fox said, looking over to him. "Since Miguel saw someone standing outside the rental where Piper and Arrow are staying while Ella was inside."

"Why would Dora decide to turn on us?" Scarlett asked, her brow furrowed in confusion. Confusion that was echoed in all the other people in the room.

"I got a weird vibe from her after Zander and I got together," Lucy said thoughtfully. "At the time, I just thought it was because it was a shock, but maybe it was more than that. She didn't seem to like that I would date one of my best friend's brother."

"While I was waiting for you guys to get here I did a little digging of my own," Ella informed them. "I remembered a few things Dora's said to me over the years that aren't suspicious in and of themselves, but put them altogether and they paint a different picture. There were some rumors about missing weapons and drug smuggling on her husband's team. He was the prime suspect, but we were able to clear him." Ella waved her hand to indicate herself and her team.

"So why would she hate us?" Cassie asked.

"Because her husband wasn't completely innocent," Ella replied. "He wasn't smuggling weapons to Raul Castillo, but he was cheating on her. Apparently, the affairs had been going on most of the marriage. She found out when he died in a car accident with one of his mistresses in the car with him. One of the reasons Dora was never on our list was because she received a huge life insurance payout after his death and a payout from the trucking company the driver of the truck that hit him worked for. She didn't need the money."

"When she applied for the receptionist job, she said it was because Prey had helped her out by proving her husband's innocence, and she wanted to be part of what we did. Said even though she had enough money to live comfortably on for the rest of her life she was young and didn't want to just sit around with nothing to do," Fox added.

"I still don't get why she'd hate us," Scarlett said.

"I don't know why," Ella said. "Maybe misplaced blame. Maybe she thought we should have discovered the affairs when we were investigating him, maybe she's just crazy. All I know is she married her childhood best friend's brother, and it caused a rift between them. She lost contact with her and the whole family. She had no family of her own, a deadbeat dad and a mom who lost custody, so she was a foster system kid. That's why she wouldn't have liked Lucy and Zander getting together. Her husband might not have been selling weapons, but she still managed to track down the dealer the weapons had been sold to. Raul Castillo. She was in a position to know everything. About the drug, when we were closing in on Raul's location. She's probably the one who tipped him off which is why we kept arriving too late. She knows all our addresses, she has access to our things at work, she knew everything we were doing and when we were going to do it."

"This is crazy," Chaos exclaimed.

"It is, and we won't have answers until we have her in custody," Ella agreed. "I want to know why she targeted us, but more than that, I want to know that she can't hurt us again. I want her found and caught."

That sentiment was echoed by every person in the room.

They all wanted this done and over with.

"If she's run, and she has enough money to stay hidden, then how will we find her?" Lucy asked.

"Actually, I have an idea on that," Miguel said, shoving off the wall he'd been leaning against and closing the short distance between himself and Ella.

"You do?" she asked, news to her since he hadn't mentioned it yet. He hadn't mentioned it to anyone, but he was positive that this would work. If he could convince his girl to go along with it. If he could keep a handle on his own fears for her safety to let her go along with it.

"Let's hear it," Fox told him.

"Dora Hibbert has been working at Prey for years now, she knows everything about you guys, and we have no way to know what else she's infected. She could have devices hidden on computer systems, phones, she could be listening in on any plans you make to try to find her," he said.

"So, we have to keep her out of the loop," King said.

"We do. Well out of the real loop," Miguel amended. "We set up a few false attempts to search for her. Keep her distracted. Make her focus be where we want it to be so she doesn't see the sneak attack coming."

"What's the sneak attack?" Ella asked, somewhat suspiciously.

"It's you," he replied. "She might know that you guys came over here today, I'm sure she knows that Ella said she'd give this a month to work out, but what if we play it up like Ella changed her mind? That she's quitting now. Ella already has a backup career, and it's one she's overdue for a performance for."

"You want me to pretend I left Prey and put on a concert?" Ella asked, wide green eyes staring up at him.

"A trap in the form of a concert," he corrected. "I want Dora thinking that you've backed away from Prey. That maybe because you did, they're not watching you as closely as they were. I want her to think that the concert would be the perfect place to try to make contact with you. If she really hates you all then she's not giving up. She might lay low until an opportunity presents itself to make a move, but she's not disappearing for good. This gives her that opportunity to strike when she thinks she can blend in and never be spotted. But only if you think you can do this, El."

It was a big risk, and a big ask. After what she'd just been through, Ella shouldn't have to play bait, but he was guessing she would if it was the only way to finally be free of the mole once and for all.

He guessed right.

Determination brimmed in those sea-green eyes of hers. "I can do it. If I have you, if I have all of you," she added, her gaze skimming over the eyes of the people determined to make it up to her for letting her down. "Then I can play bait and lure in Dora Hibbert. We're Prey, she can't beat us, she'll never even see it coming."

CHAPTER NINETEEN

February 14th
6:42 P.M.

Why had she ever thought she could do this?

Was she crazy?

Ella certainly felt like she must be as she sat backstage waiting to go on and play like nothing was wrong. Like she was just putting on a regular concert and not trying to set herself out there as a nice, juicy piece of bait and hope that Dora Hibbert was stupid enough to try to reach out and take it.

There was every chance the woman was long gone. There had been no signs of her the last few days. Her house was empty. Her car was gone. It was like she had just vanished. But they all hoped that she was still hanging around, still crazy enough to think that she could come out on top and get whatever revenge it was she thought she was entitled to.

The woman was crazy. No doubt about it. There was nothing anyone on Athena Team had ever done to her that would warrant this assault she had launched against them. They knew from the original emails that had been discovered that the Reactivator had been sold to Raul Castillo for five million dollars. Compared to the insurance policy she'd had on her husband, and the payouts she'd gotten when he was hit by a truck, she had way more money than that, so this was not about getting rich.

It seemed personal.

Which made no sense and likely wouldn't unless Dora chose to share her motivations.

If they ever caught her.

If she was there tonight.

If she decided to make a move.

There was just as much chance that she wouldn't as that she would.

What if she was out there though?

What if she was sitting in the audience of this sold-out, last-minute Valentine's Day concert they'd thrown together in a matter of days? While Ella couldn't deny it was a little boost to her ego to know that she was still popular enough to be able to sell out a concert in just days, it wasn't like that was helpful right now.

Her ego wouldn't protect her if Dora came for her.

When you were dealing with someone unstable like Dora, someone evil, someone who wouldn't think twice about hurting others to get what she wanted, you had to also accept the unpredictable. Cold and calculating people you could predict, you could look at past behavior and use it to make informed decisions about how they would likely behave in the future.

The only thing they could predict about Dora was that she would do whatever it took to achieve her goals.

Which made her so much more dangerous.

It had been a hard decision for everyone to make but no

one from Prey was in the audience tonight. If it was to be believable that she'd decided to quit, they couldn't have all the people Dora would immediately recognize sitting out there. Crazy possibly, but Dora wasn't stupid. If she saw Prey people out there, she would know this was a setup.

So instead of her Prey people it was Miguel's team sitting in the audience tonight, along with Rocco's team. She trusted these men. Knew they would do everything within their power to keep her safe. They were all wired up, in communication with one another, their eyes peeled looking for any signs of Dora.

But as much as she trusted them it didn't soothe the knot of fear in her stomach.

It sat there heavily, had for the last few days, ever since Miguel had suggested this idea and everyone had jumped all over it. It boosted her confidence to know that he hadn't shied away from putting her in the spotlight. He believed in her, he knew she could do this, could handle the pressure, it never entered his mind to wrap her in cotton wool and hide her away.

Not that he wasn't every bit as nervous about this as she was.

She knew he was and felt his fear every time they were together, but he was pushing through, knowing she had what it took to play her role in this.

Honestly, that was probably the only thing giving her the strength to be there.

If Miguel believed in her then she wasn't going to let him down.

So there she was, dressed in a black halter-neck dress and heels. Her hair was twisted up in a fancy bun with a few locks hanging free, curled to perfection. Shaking hands had made putting on her makeup almost impossible, and she was glad that Scarlett, Lucy, and Cassie had insisted on being there to help.

This was for them as much as her. They had all been targeted, had all been hurt by Dora and her games. They all needed this to be over.

A knock on the door had her about jumping out of her skin. She was so on edge, wound so tightly, that it wouldn't take much to make her snap.

Before she could say anything, the door opened, and Miguel strolled in. For a moment, her brain short-circuited and all she could see was him and how deliciously handsome he looked in his tux. Good enough to eat. Maybe if everything went off tonight the way they all hoped it would he'd let her have a taste of him when he took her home.

He'd been by her side every second of the last few days. Listening to her practice with the kind of rapt attention that made her feel like maybe people really would pay to come and listen to her play even with the short notice. Talking through everything with her so she was confident in the plan and assured that she wasn't alone, that everyone had her back. Holding her at night when her jittery fears got the best of her, coming out in nightmares.

That steady strength had helped her hold it together, and it soothed her now.

Whenever he was around, he filled her with calm. With confidence. She was falling for him a little more each day and she still had no idea what he planned to do when this was all over. For now, he seemed to just be focusing on this, on tonight, on catching the mole, but questions about what happened next kept assaulting her mind.

Stay or go?

Trust himself or not?

The ball was in his court.

"Hey, how're you doing?" he asked as he walked right to her and didn't hesitate to pull her into his arms.

Pressing her face into his neck, Ella wrapped her arms around his waist and just held onto him. Allowing herself to soak up the steady confidence she needed so desperately. "I'm all right."

"Really?"

"Really? No. But I can do this. I *will* do this," she corrected. While she knew nobody would hold it against her if she pulled out, she'd hold it against herself. This had to be done and she was the perfect person for the job.

"That's my girl. You got this, honey. I believe in you."

Grasping the lapels of his jacket, Ella pulled back and met his gaze. "And I believe in you, Miguel. Always," she whispered. Just like he wasn't leaving her alone to deal with this on her own, she would be there for him if he let her. She'd stand by his side as he worked to keep his addictions in check, fighting along with him. He didn't have to be alone. Neither of them did.

There was so much tenderness in his expression, along with a heavy dose of fear he knew was directed at himself. When he leaned down and touched his lips to her forehead she almost cried. This man had the power to ruin her and what he didn't realize was that he could wreck her just as easily by walking away as he could by staying and risking the future.

"Thank you," he whispered, then feathered his lips across hers.

The future she wanted wasn't completely out of her grasp, but it would be if the mole wasn't dealt with. So Ella shoved everything else out of her head. "Has anyone seen her?"

"Not yet. That doesn't mean she isn't out there, though."

"I hope she is. I hope she's sitting out there thinking she

won. Thinking she can come after me and no one will be there to stop it from happening. I hope that when we show her how wrong she is she breaks down and realizes that she's never going to be as strong as we are. I hope it tears her apart when she realizes that she lost."

"Bloodthirsty little thing aren't you," Miguel teased as he reached for her cello and held it out to her.

"Only when the other person deserves it," she said as she curled her hands around her instrument.

"I'll be right out there the whole time," Miguel assured her.

"I know you will be." Actually, in her heart and mind, he'd be standing on stage with her, right where he belonged.

"You ready to go and catch a mole?"

"I can't wait."

* * *

February 14TH
7:09 P.M.

"Whoa."

The whispered word came through his comms and enraptured as Miguel was by the music flowing from the stage it took him a moment to process it. Once he did a proud smile lit his lips. That was his girl up there, making music like she was born to do.

Ella wasn't just good she was out of this world phenomenal.

Every single person in the room appeared to be almost breathless as they stared at the stage, unable to tear their eyes away from the woman weaving her bow across the strings and making magic happen.

It was like with each note that tumbled from her cello she was casting a spell, locking everyone in a sort of stasis where the only thing that existed was her music.

The expression on her face was beautiful, too. There was a peace that had been lacking when he went to her in the dressing room. Then she'd been a ball of anxiety, so close to falling apart he'd been worried that she might not be able to go through with this even though he knew she wanted to.

He shouldn't have underestimated his girl.

Of course she had what it took to get up there on stage, knowing she was playing bait and yet making music like she didn't have a care in the world.

Miguel knew she'd been uncertain she could draw a big enough crowd when they threw this concert together in just a handful of days, but she shouldn't have worried. As soon as it was splashed across social media the concert sold out in a matter of hours.

Listening to her now it was obvious why. This was different than when he'd listened to her practice the last few days. Then she'd been playing just for him and for herself. There was no way he'd thought that she could be any better. But the moment she walked out onto that stage to a round of applause it was like something took over her. Somehow, she was even better tonight in the packed-out concert hall, like she was feeding off the atmosphere, taking it and drawing it into her playing.

"Whoa," Beckett "Ace" Morgan murmured again. "She's something else."

"Never heard anything like it," Mark "Bubba" Wright whispered, the awe clear in his tone even though they were spread out around the hall.

"Next time she does a concert I'm bringing Avery," Cole "Rex" Kingston said.

"Ditto," Forest "Phantom" Dalton agreed. "Kalee would

love listening to this. Anyone would. Classical music isn't usually my thing, but the way she plays, it's like she's pouring her entire heart and soul into it."

"She's amazing," Miguel said, his pride for his girl growing. He liked knowing how deeply Ella affected those around her. Still as much as she touched others, it was nothing compared to what she did to him. When she played she spoke to his soul, she soothed his fears, she filled him with confidence that he could keep himself in check and reach out and grab hold of the future he'd never allowed himself to wish for.

Unfortunately, tonight wasn't just about listening to Ella make magic.

Tonight was about putting an end to a nightmare so his girl could have the future she deserved. What he deserved was still up in the air as far as he was concerned, but Ella should have the whole world and he couldn't deny that he wanted to be the one to give it to her.

So as hard as it was, Miguel shoved the music out of his head and focused instead on the people sitting in the audience. They were all staring enraptured at the stage, their focus on the woman filling the room with musical notes. There was no indication that any of them were there for any reason other than to listen to Ella.

Was he wrong about this whole thing?

There had always been a chance that Dora Hibbert wouldn't take the bait and show up there tonight. For all they knew, maybe she really had fled town and was hiding out somewhere else, she certainly had the funds to do so.

Even though that was possible Miguel didn't believe it was likely.

Every bit of profiling they had on people like Dora said that they wouldn't give up. Just because they didn't know why she'd decided to target Athena Team there had to be a reason. People were rarely illogical, there was almost always a reason for the things they did and said. Whatever this reason was, it was important enough to Dora Hibbert for her to go to extreme lengths to target all four team members relentlessly.

There was no way she would give up.

She'd be there, he felt it in his bones.

All that was in question was when would she strike?

Surely, she wouldn't do anything while Ella was up on stage playing, that was a sure-fire way for her to get herself caught. Chances were, Dora would wait until after the concert then try to slip backstage. If she'd bought the whole thing about Ella deciding to leave Prey then she might believe that Ella was no longer under their protection, that she was fair game tonight.

It had killed every single Prey person not to be there tonight, and to keep their distance the last couple of days. They all wanted to prove themselves to Ella and there was no better way than to be watching over her. But if Dora saw one of them then she'd know she was being played, and she might decide going after Ella wasn't worth the risk.

Between his team and Rocco's there were a dozen men there tonight to have Ella's back, keep her safe. There wasn't anything he wouldn't do to protect Ella. Nothing. It was why he would walk away from her if it was the only way to keep her safe. She had to come first.

Hours ticked by.

Ella played piece after piece, keeping everyone enthralled. The energy in the room only grew with each new piece she played, and even though he was sure she must be getting exhausted, she didn't show it. The smile never left her face, and when she allowed her gaze to roam the audience, she seemed to beam that smile down to each person she saw like her music was for them personally.

It was something else, and by the time the end of the concert finally arrived Miguel was torn between being thrilled Ella had this opportunity to do something she obviously loved and disappointed that there had been no signs of Dora.

Spread as they were throughout the audience, Miguel was confident that if Dora was there then one of the men on his team or Rocco's would have seen her by now.

Maybe he had been wrong.

Maybe self-preservation had turned out to be more important to Dora than her scheme for revenge.

They'd go back to the drawing board and make sure they figured something else out. Dora didn't get to cause the kind of pain and suffering to Ella that she had and get away with it. Whatever it took they'd get her, this was not the end.

"Still no sign of her," Gumby said as the applause started to die down, people dropped back into their seats or began to gather their things.

"Doesn't mean she isn't here," Rocco's voice came down the comms. "She's proven herself to be sneaky, she could have come here in disguise."

"Prey are running facial recognition software on everyone here," Rex reminded them. "If she's here in disguise unless she was able to actually physically change her facial features, which I don't see how she would have in just a couple of days, then that will pick her up."

"If she wants to get to Ella she'll hang around for the drinks," Ace added.

That was true, this wasn't over yet, there was still time for Dora Hibbert to make her move. To give her that opportunity he was going to have to keep his distance from Ella. If he was hanging around right by her side like an angry guard dog, there was no way Dora would risk approaching.

Not that he had any intention of staying too far away.

Miguel needed to have her in his line of sight. Simple as that. The longer he was away from her the edgier he became. There was no use pretending he could keep a level head when it came to this woman, that he could stop himself from becoming obsessed with her.

It was already too late.

He was falling hard and fast.

And when he was around her he didn't even care.

"I'm going to get eyes on her," he told the others, standing and working his way through the throng of people.

"Don't get too close," Rocco reminded him.

"I know," he assured the other man. As badly as he wanted to glue himself to Ella's side, he wasn't going to mess this up. Not when the stakes were so high.

"You need one of us to stick close?" Rocco asked, understanding in his tone.

"No. I can keep it together. I'll stay close enough to keep her in my sight, but I won't get so close that it'll scare off our target," he promised.

Making quick work of heading for the backstage area, he was almost there when he saw a figure in black heading right toward Ella's dressing room. The figure was small and slim, definitely a woman, and it was dressed like one of the staff. Was that how Dora thought she could get to Ella? By pretending she was there working.

Not going to happen.

Only just as he picked up his speed, a huge group of people spilled out into the aisles blocking his way and leaving Dora Hibbert a clean shot at getting to Ella.

CHAPTER TWENTY

February 14th
   10:38 P.M.

ELECTRICITY BUZZED through Ella's bones as she walked into the dressing room and took a deep breath.

The concert was done, whether or not Dora had taken their bait and shown up remained to be seen, but regardless, it felt like tonight had been a win. It had been far too long since she last played in front of an audience, and she'd forgotten how exhilarating it was.

This was something she'd been doing since she was five years old. She'd done solo concerts and some with various members of her family, even a couple with all of them together. It was part of her, the music, the concerts, it was something she wanted to spend more time doing. As much as she loved working for Prey, and couldn't imagine not having that in her life, she needed this in her life, too.

Needed more than she'd been giving herself.

Because there was something else she needed.

Some*one* else.

When the door behind her closed with a click, she spun around expecting to find that someone standing there. Miguel would be grinning at her, and he'd pull her into his arms and spin her around, congratulating her with a kiss that would turn the electricity burning through her veins into a fire there was only one way to quench.

A way she would insist that they make happen before they went back out there to join the cocktail party.

Only when she faced the person who had entered her dressing room, she saw it wasn't Miguel. It was a woman, and she was dressed like one of the ushers. Her head was bent, hair falling down to cover her face.

It was only when the other woman slowly lifted her head and raised a hand to brush her hair back, that Ella realized who it was.

"Dora," she whispered as a manic smile took over the woman's face.

Their plan had worked. Dora was there, she'd believed the ruse that Ella was leaving Prey, believed she would be unprotected tonight, and decided to try to come after her. Even though she'd been praying this would work, that they would all finally be out from underneath the mole's thumb, it felt surreal standing face to face with someone she'd worked with, seen every day, and trusted.

Since she'd opted not to wear comms like the guys, their chatter in her ear while she was playing would be too much of a distraction, they hadn't left her alone and vulnerable. They'd suspected if she came, Dora would strike when Ella was alone, so instead of wearing a unit so she could communicate with Miguel and the others they'd given her a panic button.

All she had to do was press it and they'd all come running as fast as they could.

As surreptitiously as she could, Ella moved her hand toward the bracelet on her wrist where the small device was located.

"Whatever you're going to do I wouldn't if I were you," Dora warned, taking a step closer after locking the door behind her.

"I'm not doing anything," Ella said but stilled her hands.

"I'm not stupid, and I've worked for Prey for three years now. I know that Miguel won't have left you alone with no way for you to contact him, and whatever you were about to do was going to summon him. Nuh-uh. I don't want anyone interrupting this moment." There was a gleefulness about Dora that made Ella feel like she'd been transported into one of those old movies where the villain practically vibrated with glee about their evil plans.

While for the last three years she had believed Dora to be a nice woman who had tragically lost her husband in a car accident, a hard worker, a loyal employee, not quite a friend, but an acquaintance that she liked, it was clear she'd never seen the real Dora Hibbert.

Because the woman standing before her wasn't the same one who had greeted her each morning when she walked into the building. Who was often still there in the evenings when she called it quits after a long day.

"Why?" she asked. If she could keep Dora talking, then Miguel was going to show up sooner rather than later anyway. Even if she didn't use the panic button he would come to her as soon as he could get through the crowd and backstage to her dressing room. Not just because he wanted to make sure she was safe, but because he wanted to be with her, to celebrate with her, to hold her and tell her how proud he was of her.

"You know why," Dora said like it was obvious.

"I don't. We saved your husband, proved he was innocent of stealing and selling weapons. If it wasn't for us, he would have spent the rest of his life behind bars." It was one of the reasons that Dora had been discounted as a suspect. Of course, she'd been investigated along with everyone else, but the fact that Prey had cleared her husband's name along with the fact that she had plenty of money, had helped eliminate her.

Obviously, they'd been wrong.

They'd missed the psychosis that Dora Hibbert hid so well.

"Exactly," Dora hissed like that answered everything. Only from where Ella was standing it answered absolutely nothing.

"What do you mean?"

"Did you know that Christopher saved me one night when I was twelve?" Dora's eyes glazed over as she spoke. "My mother was dragging me toward a man she intended to give me to for sex so she could score some money for drugs and he stopped it from happening. That was the day I knew he was going to be mine. He was *meant* to be mine. My best friend's brother. My savior. She didn't understand, didn't know what it was like to grow up without a loving family. She tried to make him choose, her and their family, or me. He chose me." Glee lit Dora's face for a moment before it vanished. "He was supposed to choose me."

"And then he cheated."

Dora nodded. "You cleared him, and I thought everything was going to be okay. He was all I needed, he loved me. The first person who ever did. But then I found out the truth."

"He was cheating on you."

Fury raged in the eyes that looked back at her. "Disgusting pig."

That they could agree on. "It wasn't an accident, was it? Christopher's death?"

A slow smile curled up Dora's lips, reminding Ella of the Grinch. "Nope. It was no accident. I knew where he was going and was waiting for him, all I had to do was wait for a day when there was a truck coming in the opposite direction and then throw the spikes into the road. As soon as they pierced Chris' tires, I knew I'd done it."

"You got your revenge."

"But it wasn't enough," Dora snarled. "You had to be punished, too. If you hadn't cleared his name, he would have been in prison, I never would have learned the truth about him. I still would have had someone that loved me."

"Ella?" The door rattled as Miguel called out her name.

"Don't," Dora whispered before she could answer, pulling back her coat to reveal a suicide vest strapped to her chest. "I don't care about him, about whoever else might be here. You're the one I want revenge on not them, but I also don't care if they wind up collateral damage. It's up to you. Just you and I can go boom, or we can take out your boyfriend as well."

There was no way she was getting Miguel hurt.

This grudge Dora had was against Athena Team only, and if she had to be the sacrifice that allowed the others to be safe then she would. It wasn't how she wanted this to end, she'd wanted her shot with Miguel, but it was the better of the options.

Thankfully, the concert hall was a big place. There were passageways and corridors leading everywhere, and multiple ways out of almost every room.

Including this one.

"You never planned on getting away with it, with getting the money and building a new life, did you?" she asked Dora.

"Money means nothing to me, it was love I wanted, and

you took that away from me. All I wanted was for you to all suffer like I did. A letter to the man on Christopher's team who was the real smuggler, a promise for revenge on the people responsible for getting him put behind bars, and I got Raul's name. From there it was easy to get my revenge, so very easy."

"Ella? Why is the door locked? Are you okay, honey?" Miguel called out as the door shuddered and she suspected he was trying to knock it down.

"And now I get to take you out with me," Dora said, the creepiest smile Ella had ever seen lighting up her face like a kid who had woken up on Christmas morning to find every single item on their list to Santa sitting under their tree.

"Only if you can catch me first," Ella said, taking off toward the second door to the dressing room. If anyone was dying tonight it wasn't going to be Miguel, it wasn't going to be his team, it wasn't going to be Rocco's team, and it wasn't going to be any of the innocent people who had paid to come there tonight and hear her play.

If anyone was going to die tonight it was only going to be her and Dora Hibbert.

* * *

FEBRUARY 14TH
  10:42 P.M.

SOMETHING WAS WRONG.

There was no way Ella would lock the door to keep him out.

Even if she'd seen something that spooked her and she felt unsafe, she wouldn't just ignore him while he was calling out to her.

Why hadn't she pushed the panic button?

When she'd said she wasn't comfortable wearing comms Miguel hadn't liked the idea. He'd wanted to know that all it took was one word and he could be by her side, but he'd also respected that this whole thing had been his idea. If he wanted the concert to look believable, and Ella said having him and the rest of the guys murmuring in her ear was going to be a distraction, then he had no choice but to go along with it.

Trusting her.

Now he was wishing he'd insisted.

If he could hear Ella's voice, he could know exactly what he was up against.

It was Dora Hibbert he knew that much. The figure in black hurrying toward the dressing rooms was the mole, he felt that down to his bones. Whoever had locked the door had to be Dora, and he didn't like the idea that anyone was trying to keep him from what was his.

Regardless of his fears about himself and a future with Ella he couldn't deny that the woman already owned him. Just because it was far too soon to be even thinking about the L word it didn't mean he didn't know deep down inside, in a place he hadn't even known existed, that this woman was made for him.

Now, she needed him, and nothing was keeping him from her.

Certainly nothing as flimsy and insubstantial as a locked door.

"Mole is in the room with Ella, door locked," he said into his comms as he rammed his shoulder against the door.

The guys probably said something in response, but he heard sounds coming from the other side of the door, and his focus zeroed into one thing.

Getting to Ella.

Standing back, he slammed his foot into the door and was rewarded by a crack, and then a moment later, the broken remains parted enough that he could see inside.

A figure in black was running through the room.

No signs of Ella.

"They're on the move," he said into his comms as he shoved his body through the too-small gap. Miguel barely registered the shards of broken wood ripping at his tux, his mind was too focused on its single goal.

As soon as he was through, he started running in the direction the figure had gone, toward the other door to the dressing room. He didn't waste time checking the room for Ella's body, the mole wasn't running because they'd already achieved their goal and wanted to escape. There had been no time for Dora to kill Ella and hide the body.

The mole had to be chasing Ella.

Somehow, she'd decided running was the better option and he wished he knew why. What had Dora threatened her with? Ella knew he was right outside the door, why hadn't she called for help or pressed her panic button?

Whatever the reason, he picked up his pace. He could catch up to them. Ella was fit but she didn't spend hours every single day training. He had no idea about Dora, but Miguel was confident he could catch up to them before the mole had a chance to hurt Ella.

If she hadn't already.

He had to believe that Ella was so far unharmed because there was no blood trail. Whatever Ella's reasons for running, she was making them with a clear head, so he had to believe she knew what she was doing and had some sort of plan.

This place was like a maze, corridors heading in different directions, crisscrossing one another, leading to dozens of dressing rooms and storage rooms. If he lost them then he could lose Ella for good. All it would take was the mole to get her alone for a moment without interruption and it could all be over.

There was not a doubt in his mind that Dora was armed. Although why the woman hadn't just shot Ella and been done with it he had no idea. Maybe she'd been armed with a knife instead and hadn't been able to get close enough. Ella had self-defense training, and he knew she wasn't going to go down without a fight.

"Hey, Dora, stop!" he yelled when he spotted her up ahead.

"Miguel! Stay back!" Ella's voice screamed even though he couldn't see her.

At least he knew she was still alive.

Although she was crazy if she thought he wasn't coming after her.

Dora disappeared around a corner, and then the next thing Miguel knew the world around him blew up.

The force of the explosion was enough to take him to his knees, but not enough to pick up his body and slam it into the ground. Certainly not enough to injure him beyond making it feel like he'd been given a single-body jarring blow.

"Miguel? What happened?" Rocco's voice demanded in his ear.

"Bomb. Dora had a bomb," he replied, shoving off the shock and scrambling back to his feet, consumed with the need to get to Ella.

Just because he hadn't been injured didn't mean she hadn't.

She was a whole lot closer to the blast than he was even if he had been a mere fifty yards or so away from Dora when she set off her bomb.

Now he knew why Ella had run, why she hadn't pressed

her panic button, or answered him when he'd been on the other side of the door.

Damn, brave woman was trying to protect him.

Protect them all.

Dora must have told her about or shown her the bomb and Ella had drawn her away. It was the only reason he could think of that she would run instead of reaching out to him when she knew he was just on the other side of the door.

The closer he got to the epicenter of the explosion the more his heart dropped.

While the force of the explosion hadn't been all that powerful it was enough that parts of the walls and ceiling had collapsed, blocking him from getting to Ella.

Not acceptable.

"Ella?" he yelled, willing her to reply. If he'd lost her while he was mere yards away, he wasn't sure he'd ever be able to get over it. This woman hadn't just wormed her way into his heart, she'd barreled in without even trying or realizing she was doing it. She'd just shown him what real bravery looked like. It didn't matter to Ella that she'd been scared out of her mind and far outside her comfort zone, she'd accepted the risks and put her life on the line to protect her family, while simultaneously protecting her team and their drug.

She made him want to face his own fears and insecurities rather than trying to run and hide from them. She made him want to be a better, stronger person. She made him want to look to the future instead of constantly looking over his shoulder to the past.

Losing her before he even got a chance to tell her how much he admired her, admitted that he was falling for her, and asked her out on a real date, seemed so unfair, and yet he had no one to blame but himself. There had been nothing but himself standing in the way of doing all those things already. He'd ignored everything, his gut, his brother, Ella herself, and cowardly hidden behind his fears he might turn out to be just like his parents.

When he got no response, he called out again. "Ella? Honey, can you hear me? Call out if you can, El, I'm here, I'm coming."

There were no responses to his pleas.

Nothing.

Just silence.

Mocking silence, reminding him it could already be too late.

No.

He couldn't accept that.

Ella was there, right behind this wall of rubble and he was going to get to her.

Reaching for a piece of debris, Miguel tossed it aside then immediately reached for another. Cops and firefighters would be on the way, and the guys would be there soon. They'd get through the pile of concrete and wood and steel and through to Ella on the other side.

Seconds blurred into one another, turning into minutes.

"Ella?" Rocco asked, suddenly appearing beside him.

"Not answering."

"You sure she's in there?" Gumby asked.

"I heard her tell me to back off right before the explosion went off," he replied. "She knew Dora had a bomb, she tried to lead her away from us, from the people here for the concert." As proud as he was of her for caring about everyone else, he was furious that she thought it was okay to endanger herself in the process.

She came first.

Always.

Not him.

Not anyone else.

Just her.

245

"We'll get to her, man," Ace assured him as more men appeared around him and they began to systematically work their way through the piles of debris.

Miguel prayed that was true even as the silence on the other side of the rubble reminded him that when he got to her all he might find was a lifeless body.

CHAPTER TWENTY-ONE

February 14th
   10:47 P.M.

HER HEAD FELT like it was going to explode.

It was like someone had filled it up with dynamite and set it off.

Again and again.

The pain wouldn't go away, and Ella couldn't focus on anything else.

There was a part of her brain that knew she had to. Knew that something bad had happened, and she needed to snap to it and be aware of her surroundings because she was in danger.

But it was too hard to focus on anything around the relentless pounding inside her skull.

Groaning, she tried to look around her but all she could see was black.

Thick darkness that felt more like fog.

Turning her head to try to see if she could see something in a different direction, the arrow of pain that speared between her eyes and then directly down her entire body had her groaning and trying to stay as still as possible.

No. You have to move.

The voice whispered through her mind.

It was strong enough that Ella willed herself a little strength and managed to shift her head again. Just a fraction, but it made no difference, darkness was there too.

Everywhere.

Consuming her.

Maybe …

She'd gone blind?

Was that why her head hurt so badly?

Had she injured it and it had done something to her vision?

Fear pulsed inside her, shoving aside a little of the pain. She had to know how badly she was hurt. Had to know if there was a way to fix it.

Lifting her hand took several attempts to get it up off the … ground?

It felt like the ground. Hard and unyielding, definitely not something soft like a bed or a couch.

Somehow, she managed to lift it and bring it to her head. Pressing it to the epicenter of pain, a spot on her right temple, she felt something wet and sticky.

Blood.

Had to be blood.

Definitely injured.

But how?

Why?

Where?

What?

The questions rumbled around inside her head but there

was no answer to them. Ella had no idea what had happened to her.

Still, the persistent nagging of her subconscious urged her to wake up. To do something. She wasn't safe.

It was screaming that at her, but she still didn't know why.

"Have to move," she mumbled aloud. Her voice sounded too loud, and she winced as the sound reverberated inside her.

Using her hands, she pressed her palms to the ground and shoved herself up into a sitting position.

The world did what felt like a couple of sickening loops around her and the pain in her head was almost so bad she just sunk back down and gave up, but something urged her to keep going.

It was important.

Moving.

Waking up.

Figuring things out.

Keep going.

Balancing her weight as best she could on one of her hands, with her other hand, Ella felt around for something she could use as leverage to get to her feet. When her palm brushed across something sharp, she winced and snapped her eyes in the direction of whatever had caused her pain and startled in surprise when she could see again.

Closed.

Her eyes had been closed.

That's why she couldn't see. She wasn't blind, she just hadn't thought to check if her eyes were open.

Feeling stupid by the blunder, and also worried—if she wasn't even aware enough to know if her eyes were open or closed that could not be a good thing—Ella looked around her. It really was dark, but not the pitch black of before. She could see piles of what looked like rubble all around her, dust was in the air, and slowly memories filtered back into her mind.

The mole at Prey. The concert. The bomb. Running so no one else got caught in the explosion. Miguel calling her name. Telling him to stay back. Dora's growl that it was all over. Being lifted off her feet and then slammed back down into the ground. Then … nothingness.

When Dora set off the bomb and Ella had been caught up in the explosion, she must have hit her head.

She had a concussion.

It was the only way to explain the shooting pain between her eyes and the grogginess and confusion.

Still, she had to get up.

Had to find out if Dora was dead.

The bomb had been strapped to her so she had to be since the force of the explosion would have started right around her body. But she had to check. Had to be sure. Had to know if it really was over.

And Miguel.

What if he …?

No.

She couldn't let herself go there.

He was far enough away that he wouldn't have been killed or seriously injured when it went off.

He had to have been.

Because there was no way she could handle it if he'd been hurt or worse because he was coming to her rescue.

Somehow, Ella found the strength to get to her feet, although she swayed so badly it was a wonder she didn't fall right back down again.

Dora had been close when the bomb went off, she had to be somewhere nearby now. All she had to do was check the woman was dead and then find her way back to Miguel.

Only it felt so much harder than it sounded.

Her legs didn't want to cooperate, and she was so dizzy that remaining upright took almost all the energy she had left. Plus, debris was everywhere, and she kept stumbling over it in the dark.

It wasn't until her foot bumped into something softer than the piles of concrete and wood all around her that she realized she'd found Dora.

Even in the dark, she could see the blood.

Dead.

The woman had to be dead.

There was no way there could be so much blood and she was still breathing.

Unable to bring herself to touch the body, Ella kept moving.

Get to Miguel.

Miguel is safe.

Miguel will make everything better.

Get to Miguel.

The words ran in a loop in her mind as she shuffled slowly forward, moving barely an inch at a time.

"Ella."

Her name floated to her through the darkness.

It sounded like Miguel.

Calling to her.

If he was yelling for her then that meant he was alive. That he was okay.

Relief had her knees buckling and she threw her hands out to catch herself before she could fall. Ella knew that if she fell, she wouldn't be getting back up. Already she was hovering precariously close to unconsciousness.

"Ella, if you can hear me, I need you to answer me, honey," Miguel called out. The fear in his voice was so potent that it sank down into her, stoking her own fears.

She had to answer him.

Had to let him know she was alive.

Only when she opened her mouth, no sound came out.

No.

She had to try. Miguel was worried and she could make it better.

"Miguel," she croaked, continuing to move in the direction his voice had come from.

"Ella? Was that you, honey? Say my name again." Alongside the fear there was a command in his voice she was powerless to disobey.

"I'm h-here," she mumbled.

"I hear you, honey. I hear you. Just hold on, okay? We're getting to you as quickly as we can."

The relief in his voice gave her a small injection of strength and she reached a wall of rubble. On the other side she could hear voices. Not just Miguel's but several voices.

"Miguel," she whispered, resting her palms against the debris.

"Just here, honey. I'm coming, okay? Are you hurt?"

"My head," she murmured, sinking down to rest against the wall.

"Ambulance is already on its way. We'll get you out of here, get you to the hospital, and make you all better. All I need you to do is hold on for me a couple more minutes. Can you do that, honey?"

"Yes." At least she hoped so. Darkness was encroaching on the edges of her vision, ready to steal her sight with unconsciousness all over again.

Ella fought against it.

Clung to the knowledge that Miguel was just on the other side of the rubble and that any moment now he would be there, holding her in his arms, and everything would be okay.

Just as she almost lost her fight with the darkness, a

sudden shaft of light had her head snapping in that direction and the most beautiful sight met her eyes.

Miguel's face.

Peeking at her through a hole in the wall of debris.

"Hey, beautiful, you've never looked better," Miguel teased, even as concern danced in his dark eyes.

Ella huffed a small chuckle and went to move closer. She needed to touch him, needed to feel that he was real and not a figment of her scrambled mind.

Only she sensed something behind her.

Movement.

But she was the only one in there.

No one should be moving.

Then looking more dead than alive, Dora Hibbert appeared, a huge chunk of concrete in her hand that she was swinging directly toward Ella's head.

* * *

FEBRUARY 14TH
    10:51 P.M.

LIKE A ZOMBIE RAISED from the dead, Dora Hibbert appeared behind Ella.

In slow motion, Miguel was forced to watch as the woman raised a huge chunk of concrete and swung it toward Ella's head.

Another blow after the one she'd already taken could easily be enough to end the life of the woman who had so tenderly reached into his chest and taken hold of his heart.

There was no way he could stop this from happening.

Ella was between him and Dora, there was no way he could get his weapon in his hand and line up a shot where he wasn't going to hit his woman before Dora could take Ella out.

It was her intention.

He could see that in the manic eyes that seemed to glow in the light filtering into the cavern where Ella and Dora were trapped.

"Dora, don't!" he screamed, knowing the woman wasn't going to listen.

Ella whimpered and he was sure the sound would stay with him for the rest of his life. The last sound he would ever hear her make.

There was nowhere for Ella to go.

She was trapped.

Even with a dozen men digging through the rubble, they couldn't get to her in time.

No moment in his life had ever been this horrific. Miguel would take being nine years old and getting shot every single time over this.

The concrete swung closer to Ella's head, seconds away from making contact. Miguel screamed Ella's name as he frantically tore through the wall of rubble preventing him from getting to her.

Then, at the very last second, just as he was sure he was about to watch his girl take her final breath as the blow to the head stole her from him, Ella sprang into action.

Somehow, she'd found her own weapon, and she swung it as she launched at her would-be murderer.

Moving quicker than Dora, and catching the other woman off-guard, Ella slammed the concrete she held in her hand into Dora's head.

The sickening crunch was another sound that would stay with him for the rest of his life.

At least the sound of concrete hitting bone, splintering it, wasn't his girl's skull being shattered.

Functioning clearly in a terror-fueled autopilot, Ella didn't stop after one strike.

Again and again, she slammed the concrete into Dora's head.

Following the woman to the ground, she kept going.

Blow after blow.

Desperate to get to his girl, Miguel renewed his efforts to get through the rubble, and as soon as there was a hole big enough for him to scramble through that was exactly what he did.

"Honey, I'm here now. You can stop, Ella," he said softly, reaching out to grasp her wrist to still her.

While he'd been worried she might fight him, fueled by fear and survival as she was, Ella didn't. As soon as his fingers circled her wrist, she dropped the bloody chunk of concrete and all but collapsed into his arms.

Breathing hard, shaking all over, huge violent shudders, Ella sobbed in his arms as he pulled her close and held her tight against his chest. She felt every bit as good as he'd been imagining. Not just good, holding her felt right.

Almost too right.

Because even though he could acknowledge Ella as his, that didn't magically solve all his problems. He still had to find a way to make sure that he was never going to be a threat to this beautiful, brave woman he clutched against him like the precious thing she was.

"Is ... is she ... d-dead?" Ella asked through her tears.

"She'd dead," Rocco answered for him as the other man knelt beside Dora Hibbert.

"You killed her, honey," he told his trembling woman.

"Killed the mole *and* a weapons trafficker. Girl, you are on fire," Rocco teased, and Ella hiccuped a laugh.

"You're amazing," Miguel agreed, smoothing a hand down Ella's tangled locks.

When she looked up at him, he knew he was done for. Whatever it took he would find a way to be with this woman. Whatever personal demons he had to exorcise he would do. Anything. Walk through the fires of Hell themselves if he had to.

But he couldn't walk away from her.

Couldn't not give this thing between them a chance.

"I-I was s-scared," Ella stammered. "I thought … I th-thought you w-were d-dead."

That right there was why he had no choice but to find a way to be with her. Even though she was the one blown up, the one trapped with a deranged would-be killer, she had been more worried about him.

"No, honey. I'm okay, and now you're safe, too. Dora won't ever hurt you again." Neither would anything else. He was never letting his girl get hurt again. For the rest of his life, he would find a way to protect her from pain.

"Ambulance is just pulling up outside," Phantom said through the slowly enlarging hole in the wall of rubble that had kept him from his girl for what felt like hours.

"Time to get you to the hospital," he told Ella, palming her cheek and letting his fingertips caress her soft skin. Blood coated the other side of her face, and various other places on her exposed arms. Her dress was torn, even in the thin light he could see bruises beginning to form, and she'd lost both her shoes. Still, she was the most beautiful thing he had ever laid eyes on, and for some reason, she seemed to be interested in him.

A miracle.

No other way to describe how a woman like Ella could want a man like him.

"Miguel?"

"Yeah, honey?"

"I think I'm going to pass …"

Ella's voice trailed off as she did indeed pass out, collapsing against him. Catching her weight as she fell, Miguel swung her up into his arms. His heart raced in his chest, head injuries could be tricky. Just because she'd been awake, talking, walking, and reacting, didn't mean that she was out of danger. Didn't mean she was going to be okay.

"Here, let's get her out of here," Rocco said with more calm than Miguel could muster as he guided them toward the hole.

Big enough now to easily pass Ella through into Phantom's waiting arms, the seconds where someone else was holding what was his while he also climbed through to the other side felt far too long. There was no way he could go the rest of his life without Ella by his side.

As soon as he was on his feet on the other side of the remains of the wall of rubble Phantom handed Ella back to him. With a nod of thanks he took off toward the nearest door, desperate to get Ella the medical attention she needed.

Handing her off to the paramedics was hard. If it wasn't for Rocco informing them that Miguel would be riding with her, he was sure he would have been denied. If that had happened he would have lost it.

Just not holding her was enough to have his heart hammer painfully in his chest.

This woman consumed him, and it was both a blessing and a curse.

Staying by her side as she was treated in the emergency room, taken for tests and scans, then finally settled in a quiet, dark private room where she could rest, his mind was constantly running through scenarios, trying to figure out how he could keep Ella in his life but also ensure he would never be a threat to her.

In the end, the only answer he could come up with was one he didn't like.

One Ella might not be able to accept.

How was he going to convince her that this was the only way?

Being an addict was for life. It wasn't something you just got over, something that just went away on its own. It was a battle you would fight every single day.

It was a battle he *wanted* to fight.

Would fight the best way he knew how.

Which was why he knew that this was something he was going to have to do whether Ella could understand why or not.

Hurting her wasn't an option. Risking her safety and her happiness was not something he was prepared to do. This was the best way he could think of to make sure it didn't happen.

The problem was in doing it, he was going to risk losing his girl anyway.

No.

He had to believe that Ella would trust him to know what he had to do, that she would be willing to go along with this so they could have the future he was sure they both wanted.

Leaning over the bed where his girl was sleeping peacefully, Miguel brushed his knuckles across her cheek, then touched his lips to her forehead. "Please understand, honey. Please know I don't want to do this, but I have to. Please forgive me."

Then he touched his lips to hers in a soft kiss and prayed it wouldn't be the last one he ever got to give her.

CHAPTER TWENTY-TWO

March 1ˢᵗ
   9:35 A.M.

ELLA HATED THIS.

It was perhaps one of the hardest things she'd ever had to do, and she was only one week into the month-long ordeal she was going to have to find a way to endure.

Agreeing to go along with this hadn't been easy, but how could she deny Miguel when it was clear this was what he believed he needed in order to be able to commit to any sort of future with her?

Wasn't like he'd done it in a blackmailing kind of way. Agree to do this or I won't be with you. He'd explained his reasoning, his fears and concerns, why he thought this would be helpful for him, and while she didn't necessarily agree that this was what he needed to move forward, how could she tell him that she knew better than he did what he'd been through?

So she'd agreed.

To one month apart before they officially became a couple.

One month.

One very long month that right now she had no idea how she was going to survive.

When he'd first told her that he needed to prove to himself that he wasn't so obsessed with her and a life with her that he could spend a month away from her without being consumed with the need to turn to drugs it hadn't sounded all that bad. A month was only thirty days long—well, technically, thirty-one, but the extra hadn't seemed so bad—it should be easy enough to not see him for that amount of time.

Texting was supposed to be out as well, but she'd negotiated it in, saying that she understood why he felt he needed this time to prove things to himself, but she had needs, too, and one of them was contact with him. So they texted a little, not as much as she would have liked, but enough to get through each day knowing she at least got to tell him she was thinking of him and know he was thinking of her in return.

That helped enough to make the separation bearable, and she did have a lot to keep her occupied. Medical appointments, counseling sessions with Piper, debriefing and several meetings with the cops and Prey as she gave her statement several times over. There had also been a lot of spending time with her team and trying to rebuild those bonds that had been the foundation of her whole life these last several years since they joined Prey.

Spending time each day with her Athena Team girls, and the guys was actually helping. They'd all stepped up to be there for her, but she still missed Miguel.

The first week he hadn't left her side. Although he'd told her about his need to spend an entire month away from her as soon as she'd regained consciousness in the hospital, he'd assured her he wasn't bailing right away. He'd stayed with her in the hospital, taken her home when she was discharged, and looked after her those first few days. It wasn't until she was able to do things for herself again that he kissed her goodbye and promised that once he was confident he was never going to put her in danger from his addictions he'd be back.

There was a little thread of anger at him leaving when she still needed him, Ella couldn't deny that. But there was also compassion and understanding because she recognized that Miguel was trying to do the best he could with what he had. She also understood that he truly believed this was something he needed to do.

It just sucked.

With a sigh, she shoved off the couch and wandered over to the kitchen. Ella wasn't really hungry, she still hadn't reclaimed her appetite, but she wasn't sure if it was the lingering effects from the concussion or just because she was missing Miguel so much.

Still, she grabbed a bar of chocolate and wandered back over to the couch, flopping down onto it. A headache still pulsed at the back of her head most days, but nothing compared to how bad it had been those first few days. There were other bruises and several gashes, including a couple that had needed stitches, littering her body, but most of the pain from them had been overshadowed by her head.

At least the dizziness was gone now, that had been a nightmare.

Not that she was really regretting those few days she and Miguel spent mostly snuggled up side by side in her bed as she slept off the worst of the concussion symptoms. Even as exhausted as she'd been, as bad as the pain, nausea, and dizziness had been, she wouldn't take back those days for anything.

Now, all she had to do was get through the next three weeks and then she could have a whole lifetime of moments just like that.

Of course, they'd had the discussion before Miguel went that there were no guarantees about the future. They were right at the very beginning of a relationship and hadn't even officially put a foot on the track yet. Despite all of that, they both felt what was between them, both knew it had the potential to become an all-consuming love affair that would last until they took their final breaths.

Even then she believed their souls would find one another in the afterlife. That she and Miguel were destined to be together for all eternity.

"It's only another three weeks," she reminded herself aloud.

Three weeks.

More than actually.

It felt like a lifetime.

A knock on her door had her dragging herself back to her feet, the forgotten chocolate bar tumbling to the floor as she stood. Not bothering to retrieve it she headed for the front door, already knowing who would be there.

Her Athena Team girls.

They came every morning. Not too early as she still found herself needing a solid ten hours of sleep minimum, but early enough that she wouldn't be tempted to make herself lunch. That was their job now, well apparently, it certainly seemed like it since they'd been there around ten every single morning. One of them would drive her to her appointment with Piper in the afternoon, and then they'd all eat dinner together.

Athena Team was temporarily on leave from Prey, and they all needed it.

All of them had been victimized by Dora Hibbert and

Raul Castillo, and they all needed to heal. Individually and as a team. They'd allowed the mole to come between them, and while things might not ever be exactly the same as they'd been before, Ella was confident that she could move forward and keep working at the job she loved with the people she loved even if they'd hurt her when they doubted her.

As predicted, when she opened her door all three of her friends were standing on her doorstep, along with their guys. It hurt a little to see the happy couples, but even though she missed him, Ella was still proud of the fact that Miguel was so determined not to repeat his parents' mistakes.

"You guys are a little early today," she said as she stepped back to allow them all to enter.

"We missed you," Cassie said, giving her a gentle hug.

"I missed you, too," Ella admitted. It was true as well. Miguel wasn't the only one she was missing these days.

"You did?" Scarlett asked, eyes lighting up.

"I did," she confirmed. "I'm glad we've got this time to spend together, I think we need it."

"We definitely do," Lucy said, hobbling into the room, her foot still in a moon boot.

"You heard from my idiot brother today?" Luis asked as they all headed for the living room.

Protectiveness swirled inside her. Miguel wasn't an idiot. He was trying to do the right thing, he was trying to protect her from pain. Just because she wished he was there didn't mean she would stand for anyone speaking bad about him. "He's not an idiot. He's honorable and noble, and doing what he has to do to keep me and himself safe."

"Little brother picked good," Luis said, beaming at her like she hadn't just told him off.

Ella huffed. "And to answer your question, yes I have. I hear from him every day."

"Hey, Ella." Luis grabbed her hand, stopping her before

she could drop back down onto the couch. "I get why he's doing it. I think he's wrong, he's nothing like our parents, but I respect him wanting to make sure he can trust himself."

"It's important to him, and that makes it important to me," she said.

"Which is exactly why I think my brother did a good job when he picked you."

"I think it was more like the universe picked us for each other," she said, offering him a smile.

"I know the feeling," Cassie said, snuggling into Luis' side when the two of them sat down side by side.

"Ditto," Lucy agreed, all smiles when Zander fussed around her helping her get comfortable.

"I think the universe did some excellent matchmaking," Scarlett said, sliding her hand into Tate's.

Looking around at the three happy couples, Ella couldn't agree more. Fate might have dealt them all a rough hand this last couple of months, but it had also brought them all plenty of good.

Now all she had to do was wait for Miguel to come home, and the next chapter of her life could begin.

* * *

March 21ST
    6:13 P.M.

Finally.

Feeling like he'd been deprived of oxygen and was about to take his first breath in a month, Miguel walked down the front path toward Ella's front door.

That was exactly what the last four weeks had felt like.

Like he couldn't breathe.

Like a piece of himself had been amputated.

All he'd wanted was to see Ella, be able to pull her into his arms, hold her, kiss her, and make love to her. If his team hadn't been called out on a mission and been out of the country for the last ten days, he very well might have caved and gone to her early.

In a way, this last month had proven to him that if the worst happened and he wound up losing Ella, or something else equally as terrible happened in his life, he'd be able to resist the temptation to turn to drugs as the answer. In another way, it had proven to him he couldn't live without this woman.

Didn't want to.

Ella was his, and he was hers.

Simple as that.

Having her around was being at peace, it was feeling complete, it was knowing what it felt like to find your place in the world.

Finally, he could come home to his girl, knowing that he truly had his addictions under control, that he was no threat to her, that he would never wind up inflicting on her—or any children they might have—the same kind of life his own parents had given him and his brother.

He was home for good.

Because nothing could make him leave Ella again.

Nothing.

While she knew this was the day he was supposed to come home to her, Ella also knew that his team had been called out and he hadn't texted to let her know he was back. He wanted to surprise her, because at the back of his mind was a tiny little niggling voice of doubt that kept wondering if things had changed for Ella over the past month.

Just because he had learned he didn't want to live without her didn't mean she felt the same way.

Maybe a little distance had given her a different perspective.

Especially now that she was safe and working things out with her team.

The knot of fear in his gut worsened as he knocked on the door and waited.

It might have been a month since he last saw her, the longest month of his life, but these last few moments felt like an eternity.

When she threw open the door, Ella's mouth dropped open, and she stared at him like she'd just seen a ghost.

Good or bad?

Reading her expression was impossible, or maybe it was just his own fears and insecurities clouding his judgment.

Because when she suddenly launched herself at him, he was caught completely by surprise.

His arms automatically moved to catch her, and Ella attached herself to him, arms wrapped tightly around his neck, legs wrapped around his hips, clinging to him with her face pressed into the crook of his neck.

Just like that, his heart began to beat normally again.

"Are you really here?" Ella asked, her voice muffled as it pressed tighter against his skin.

"I'm really here, honey." One of his hands palmed the back of her head, the other curled tightly around her waist, clutching her against him. Damn, he never wanted to let her go again. Miguel could quite happily stand there, just like this, holding his girl in his arms, for the rest of his life.

"I missed you so much," Ella murmured as her tears began to wet his skin.

"Oh, honey, not more than I missed you," he assured her. Knowing he'd inflicted pain on this beautiful, brave woman hurt, but not more than hurting her worse down the line

own release. He needed her to know how much he adored her, how lost on her he was.

Her ecstasy-filled cries filled the room as he gave her her first orgasm of the night.

Without letting her come down from her high, Miguel moved up her body, his lips finding hers as his fingers took the place his tongue had just vacated. Again, he alternated between stroking deep inside her, making sure to curl his fingers at just the right angle to catch that spot he knew he could use to make her fall apart, and working her sensitive bud.

His responsive girl was quickly rushing toward a second orgasm. He could tell in the desperate way her tongue dueled with his, in the way her body writhed beneath him, the way her fingers clawed at his back, drawing him closer even though his body covered hers.

When she came, clamping around his fingers as his thumb worked her bundle of nerves, he swallowed her scream, making it part of him. Her pleasure was his because there was no sweeter feeling in the world than knowing you made your girl come so hard she forgot her own name, anything less was unacceptable.

"My Ella," he murmured as he lined himself up and thrust into her in one smooth move.

Ella cried out, her already fluttering internal muscles clamped around him, and he groaned, almost losing his control and coming too soon. Not until his girl was riding that high with him.

"Move, honey, move with me. Take what you need. Whatever it is I'll give it to you, always."

"You," Ella said, lifting her head to press her lips to his. "All I need is you."

"You have me, honey. All of me."

Together they set a steady pace, climbing higher and

higher as one, and when Miguel knew he couldn't hold off a second longer, he reached between them, took Ella's bud between his fingers, and tweaked it, setting off a chain reaction as her orgasm triggered his own.

It exploded around him with a force he'd been unprepared for, picking him up and sweeping him away into a galaxy he hadn't even known existed.

This was what it felt like to be falling in love. To be so consumed with another person that you quickly forgot where you ended, and they began.

As terrifying as it was, it was also the most exhilarating feeling in the world.

Whatever it took he was going to keep his addictions in check because there was no way he was ever going to risk causing this amazing woman even an ounce of pain.

CHAPTER TWENTY-THREE

March 21ˢᵗ
    10:08 P.M.

THIS WAS her favorite place to be.

Right here in Miguel's arms.

Too bad it wasn't possible to stay right where she was for the rest of her life. She didn't really need to go to work, did she? Or eat? Or shower? Or do anything other than this?

Since she had bills to pay, of course, she was going to have to get out of bed sooner or later, but Ella didn't want to think about that yet. Nor did she want to think about how being with Miguel wouldn't mean falling asleep in his arms every night or waking up each morning with the heat of his body soaking into hers.

Reality was that with his job, Miguel would be away a lot. Sometimes for months at a time. There were special days he'd miss, birthdays and holidays, and if they had kids then sometimes, she'd feel like a single mom. It would suck not to be able to be with him every single day, but she knew who he was and what he did when she fell for him, and having spent this past month without him Ella knew for certain she'd rather have him as much as she could than not at all.

"I can hear you thinking," Miguel's voice rumbled through the chest she was using as a pillow. "Second thoughts?"

The vulnerability in his voice made her sad. Miguel hadn't conquered his demons for her, he'd done it years ago for himself because he wanted a better life than his parents had, but he'd solidified his faith in himself for her. So, he never let her down by letting his issues touch her, and she wanted to do the same for him, wanted to never let him down, so he always knew how much he was appreciated and cared for.

Shifting so her chin was propped up on his chest she met his gaze. "I'm not having doubts about you, Miguel. Not now, not ever. I was just thinking of how much I'm going to miss you when your team gets called out and you're away. I know it'll be hard at first, but we'll figure out a system that works for us and our kids."

"Kids?" Miguel asked with a lazy smile that made her stomach flutter.

"I've always wanted a big family, at least four kids, so now's the time to speak up if you only want one or two," she informed him.

The smile grew bigger. "I don't care how many kids you want, honey. I'll have a dozen if it makes you happy." His smile faltered. "It is going to be rough being with me though, El. I will be away a lot. Sometimes, I won't even be able to give you a warning first. I'll just get a call and have to go. I could be away a couple of days or a couple of months, and I won't ever be able to talk to you about it."

It was clear Miguel was concerned about this, and while

she was absolutely not looking forward to it, she also absolutely believed they would find a way to make the best of it. "Miguel, as long as you are one hundred percent present when you're home that's all I'm ever going to ask of you. I know your job, I work at Prey so I'm familiar with security clearances, and I do believe we can make this work. I'm all in."

"All in," he said softly like he enjoyed the sound of the words and what they represented. "I'm all in, too, honey. And I promise you here and now that when I'm home you'll get all of me."

"That's all I ask," she assured him.

"And you have it." Miguel touched a kiss to the tip of her nose. Then his hand, which had been resting on her hip, dipped a little so his fingers could brush across her center. "So you really want a whole lot of kids?"

"Mmm," she moaned as he found her bud and began to circle it slowly, teasingly. "Yeah. A whole bunch. I loved having three sisters and always knew I wanted at least the same number of kids my parents had."

"By the time Luis and I went to live with our foster parents, their four biological kids were already adults, so it's always just been the two of us. I think I like the idea of a big family though."

"Big families mean always having company, someone to play with and talk to." Ella sucked in a breath when the tip of his finger edged inside her only to disappear as he resumed trailing lazy circles over her bundle of nerves.

Two could play that game.

"If we want a big family we should probably get in lots of practice," she told him as she grasped his erection and began to slide her hand up and down his length, loving the way it jerked at her touch.

"Oh yeah, honey, I agree. *Lots* of practice." Miguel's hands moved to grasp her hips, and he lifted her up so she was straddling his thighs.

"Mmm," she moaned again as his tip nestled against her entrance, teasing her, teasing them both if Miguel's expression was anything to go by. "All positions."

"Definitely." Miguel sucked in a breath as she sank down just enough to take the first inch of him inside her. "Should probably try out different locations in the house, too."

"I'm down for that." Ella's head tipped back as she took another inch.

"Different times of the day, too."

"Maybe we should just stay here and keep practicing."

"I'm down for that. Who needs jobs anyway?"

Ella giggled. "I'm thinking we do if we want a dozen kids." A dozen was really too many, but she'd take four or five, even six. Cute little boys with dark hair and eyes, loyal and strong, protective just like their daddy. And adorable little girls with her blonde hair and green eyes, ready to conquer the world because they'd know from day one that they could do anything they set their minds to.

With a house filled with love, laughter, and a whole lot of noise, she'd never feel lonely again. Hadn't felt lonely since Miguel had appointed himself her friend and protector, then grown to be so much more.

"Let's start trying," she said, sinking the rest of the way down until Miguel was buried deep inside her.

"For real?" His hands—still on her hips—stilled her when she tried to roll them to create the friction she needed. "You want to start trying for a baby?"

"As soon as I go off birth control."

"We've only known each other a couple of months and spent hardly any time together. You really want to try to get pregnant this soon?"

"Not if you're not ready, but who gets to decide what's

soon and what's not?" Had it been a short amount of time? Sure. But so what? What was the appropriate amount of time to wait before starting a family? "Besides, by the time I go off birth control and we actually get pregnant, it would likely be several months maybe even more than a year. Then nine months of cooking before we'd actually have a baby. But we both have to be ready before we start trying."

"All in."

"All in," she agreed.

"I'm ready to start trying any time you are, honey." Then Miguel finally released his grip on her hips and she began to move.

Meeting her thrust for thrust, the fingers of one of his hands working her bud while his other played with her nipples, Ella quickly felt pleasure ignite. Each time she lifted her hips then sunk back down again, that pleasure began to grow.

But in the end, it wasn't the feel of Miguel inside her, wasn't the way he circled her bundle of nerves, wasn't the tweaking of her nipples that had her orgasm exploding inside her, it was the look in his eyes.

Love.

Whether they'd said the words out loud or not, she felt it, saw it in the way he watched her, and she made sure her own eyes conveyed the same emotion.

As the powerful orgasm began to ebb, Ella rested against Miguel's chest, keeping his length snug inside her, not ready yet to lose that connection.

"It feels wrong to say but I'm kind of glad Dora Hibbert went off the deep end, decided to blame my team for finding out about her husband's affairs, and decided she wanted revenge," Ella whispered as she nuzzled her face against Miguel's neck. "If she hadn't, I never would have been threatened and gone to Mexico and you never would have come after me, and we wouldn't be here right now."

"I never knew this level of happiness existed," Miguel said as he wrapped her tightly in an embrace.

"Me either," she agreed. For as long as she could remember, Ella had known she'd wanted to find someone to love, marry them, have kids, and spend a lifetime enjoying one another, growing old side by side. There had been times it had felt like a fairytale, something that shimmered constantly out of reach, something that could never become a reality.

Now she'd found it, and it was infinitely better than she had ever imagined.

When Ava is rescued by Nathaniel after falling victim to a human organ trafficking ring she's determined to shut them down in the first book in the action packed and emotionally charged Prey Security: Cyber Team series!

Rescuing Nathaniel (Prey Security: Cyber Team #1)

ALSO BY JANE BLYTHE

<u>SAVAGE RISK</u>

Prey Security: Bravo Team Series
<u>VICIOUS SCARS</u>
<u>RUTHLESS SCARS</u>
<u>BRUTAL SCARS</u>
<u>CRUEL SCARS</u>
<u>BURIED SCARS</u>
<u>WICKED SCARS</u>

Prey Security: Charlie Team Series
DECEPTIVE LIES - 1/2025

Saving SEALs Series
SAVING RYDER
SAVING ERIC
SAVING OWEN
SAVING LOGAN
SAVING GRAYSON
SAVING CHARLIE

Candella Sisters' Heroes Series
LITTLE DOLLS
LITTLE HEARTS
LITTLE BALLERINA

<u>Broken Gems Series</u>
CRACKED SAPPHIRE
CRUSHED RUBY
FRACTURED DIAMOND
SHATTERED AMETHYST

SPLINTERED EMERALD

SALVAGING MARIGOLD

NINE

TEN

Storybook Murders Series

NURSERY RHYME KILLER

FAIRYTALE KILLER

FABLE KILLER

Christmas Romantic Suspense Series

CHRISTMAS HOSTAGE

CHRISTMAS CAPTIVE

CHRISTMAS VICTIM

YULETIDE PROTECTOR

YULETIDE GUARD

YULETIDE HERO

HOLIDAY GRIEF

HOLIDAY LOSS - 12/2024

Conquering Fear Series

(Co-written with Amanda Siegrist)

DROWNING IN YOU

OUT OF THE DARKNESS

CLOSING IN

ABOUT THE AUTHOR

USA Today bestselling author Jane Blythe writes action-packed romantic suspense and military romance featuring protective heroes and heroines who are survivors. One of Jane's most popular series includes Prey Security, part of Susan Stoker's OPERATION ALPHA world! Writing in that world alongside authors such as Janie Crouch and Riley Edwards has been a blast, and she looks forward to bringing more books to this genre, both within and outside of Stoker's world. When Jane isn't binge-reading she's counting down to Christmas and adding to her 200+ teddy bear collection!

To connect and keep up to date please visit any of the following

Email – mailto:janeblytheauthor@gmail.com
Facebook – https://www.facebook.com/janeblytheauthor
Instagram – https://www.instagram.com/
jane_blythe_author
Reader Group – https://www.facebook.com/groups/
janeskillersweethearts
Twitter – https://www.twitter.com/jblytheauthor
TikTok - https://www.tiktok.com/@janeblytheauthor
Website – https://www.janeblythe.com.au

There are many more books in this fan fiction world than listed
here, for an up-to-date list go to www.AcesPress.com

You can also visit our Amazon page at:
http://www.amazon.com/author/operationalpha

Special Forces: Operation Alpha World
Christie Adams: Charity's Heart
Elizabella Baker: Challenging Luke
Linzi Baxter: Dangerous Rescue
Misha Blake: Flash
Anna Blakely: Rescuing Gracelynn
Julia Bright: Saving Lorelei
Cara Carnes: Protecting Mari
Kendra Mei Chailyn: Beast
Melissa Kay Clarke: Rescuing Annabeth
Gia Cobie: Saved from Revenge
Samantha Cole: Handling Haven
KaLyn Cooper: Spring Unveiled
Jordan Dane: Redemption for Avery
D.M. Earl: Claire's Guardian
Riley Edwards: Protecting Olivia
Dorothy Ewels: Knight's Queen
Lila Ferrari: Protecting Joy
Nicole Flockton: Protecting Maria
Amy Gamet: Guarded by the SEAL
Lea Griffith: Finding Ava
Desiree Holt: Protecting Maddie
Danielle M. Haas: Crossroads of Betrayal
Bree Hera: Trusting the Team
Jesse Jacobson: Protecting Honor
Rayne Lewis: Justice for Mary
Ireland Lorelei: The Detective

Kristin Lynn: Worth the Risk

JM Madden: Rescuing Olivia

A.M. Mahler: Griffin

Ellie Masters: Sybil's Protector

Trish McCallan: Hero Under Fire

Naomi McKay: Twist

KD Michaels: Saving Laura

Olivia Michaels: Protecting Harper

Annie Miller: Securing Willow

MJ Nightingale: Protecting Beauty

C.K. O'Connor: Delaney's Bodyguard

Melinda Owens: Betraying Katie

Victoria Paige: Reclaiming Izabel

Danielle Pays: Defending Sarina

Lainey Reese: Protecting New York

KeKe Renée: Protecting Bria

Taryn Rivers: Savage Cove

TL Reeve and Michele Ryan: Extracting Mateo

Ariana Rose: Chasing Paige

Deanna L. Rowley: Saving Veronica

Angela Rush: Charlotte

E.M. Shue: Discovering Tyler

Rose Smith: Saving Satin

Tyler Anne Snell: Cowboy Heat

Dee Stewart: Fighting for Brielle

Lynne St. James: SEAL's Spitfire

Bella Stone: Rexar

Jen Talty: Protecting Ainsley

Reina Torres, Rescuing Hi'ilani

LJ Vickery: Circus Comes to Town

R. C. Wynne: Shadows Renewed

Delta Team Three Series
Lori Ryan: Nori's Delta

Becca Jameson: Destiny's Delta
Lynne St James, Gwen's Delta
Elle James: Ivy's Delta
Riley Edwards: Hope's Delta

Police and Fire: Operation Alpha World
Freya Barker: Burning for Autumn
B.P. Beth: Scott
Jane Blythe: Salvaging Marigold
Julia Bright: Justice for Amber
Gia Cobie: Saved from Revenge
Hadley Finn: Exton
Danielle M. Haas: Crossroads of Betrayal
Deanndra Hall: Shelter for Sharla
Jenna Harte: Dead But Not Forgotten
India Kells: Game Master
Amber Kuhlman: Protecting Paisley
Reina Torres: Justice for Sloane
Aubree Valentine, Justice for Danielle

Tarpley VFD Series
Silver James, Fighting for Elena
Deanndra Hall, Fighting for Carly
Haven Rose, Fighting for Calliope
MJ Nightingale, Fighting for Jemma
TL Reeve, Fighting for Brittney
Nicole Flockton, Fighting for Nadia

As you know, this book included at least one character from Susan Stoker's books. To check out more, see below.

SEAL of Protection: Alliance Series
Protecting Remi
Protecting Wren (Nov 5, 2024)
Protecting Josie (Mar 4, 2025)
Protecting Maggie (Apr 1, 2025)
Protecting Addison (May 6, 2025)
Protecting Kelli (TBA)
Protecting Bree (TBA)

The Refuge Series
Deserving Alaska
Deserving Henley
Deserving Reese
Deserving Cora
Deserving Lara
Deserving Maisy
Deserving Ryleigh (Jan 7, 2025)

SEAL Team Hawaii Series
Finding Elodie
Finding Lexie
Finding Kenna
Finding Monica
Finding Carly
Finding Ashlyn
Finding Jodelle

Eagle Point Search & Rescue
Searching for Lilly
Searching for Elsie

Searching for Bristol
Searching for Caryn
Searching for Finley
Searching for Heather
Searching for Khloe

Delta Team Two Series

Shielding Gillian
Shielding Kinley
Shielding Aspen
Shielding Jayme (novella)
Shielding Riley
Shielding Devyn
Shielding Ember
Shielding Sierra

SEAL of Protection: Legacy Series

Securing Caite (FREE!)
Securing Brenae (novella)
Securing Sidney
Securing Piper
Securing Zoey
Securing Avery
Securing Kalee
Securing Jane

Delta Force Heroes Series

Rescuing Rayne (FREE!)
Rescuing Aimee (novella)
Rescuing Emily
Rescuing Harley
Marrying Emily (novella)
Rescuing Kassie
Rescuing Bryn

Rescuing Casey
Rescuing Sadie (novella)
Rescuing Wendy
Rescuing Mary
Rescuing Macie (novella)
Rescuing Annie

Badge of Honor: Texas Heroes Series

Justice for Mackenzie (FREE!)
Justice for Mickie
Justice for Corrie
Justice for Laine (novella)
Shelter for Elizabeth
Justice for Boone
Shelter for Adeline
Shelter for Sophie
Justice for Erin
Justice for Milena
Shelter for Blythe
Justice for Hope
Shelter for Quinn
Shelter for Koren
Shelter for Penelope

SEAL of Protection Series

Protecting Caroline (FREE!)
Protecting Alabama
Protecting Fiona
Marrying Caroline (novella)
Protecting Summer
Protecting Cheyenne
Protecting Jessyka
Protecting Julie (novella)
Protecting Melody

Protecting the Future
Protecting Kiera (novella)
Protecting Alabama's Kids (novella)
Protecting Dakota

New York Times, *USA Today* and *Wall Street Journal* Bestselling Author Susan Stoker has a heart as big as the state of Tennessee where she lives, but this all American girl has also spent the last fourteen years living in Missouri, California, Colorado, Indiana, and Texas. She's married to a retired Army man who now gets to follow *her* around the country.

www.stokeraces.com
www.AcesPress.com
susan@stokeraces.com

Made in the USA
Monee, IL
19 November 2024

70582450R00167